8-85-√ √

D0162782

√

FIC
WEL
Wells, H. G.
(Herbert George),
1866-1946.

The man with a nose

DATE			

© THE BAKER & TAYLOR CO

The Man with a Nose

and the Other Uncollected Short Stories of H. G. Wells

The Man with a Nose

and the Other
Uncollected Short Stories of

H.G. Wells

*edited and
with an Introduction by J.R. Hammond*

THE ATHLONE PRESS

LONDON

First published 1984 by The Athlone Press Ltd
44 Bedford Row, London WC1R 4LY

British Library Cataloguing in Publication Data

Wells, H.G.
The man with a nose and other uncollected
short stories of H.G. Wells.
I. Title
823'.912 [F] PR5770
ISBN 0-485-11247-7

Library of Congress Cataloging in Publication Data

Wells, H. G. (Herbert George), 1866–1946.
The man with a nose.
I. Title.
PR5774.M24   1984   823'.912   84-14624
ISBN 0-485-11247-7

Typeset by Inforum Ltd, Portsmouth
Printed and bound in Great Britain by
Biddles Ltd, Guildford and King's Lynn

Contents

Introduction *by J.R. Hammond*   vii

1   The Man with a Nose   1

2   A Perfect Gentleman on Wheels   5

3   Wayde's Essence   16

4   The Queer Story of Brownlow's Newspaper   25

5   Walcote   43

6   The Devotee of Art   50

7   A Misunderstood Artist   61

8   Le Mari Terrible   65

9   The Rajah's Treasure   69

10 The Presence by the Fire   81

11 Mr. Marshall's Doppelganger   87

12 The Thing in No. 7   97

13 The Thumbmark   104

14 A Family Elopement   111

15 Our Little Neighbour   117

16 The Loyalty of Esau Common   126

17 The Wild Asses of the Devil   142

18 Answer to Prayer   153

19 The New Faust   156

Bibliography   212

Introduction

THE NAME H.G. WELLS requires no introduction to the reading public. For fifty years, from the publication of *The Time Machine* in 1895 to his last book *Mind at the End of its Tether* in 1945, his novels, short stories and forecasts of the future delighted and entertained an audience of millions throughout the world. Today, forty years after his death, his stature as a novelist and prophet is increasingly being recognised.

Wells's popularity as a short story writer shows no sign of abating and collections of his stories continue to sell in a variety of editions. When *The Complete Short Stories of H.G. Wells* was compiled in 1927 the stories now before the reader were omitted. There were various reasons for this. Three of them — "The Queer Story of Brownlow's Newspaper", "Answer to Prayer" and "The New Faust"— had not then been written. Of the remainder, it was apparently felt that they were not of a sufficiently high standard to merit republication in book form. Reading the stories today it is difficult to agree with this judgment. A careful appraisal reveals that the uncollected stories contain much that will bear comparison with Wells at his best.

"Walcote" and "The Devotee of Art" were originally published in the *Science Schools Journal*, founded by Wells himself when a student at the Normal School of Science (now the Imperial College of Science and Technology). "The Devotee of Art" is an ambitious piece of work which was later revised under the title "The Temptation of Harringay". "Walcote" is an early exercise in the Poe manner; his biographer Geoffrey West records that it is "certainly not without incipient narrative and dramatic ability."

"A Misunderstood Artist" and "The Man with a Nose" were both included in *Select Conversations with an Uncle* (1895), a collection of stories and essays which appeared in the same year as *The Time Machine*. Each illustrates the extraordinary range of themes at his command as well as his ability to engage the reader's attention with an apparently casual incident or encounter, as does the next story, "A Family Elopement." "The Thing in No. 7", "Wayde's Essence" and "The Thumbmark" first appeared in the *Pall Mall Budget* in a series of tales published under the title "Single Sitting Stories". It was this series, under the editorship of C. Lewis Hind, which first launched Wells on his highly successful literary career. He recorded later: "I set myself, so encouraged, to the experiment of inventing moving and interesting things that could be given vividly in the little space of eight or ten such pages as this, and for a time I found it a very entertaining pursuit indeed. Mr. Hind's indicating finger had shown me an amusing possibility of the mind."

The next group of stories, by date— "Our Little Neighbour", "The Presence by the Fire", "The Rajah's Treasure", "Le Mari Terrible" and "Mr. Marshall's Doppelganger" — illustrate diverse facets of his skill as a storyteller. They date from the years 1895–7, one of the most creative periods in Wells's life, when he was (in his own words) "writing away for dear life" in order to establish himself on the London literary scene. "The Rajah's Treasure" and "Le Mari Terrible" were included in *Thirty Strange Stories* (1897), a collection published in the United States but not in Britain. "The Presence by the Fire" illustrates Wells's gift for creating an atmosphere of haunting suspense, while "Mr. Marshall's Doppelganger" reveals his abiding affection for the rural England he knew so well as a young man. The setting is probably Midhurst, Sussex, where he lived from 1883–4.

"A Perfect Gentleman on Wheels" is a reminder of his enthusiasm for cycling and should be compared with *The Wheels of Chance* (1896) as an impression of cycling before the advent of the motor car. "The Loyalty of Esau Common" was originally intended as part of a series of critical short stories about the British Army. The project was later abandoned, although in addition to "Esau Common" it yielded another interesting story, "The Land Ironclads". "The Wild Asses of the Devil" illustrates the darker side of Wells's mind. Originally included in *Boon* (1915), though probably written much earlier, it is an entirely characteristic fantasia on the theme of human fallibility. The setting is recognisably Sandgate, near Folkestone, where he lived from 1899–1909.

"The Queer Story of Brownlow's Newspaper", one of the finest stories in this collection, was written in 1932, when his thoughts were turning increasingly to the future. It belongs to the same period as *The Shape of Things to Come* (1933) and indeed is discussed in the preface to that book. Reading the story today, fifty years after it was written, it is fascinating to speculate on Wells's predictions. "Answer to Prayer", written in 1936, is an interesting example of his lifelong preoccupation with matters of belief. Other examples of the genre are "The Story of the Last Trump" and "A Vision of Judgment".

The final story in this collection, "The New Faust", is a reworking of the basic theme of "The Late Mr. Elvesham" (1896). Subtitled "A Film Story", it illustrates his deep interest in the cinema as a medium of expression. Other film scenarios written at this time include *Things to Come* and *Man Who Could Work Miracles*. No film version was made of "The New Faust" though it remains a fascinating example of the visual and dramatic qualities of Wells's fiction.

The publication of the *Uncollected Short Stories of H.G. Wells* is an exciting literary event. Within these nineteen tales there is abundant evidence of his powers as a storyteller and of that unusual combination of imagination and compassion which made him one of the foremost writers of his times.

J.R. Hammond.
Vice-President, H. G. Wells Society

I

The Man with a Nose

"I never see thy face but I think upon hell-fire, and Dives that lived
in purple, for there he is in his robes, burning, burning."

"My nose has been the curse of my life."

The other man started.

They had not spoken before. They were sitting, one at either
end, on that seat on the stony summit of Primrose Hill which
looks towards Regent's Park. It was night. The paths on the
slope below were dotted out by yellow lamps; the Albert-road
was a line of faintly luminous pale green — the tint of gaslight
seen among trees; beyond, the park lay black and mysterious,
and still further, a yellow mist beneath and a coppery hue in the
sky above marked the blaze of the Marylebone thoroughfares.
The nearer houses in the Albert-terrace loomed large and black,
their blackness pierced irregularly by luminous windows.
Above, starlight.

Both men had been silent, lost apparently in their own
thoughts, mere dim black figures to each other, until one had
seen fit to become a voice also, with this confidence.

"Yes," he said, after an interval, "my nose has always stood
in my way, always."

The second man had scarcely seemed to notice the first
remark, but now he peered through the night at his interlocutor.
It was a little man he saw, with face turned towards him.

"I see nothing wrong with your nose."

"If it were luminous you might," said the first speaker.
"However, I will illuminate it."

He fumbled with something in his pocket, then held this
object in his hand. There was a scratch, a streak of greenish
phosphorescent light, and then all the world beyond became
black, as a fusee vesta flared.

There was silence for the space of a minute. An impressive
pause.

"Well?" said the man with the nose, putting his heel on the
light.

I

"I have seen worse," said the second man.

"I doubt it," said the man with the nose; "and even so, it is poor comfort. Did you notice the shape? the size? the colour? Like Snowdon, it has a steep side and a gentle slope. The size is preposterous; my face is like a hen-house built behind a portico. And the tints!"

"It is not all red," said the second man, "anyhow."

"No, there is purple, and blue, '*lapis lazuli*, blue as a vein over the Madonna's breast,' and in one place a greyish mole. Bah! The thing is not a nose at all, but a bit of primordial chaos clapped on to my face. But, being where the nose should be, it gets the credit of its position from unthinking people. There is a gap in the order of the universe in front of my face, a lump of unwrought material left over. In that my true nose is hidden, as a statue is hidden in a lump of marble, until the appointed time for the revelation shall come. At the resurrection — But one must not anticipate. Well, well. I do not often talk about my nose, my friend, but you sat with a sympathetic pose, it seemed to me, and to-night my heart is full of it. This cursed nose! But do I weary you, thrusting my nose into your meditations?"

"If," said the second man, his voice a little unsteady, as though he was moved, "if it eases your mind to talk of your nose, pray talk."

"This nose, I say then, makes me think of the false noses of Carnival times. Your dullest man has but to stick one on, and lo! mirth, wit, and jollity. They are enough to make anything funny. I doubt if even an Anglican bishop could wear one with impunity. Put an angel in one. How would you like one popped on to *you* now? Think of going love-making, or addressing a public meeting, or dying gloriously, in a nose like mine! Angelina laughs in your face, the public laughs, the executioner at your martyrdom can hardly light the faggots for laughing. By heaven! it is no joke. Often and often I have rebelled, and said, 'I will not have this nose!' "

"But what can one do?"

"It is destiny. The bitter tragedy of it is that it is so comic. Only, God knows, how glad I shall be when the Carnival is over, and I may take the thing off and put it aside. The worst has been this business of love. My mind is not unrefined, my body is healthy. I know what tenderness is. But what woman could overlook a nose like mine? How could she shut out her visions of it, and look her love into my eyes, glaring at her over

2

its immensity? I should have to make love through an Inquisitor's hood, with its holes cut for the eyes — and even then the shape would show. I have read, I have been told, I can imagine what a lover's face is like — a sweet woman's face radiant with love. But this Millbank penitentiary of flesh chills their dear hearts."

He broke off suddenly, with loud ferocious curses. A young man who had been sitting very close to a young woman on an adjacent seat, started up and said "Ssh!"

He whom the man with the nose had addressed now spoke. "I have certainly never thought before of a red nose as a sorrowful thing, but as you put it. . . ."

"I thought you would understand. I have had this nose all my life. The outline was done, even though the colour was wanting, in my school days. They called me 'Nosey,' 'Ovid,' 'Cicero,' 'Rhino,' and the 'Excrescence.' It has ripened with the slow years, as fate deepens in the progress of a tragedy. Love, the business of life, is a sealed book to me. To be alone! I would thank heaven. . . . But no! a blind woman could feel the shape of it."

"Besides love," interrupted the young man thoughtfully, "there are other things worth living for — duty. An unattractive nose would not interfere with that. Some people think it is rather more important than love. I admit your loss, of course."

"That only carries out the evidence of your voice, and tells me you are young. My dear young fellow, duty is a very fine thing indeed, but believe me, it is too colourless as a motive. There is no delight in duty. You will know that at my age. And besides, I have an infinite capacity for love and sympathy, an infinite bitterness in this solitude of my soul. I infer that you would moralise on my discontent, but I know I have seen a little of men and things from behind this ambuscade — only a truly artistic man would fall into the sympathetic attitude that attracted me. My life has had even too much of observation in it, and to the systematic anthropologist, nothing tells a man's character more than his pose after dark, when nobody seems watching. As you sit, the black outline of you is clear against the sky. Ah! *now* you are sitting stiffer. But you are no Calvinist. My friend, the best of life is its delights, and the best of delights is loving and being loved. And for that — this nose! Well, there are plenty of second-best things. After dark I can forget the monster a little. Spring is delightful, air on the Downs is delightful; it is

3

fine to see the stars circling in the sky, while lying among the heather. Even this London sky is soothing at night, though the edge is all inflamed. The shadow of my nose is darkest by day. But to-night I am bitter, because of to-morrow."

"Why, to-morrow?" said the younger man.

"I have to meet some new people to-morrow," said the man with the nose. "There is an odd look, a mingling of amusement and pity, I am only too familiar with. My cousin, who is a gifted hostess, promises people my nose as a treat."

"Yes, that must be bad for you," said the young man.

And then the silence healed again, and presently the man with the nose got up and passed into the dimness upon the slope of the hill. The young man watched him vanish, wondering vainly how it would be possible to console a soul under such a burthen.

2

A Perfect Gentleman
on Wheels

It was the stirring of spring, the tendency of fashion, and the ghost of a sneer drove him to do it. More particularly the ghost of a sneer. It was the tragedy of his life that he admired her, and he struggled against her in vain. She was frankly— antipathetic. You might have called her anything before you would have called her *chic*; at times he had to admit that she was— to tell the dreadful truth— "robust." Moreover, the most exquisite epigrams, the prettiest turns of wit, would often as not simply make her stare and laugh— only too evidently *at* him. And yet when the healthy Philistine school-girl asked him, "Do you ever venture beyond the Park, Mr. Crampton?" it sufficed. He told his mother plainly his honour was involved. And an irreverent porter saw him — already heated — wheeling his machine upstairs from the Sutton platform — and there are few things less adapted to go upstairs with any pretence to grace — on his way to Brighton and her.

His machine, like himself, was a little overdressed— we are far from a sound criticism of bicycles— chocolate enamelled it was, with translucent mudguards and the daintiest white handles, and the gear case was of filmy celluloid, with a sort of metal dab like a medal upon it. He wore a cocked hat— or at least one of those brown felt hats that ought to be called cocked hats, whatever the proper name for them may be — and to distinguish himself from the common cycling cad, among other reasons, he wore trousers. The brown of his clothing was apt to his machine, and his tie white and pretty. And when the vulgar cabman outside Sutton station called "New Woman" after him, he pretended not to hear, and went on mounting his machine all across the road. He was quite a sight to see riding up the road towards Belmont, and the sun was so struck by his spick-and-span appearance that he picked out every line of enamel and metal on him and dazzled the passer-by therewith. "Something like a thing to shine on!" said the sun. "Just look at this!" and "Did you ever?" in the excess of his admiration.

He had begun his ride from London to Brighton at Sutton — which was generous treatment for London in the geographical sense. His mother — he was her only son — had gone to Brighton by train. The Fentons were there also, and the juxtaposition had its quality of design. His mother had devoted her life to him; she held that he was delicate, and knowing the dreadfulness of public schools almost as well as Mr. Oscar Browning, had kept him by her under a progressive series of amenable tutors — making a perfect gentleman of him according to her lights. And Madge Fenton, with her half-share in Fenton's Safe Cure, was just the fit mate for the sole proprietor of Crampton's Meat Juice. It was quite a mother's plan, to marry her son and yet keep him in the family. And certainly he appreciated Madge, though *her* attitude was a little doubtful. Yet the steady pressure of her elders was bound to win in the long run, and she was a good girl — as times go.

The road from Sutton to Burgh Heath looks like any other road on a map. But unlike the generality of roads known to Mr. Crampton, it persistently went up hill. It was already going up hill at Sutton station, and it went on pretty steeply for a space, but with an air of its being a last effort. Then round a bend came a view of a huge Industrial Home, and another last effort. Then a clear interval, even down hill, to Belmont station, and then it started off again fresh as a daisy. It went up hill visibly for a mile to Banstead station, and then, masked by trees, it continued to go up hill. Mr. Crampton was surprised, but the day was young and his man had oiled and adjusted his machine to a nicety. So he stuck to it — riding steady, and swinging a cigarette in the disengaged hand. Until presently a Bounder, with a machine that went clank, became audible behind him.

To Mr. Crampton the idea of being overhauled by a member of the lower classes was distasteful, and relying on the clank and the excellence of his machine, he threw away the cigarette and quickened his pace. Thereupon the Bounder rang his bell — it was a beast of a cheap bell — and the clanking grew more frequent and louder, until it was close behind Mr. Crampton. After a sharp spurt, Mr. Crampton decided that he would not race after all, and the Bounder drew alongside. He was quite the most dreadful type of Bounder, with a machine with a loose mudguard and a peckled bell; he had a very dirty suit of C.T.C. grey, and a perspiring red face with a strip of damp hair across

6

his forehead. And he had the cheek to speak to Mr. Crampton!

"Pretty Jigger!" said the Bounder.

Mr. Crampton was so startled, he wobbled, and almost collided. "I beg your pardon!" he said, in a repressive tone.

"Nice-looking machine you've got."

Mr. Crampton was quite at a loss for words. But he was determined to shut the fellow up promptly. "I'm afraid I can't say the same of yours," he said at length.

"No, it isn't up to much," said the Bounder cheerfully. "Are you going far? Because, if so —"

Two Girls (possible Nice Girls) appeared riding down towards them. They might think that he and the Bounder were travelling together! "It's no business of yours," said Mr. Crampton, "where I'm going." And something indistinct about "damned impertinence!"

"Lord!" said the Bounder. "No offence." It took him a minute to digest. Then he said something over his shoulder to Mr. Crampton that was lost, and putting his head down below his shoulders, went clanking off at a great pace, his shoulders moving with his feet in a manner entirely despicable.

Mr. Crampton rode quite erect, and with only one hand on the handle, to show that he was not racing, until the girls were well past him, and then he dismounted. This eternal hill was tiresome, and he did not want to overtake the Bounder. Walking, one could notice the fine growth of green with which the hedges were speckled, and the gum-exuding chestnut buds; and the dead nettles were all in flower. In fact, it was a pleasant change from the saddle for a man who was not a scorcher.

And at last he came to Burgh Heath. As this seemed to be a sort of village green, he mounted again. Some way along was a little sweetstuff shop, and outside was the Bounder's machine. The Bounder was in the doorway, with his hands in his pockets, eating. He looked round at Mr. Crampton, and immediately looked away again, with a hollow pretence of self-esteem.

And away down a hill, Mr. Crampton was passed by a tandem bicycle. He overtook its riders, a girl and a man, walking the next ascent. They seemed to be father and daughter, the father a sturdy red-bearded man with very fat legs, and the daughter decidedly pretty. She was dressed in greenish grey, and had red hair. Mr. Crampton was very glad indeed that he had got rid of the Bounder forthwith. He had to set his teeth to get up the hill, but of course it was impossible to dismount, and then came a run down, and then a long gentle slope that was rather trying, with a pretty girl on a tandem behind, that is, to keep one in the saddle. Reigate Hill came none too soon to give Mr. Crampton a decent excuse for dismounting. So he put the machine carefully where it looked well on the turf, and took out his silver cigarette case, and was in his attitude ready, looking over the clustering town and broad blue Weald, as the tandem couple came walking down the hill. So far the ride had been very pleasant.

After that the Bounder, hot and panting. He came towards the turf as if contemplating a lounge, and his eye caught the chocolate bicycle. He glanced swiftly up at Mr. Crampton, and went incontinently down the hill towards the town, visibly discomfited.

Mr. Crampton lunched in Reigate. It was in the afternoon that his adventures really began — as he rode towards Crawley. The morning's ride had told on him, and three gates had the honour of supporting him for leisurely intervals between Reigate and Horley. Cyclists became frequent, and as they went by during his sessions on the gate, he smoked ostentatiously or (after he had smoked sufficiently) sketched in a little morocco-bound sketch-book — just to show he was not simply resting. And among others a very pretty girl flashed by — unaccompanied.

Now Mr. Crampton, in spite of his regard for Madge, was not averse to dreams of casual romance. And the bicycle in its earlier phases has a peculiar influence upon the imagination. To ride out from the familiar locality, into strange roads stretching away into the unknown, to be free to stop or go on, irrespective of hour or companion, inevitably brings the adventurous side uppermost. And Mr. Crampton, descending from his gate and mounting, not two minutes after she had passed, presently overtook her near the crossroad to Horley, wheeling her machine.

She had a charmingly cut costume, and her hair was a pleasant brown, and her ear, as one came riding up behind her, was noticeably pretty. She had punctured the tyre of her hind wheel; it ran flat and flaccid — the case was legible a hundred yards off.

Now this is the secret desire of all lone men who go down into the country on wheels. The proffered help, the charming talk, the idyllic incident! Who knows what delightful developments?

So that a great joy came to Mr. Crampton. He dismounted a little way behind her, advanced gracefully, proffered the repair outfit in his wallet. He had never attempted to repair a tyre before, and so he felt confident of his ability. The young lady was inclined to be distant at first (which was perfectly correct of her), but seeing that it was four miles to Crawley, and Mr. Crampton a mere boy and evidently of a superior class, she presently accepted his services. So coming conveniently to a convenient grassy place at the cross-road, Mr. Crampton turned the machine over on its saddle and handles, severely bruising his knee as he did so, and went quietly and methodically to work — it being then about three o'clock in the afternoon, and the sun very bright and warm.

He talked to her easily. Where had she punctured? She did not quite know, she had only just noticed that the tyre was "all flabby." "A very unpleasant discovery," said Mr. Crampton. "We must see just precisely what is the matter."

"It's very kind of you," she said. "Are you sure you can spare the time?"

"I'm merely running down to Brighton," he said. "I couldn't think of leaving you in this predicament."

Mr. Crampton had of course no mechanic's knowledge of bicycles, but he knew the things were very simple. He knew he had to remove the tyre, and it did not take him long to discover that in order to remove the tyre he would have to remove the wheel. How to get the wheel off was a little puzzling at first — it was evident the chain would have to come away. That involved operations with a dress guard and a gear case. "It's an inductive process," said Mr. Crampton lightly — concealing a faint qualm of doubt, and setting to work on the gear case.

"They're frightfully complicated things," she said.

"These machinery people make them rather stupidly," said Mr. Crampton.

"*I* shouldn't *dare* take the thing to pieces as you are doing."

"It's very simple, really."

"I think men are *always* so much cleverer than girls at this sort of thing."

Mr. Crampton did not answer for a second.

"You've blackened your fingers!" she said.

It was very nice and friendly of her, but a little distracting. She kept stepping about on the growing circle of nuts, chains, screw-hammers, washers, and so forth about Mr. Crampton, and made many bright, intelligent little remarks that required answering. And she really was pretty. Mr. Crampton still continued to enjoy the incident in spite of his blackened hands, and the heat of the day, and the quite remarkable softness of the nuts on her machine. "If we *are* better at machine-mending and that sort of thing," he said, "you have your consolations."

"I don't think so."

"The emotions," said Mr. Crampton.

"But men have emotions."

"As girls have bicycles," said Mr. Crampton, with the air of a neat thing, mislaying the pin of the chain, and proceeding to pull out the wheel.

The removal of the tyre was the turning-point of the affair. It simply would not come off the rim. "*These* detachable!" said Mr. Crampton. He had to ask her to pull, and the struggle was violent for a moment, and a spoke got bent. Then he pinched her finger very severely. He knew the operation depended upon a knack, and as he was ashamed of not knowing the knack, he pretended to be doing something else when a man cyclist went by. Three little children came by and seemed profoundly interested until Mr. Crampton stopped and stared steadily at them. Then each began edging behind the other, and so they receded. And a tramp offered ingenious but impracticable suggestions until Mr. Crampton gave him sixpence to take them away. Then came the Tandem he had seen in the morning going Londonward, and the old gentleman insisted on knowing what was the matter. Beastly officious of him! "We can't remove the tyre," said the young lady — a little needlessly, Crampton thought.

"Simple enough," said the old gentleman, in abominable taste. It *was* simple — in his hands. In a minute the tyre lay detached.

"*I* can manage now, thanks," said Mr. Crampton, rather stiffly.

"Quite sure?" said the old gentleman.

"Quite," said Mr. Crampton, with a quiet stare, and the old gentleman mounted his machine. For of course Mr. Crampton trusted to the directions on his repair outfit, as any one would.

"Thank you very much indeed," said the young lady.

"No trouble at all," said the old gentleman, and off he rode.

The next misunderstanding was entirely due to the silly, vague way in which the directions on the box were given. Really you had to stick the round patch thing on to the puncture, but Mr. Crampton read rather carelessly, and first of all cut out a circular place in the air chamber, and seeing it was not quite round, he cut it a little larger, and so on, until it was a little too big for the patch thing. The young lady had been silent for the last ten minutes or so, watching Mr. Crampton's face, but now she asked suddenly, "Are you sure that is the right thing to do?"

"It says so on the box," said Mr. Crampton, looking up with a smile. "But really I don't see how we are to manage it quite."

"Do you know," said the young lady, "I wanted to be in Crawley by four."

It was a little rude of her, but Mr. Crampton looked at his watch — it was five minutes past four! "Dear me!" he said agreeably; "the time *has* flown." And suddenly he remembered he was twenty-six miles from Brighton.

"I think, do you know," said the young lady, "if you don't mind, I will wheel my machine, after all. It seems such a long job mending it. And really, in Crawley the Man —"

"These Local Fellows aren't always quite reliable. I'm frightfully sorry, you know, not to have got it right just at once, but —"

"It was very kind of you to try," she said.

"Do you know," said Mr. Crampton, "even now —" For the thing really interested him. His idea was to try a piece of paper smeared with solution, but it did not work, and at a quarter past four he began putting the machine together, with nothing but a neat circular opening cut in the air-tube of the tyre to show for his wasted hour. His interest was fading, and the girl's manner was not so nice as it had been. And curiously enough the wheel would not go on right, and there was a difficulty about the chain. One or two of the little nut things may have lost themselves in the grass, and — trivial though they were — this complicated the business. Mr. Crampton was becoming painfully aware that his hands were black and his cuffs crumpled. He suddenly felt tired and disgusted at the whole absurd incident, and seeing the growing impatience of the girl, he hurried the rebuilding indiscreetly, using his wrench as a hammer when necessary. The eyes of passers-by seemed ironical.

Bicycles are odd things. He made it look all right — except the gear-case, which he had trodden on, but when he stood it up, right way up, the chain flapped about on the gear-case, and the wheel would not go round.

He tried what a little force would do, but it only produced curious clanking noises.

It was a most disappointing incident, and although the girl was indisputably pretty, curiously devoid of any real romantic quality. "It doesn't seem right, quite, *yet*," she said.

"I'm afraid not," said Mr. Crampton rather red in the face, holding the machine by saddle and handle, and looking at it in a speculative way. It was really rather a difficult situation, and he was trying to think what to do next. It came of being a gentleman, of course, and chivalrous. Bounders would have ridden by in the first place, without attempting to help. He wanted very badly to swear, and it was very clear indeed in his mind that he ought to be riding on.

His self-control was admirable. "I'm afraid it's no go," he said, looking up and smiling.

She was looking quite straightly at him. There was no appearance of anger in her manner, but she remarked quietly: "I don't think you ought to have touched my machine. I'm afraid you know very little about them."

Mr. Crampton perceived at once that she was not a lady.

All the more reason, he told himself, that he should assert himself a gentleman. "It seems to me," he said, "that I can do very little good in this case."

"It seems so to me," she said, annoyed to find him not humiliated.

There came a rhythmic clanking on the road, and the red, damp-haired Bounder in grey, whom Mr. Crampton had snubbed at Banstead, going Londonward now, and riding laboriously, drew up. "Ullo!" he said, softly, to himself, and as he passed, "Nothing wrong?"

Positively she answered him. Mr. Crampton did not notice it, because he was looking at the machine, but she must have done so.

The Bounder was already some yards down the road, but he dismounted with such alacrity that he almost tumbled over. He flung his machine into the hedge in a fine careless way, and came back. "What is it?" he said.

"Nothing," said Mr. Crampton, full of angry shame.

"Had a tumble, Miss?" said the Bounder, not at all abashed, with his eye on the bent mudguard.

"I can manage very well, thank you," said Mr. Crampton.

"Let's have a look at the Jigger," said the Bounder,

12

advancing; and suddenly became aware that he had met this obstructive person in brown before. He looked at the girl.

"Please let the gentleman see," said the young lady quietly.

At that Mr. Crampton's temper gave way entirely. "Very well," he said quite crossly. "I understood *I* was to mend your machine. I've wasted an hour on it."

"Steady on," said the Bounder very quietly, bending down and looking at the machine.

"I didn't know you wanted to stop every man that came along," said Mr. Crampton, suddenly exasperated to insult.

"Steady on," said the Bounder again.

Mr. Crampton replied with a look of freezing contempt.

"When you were rude to me," said the Bounder, looking up, "I let you alone. But if you're going to be rude to this Young Lady, I shall just punch your 'ead. See? I'm an engine-fitter, and it don't take *that* to see you've been pretty near knocking all the quality out of a vally'ble machine."

Mr. Crampton was breathless with anger.

"I'm quite prepared to *pay* for any damage I've done," he said.

Neither of them had the manners to answer, though he stood quite a minute. Trembling with indignation, Mr. Crampton picked up his machine, mounted a little clumsily, and rode off. He rode very fast until he was round the bend — just to show how angry he was. For a space he was boiling with rage. Then he laughed aloud in a sardonic fashion. "Of all possible experiences!" he said. "Ha-ha! And this comes of trying to help a fellow-creature!"

The sardonic mood remained. He hated every human being on the road and every human being in Crawley, both on the right-hand side and on the left. Most of them, from their manner, seemed to be aware of his recent indignities. He rested at Crawley an hour, hating people quietly but steadily, and thinking of alternatives to his sayings and doings with the Bounder and the Young Lady. It was six when he rode on again, and the sun was setting. A mile out of Crawley he came to a long dark hill. Twilight came as a surprise, and with it came an acute sense of fatigue. He dismounted. Presently he mounted again. It was difficult to decide which progress was most tiring — afoot or awheel. And this was pleasure! An acute realisation of the indescribable vulgarity of cycling came into his mind. A dirty, fatiguing pursuit that put one at the mercy of every impudent Cad one met. He began to stamp with his feet, and use words that even his mother's care had not prevented his learning. The road before him was dark, interminable, impossible. He saw a milestone dimly, and went to it with a lingering hope that Providence might have interposed on his behalf and cut out a dozen miles or so, but there it was: "Brighton 20 miles."

And then comes a mystery. Within ninety minutes Mr. Crampton was alighting outside the Best Society Hotel at Brighton. There is a railway station at Three Bridges, but I hold that an author should respect the secrets of his characters. There was no incriminatory ticket on his machine, and he never gave any one the slightest ground for supposing that he did anything but cycle the whole way. His hat was awry, his clothes dirty, his linen crumpled, and his hands and his face and his tie were defiled with black from the young lady's chain.

His mother received him with effusion. She had grown nervous with the darkness. "My dear, dear Cecil," she said, advancing. "But how white and tired you look! And the dust upon you!" She laid caressing fat hands upon his shoulder.

"*Don't*," said Mr. Crampton briefly, and flung himself into a chair — scowling.

"You might give a chap something to drink," he said, "instead of standing there."

But after dinner he recovered, and talked to her. Among other things he admitted he liked Madge, and seemed to take his mother's timid suggestions in a sympathetic spirit. "But I wish she didn't bicycle," he said; "it's a bit — common."

They lunched next day with the Fentons. He waited for his opportunity to score his point, making no attempt to lead up to it, and so it did not come off until late in the afternoon. Mrs. Crampton would have boasted to Madge of his manliness in riding the Whole Way, but for his express prohibition.

"No," he said quite calmly, in answer to some remark. "I didn't train. I wheeled down."

Madge looked quite surprised. "Fifty-two miles!" she said.

"I don't know the distance," said Mr. Crampton. "It didn't seem so exceedingly long."

The increase in her respect was swift and evident. "How long did it take you?"

"Six — seven hours. I started about midday. But I didn't scorch, you know. And I stopped about half an hour mending a girl's tyre."

He tried to look as though he had done nothing extraordinary.

"Here's Ethel, of all people!" said Mrs. Fenton, rising. "My dear!"

Mr. Crampton looked up, and there in the doorway was the heroine of the punctured tyre. . . . Madge rose, too, to welcome her friend, and missed his expression. "And here is Cousin Cecil," she said, introducing Mr. Crampton. The new-comer advanced brightly, stared, hesitated, and bowed coldly.

Mrs. Crampton never quite understood the business, because her son was not only reticent, but extremely irritable when questioned. Evidently the young people had met before, and were under considerable constraint. She is inclined to think, from the subsequent incidents, that Ethel was a designing sort of girl, who set Madge against him with the idea of securing him for herself. In that, at any rate, she was disappointed. But the Brighton gathering was certainly a failure, and Mr. Crampton is still not engaged. Yet, seeing his position, it is odd some girl has not snapped him up. Madge (silly girl!) married a young doctor three months ago.

3
Wayde's Essence

WAYDE was a man greatly envied. For seventeen years his life had been success — not that common success that consists only in a run of favourable accidents, but success honestly worked for; success that came to him of his own compulsion; the success of a strong and capable man. He had written well, married well — the girl was at once the sensation and heiress of her year — won a hopeless election; and though notoriously a poor man of mediocre birth, secured a place at last — the only man of mediocre birth therein — in an advanced Radical Ministry. No wonder all those other poor men of mediocre birth who chanced to be writing political leaders found much that was fortuitous in his ascent. But the fact remains that Wayde was a very brilliant man, and fully deserved his winnings. He sat before the fire, staring into the red coals, and admitted as much to himself. His left hand, resting on the table, held a little white glass bottle full of a mobile, fluorescent, lavender-tinted liquid.

"Wonderful stuff!" he said to old Manningtree, with a faint smile; "I wonder what you put into this Water of Success."

"You might wonder all day," said Manningtree, "and still be surprised, at the end of it, when I told you."

The two men relapsed into a comfortable silence. It is the true test of friendship, that comfortable silence, when the bothering battledore and shuttlecock of conversation are put aside, and we enjoy a companionable solitude. Wayde's mind went back through the past seventeen years, a pleasant flight of reminiscence. Tomorrow he had to introduce a much-ridiculed Bill prohibiting the nude in art. It was an absurd Bill, not intended to pass, but introduced to satisfy a serious and important faction; and the task of producing it was, he understood, a compliment to his dexterous insincerity. He was the only man on his side capable of the necessary blend of epigram — which the serious faction would not understand, and earnestness — which they did — and he intended to astonish his rivals by making on this unpropitious occasion a brilliant display, changing from poking fun to propitiation with the

16

perplexing swiftness of the colour changes in shot silk. He knew exactly how he would do it. And on Tuesday he had to receive three deputations, mutually hostile, on the Rayner's Den question. He had no doubt he should dispose of them successfully and satisfy them all. Wednesday he dined with the Premier — he smiled to think with what trepidation he would have contemplated such a festival twenty years ago. Then Thursday — Thursday was really a great day. Thursday would raise him a step in the estimation of several millions of people, for on Thursday he had to smash and pulverise Braun, and he had not the slightest doubt he would smash and pulverise Braun, who was going to make trouble upon the foreign policy of the Government. Possibly the Government had erred in one or two little matters — Wayde was not Foreign Secretary — but the Opposition had certainly erred far more seriously in putting up Braun— against *him*. "Yet, twenty years ago!" thought Wayde. He tried to imagine himself smashing Braun twenty years ago.

And that, indeed, brings us at once to the gist of the story. The curious thing is that eighteen years ago Wayde had been, in his own opinion, a conspicuous failure in life, a man of thirty-one who had done nothing — or rather, what is worse, done many things very poorly. Judicious people had pronounced him clever, an eminent critic who had met him by accident had suspected him of genius, and his sisters believed in him. That much, and a double second at Cambridge, a third place in a chess tournament, a novel that had sold to the extent of two thousand copies, a volume of critical essays, some unsuccessful Extension lecturing, and some futile appearances upon the local political platform, completed his record— respectable, no doubt, but scarcely augury of the Cabinet Minister at forty-eight. Wayde looked affectionately at the little bottle in his hand.

In those days Wayde had been anything but a success— not even a social success. The fact was he lacked "nerve," suffered, as we might say, from constitutional Doubt. Old ladies considered him a nice young man, but shy, new young ladies called him weedy. His conversation was an epitome of his life, a series of hesitations, punctuated by good things ill said. His book had been a vivid work in the manuscript; in the proof he refined all his points and altered the plot until it was so subtle that nobody appreciated it. He was a profound chess scholar, and had succumbed chiefly, he averred, to an odour of garlic that emanated from Botch, the Teutonic champion. At thirty Wayde seemed already inclined to take a diminishing interest in life, and a spinsterhood of natural history, local chess, and refined criticism seemed his destiny rather than the Cabinet.

It was old Manningtree who had saved him. Salvation fell upon him suddenly, seventeen or eighteen years ago, in a billiard-room. Wayde missed an elongated but easy cannon by a hair's-breadth. He bit off the head of a weak curse.

"That's it," said Manningtree.

"I beg your pardon," said Wayde — he was always begging someone's pardon in those days.

"Not the slightest doubt of it," said Manningtree. He stood chalking his cue and regarding Wayde with a critical eye. "You are a very interesting case, Wayde."

Wayde detested being looked at. "What do you mean?" he said. "No new disease, I hope."

"A constitutional disproportion," said Manningtree. "If — between ourselves — I might commit a breach of professional etiquette, trench on your proper cherub's province, and proffer advice . . ."

"Whaddy says I'm as sound as a roach," said Wayde.

Manningtree struggled into a sitting position upon the edge of the board and took delicate aim. "You know" — cannon — "I take rather an interest in you, Wayde. You're curious. That Botch, for instance, wasn't your master at chess. I've studied his games." Manningtree remained sitting on the board and seemed to meditate chess for a moment. "Confound it! You could have knocked him into a cocked-hat."

"So I thought," said Wayde. "Only . . ."

"That's it," said Manningtree again. "That's precisely it."

"What?" said Wayde. "I was going to say his garlic . . ."

"But it wouldn't be true. The trouble is, to put it frankly, the disproportion of your character and capacity. You suspect as much yourself. You are always tripping yourself up. Some subtle doubt is always arising just at the wrong moment and spoiling your stroke. You lost every one of those games because at a critical point in each one of them you tried to hedge. You think, 'I may miss.' That means missing for anyone. It kills your action, takes all the spirit out of it, and leaves the corpse of it for your performance. If it were not for *that*, Wayde . . ."

"Well?"

"You would be a brilliantly successful man. In fact, without any flattery, I honestly believe you a man of very exceptional capacity."

"But not of exceptional character," said Wayde, smiling. "It's a pity about the character."

"It's not a hopeless one by any means. Capacity is a question of brains; character —, well, it's physiological, chiefly circulation and digestion. That, indeed, is why I am talking to you." He paused. "I should not talk to a hopeless case."

Wayde stared at him. It was an unusual occasion. He was taken aback, failed to grasp the situation all at once.

"You've left yourself comfortably off," he said, looking at the board. Manningtree got down and walked round the table.

For perhaps three minutes neither spoke a word. Manningtree went on serenely with a fine healthy break. Then Wayde coughed. "I've never looked at this hesitation of mine before in the light of a disease. I know perfectly well what you mean. I've felt it lots of times, though I've never seen it quite so clearly as you put it. Just before I'm going to do anything I feel that I shall muddle it, and then — I'm hanged if I don't muddle it. The brutal confidence of that German Botch knocked me to pieces. The thing's grown on me. Whenever I set out to do anything I begin to anticipate the moment of hesitation, and down I go. I was better at school, but even there I began to muff my bowling in my last year. But, as I say, I regarded it as a kind of mental curse . . ."

"Nerves," said Manningtree — "solar plexus."

"Then do you really mean to say?" . . . began Wayde.

"Yes, I do," said Manningtree. "It's amenable to physic. Why it should be I don't know, but there is a certain drug —"

"Faith pilule!" said Wayde.

"It's not a pilule at all. The stuff is an alkaloid — chiefly. Anyhow, there's not the slightest doubt that it smooths out that particular mental rut that jolts your springs, chokes the thought that trips you before it can get born; substitutes I CAN, loud and clear, for 'I'm afraid — presently — I shall falter — or twist. . . .'"

"I can scarcely believe it," said Wayde.

"You have a patient before you," said Manningtree. And he resumed his easy procession to the end of the game.

"I say," said Wayde, after another gap in the conversation. "Well?"

"I would like to try that medicine, anyhow."

"Unhappily, you can't."

"But I thought you told me because . . ."

"I don't know how to prepare it quite," said Manningtree. "I have precious little left. The way I came by it is peculiar . . . ninety-eight, game."

"Surely you hope?" said Wayde. "Or . . ."

"I hope," said old Manningtree replacing his cue in the stand, and fixing his bright little eyes for a moment on Wayde's face. "And I am more than half disposed to let *you* have some if I do hit upon it." He surveyed Wayde in silence. "But" — he spoke with measured emphasis — "*it is scarcely the drug one feels disposed to sell for a guinea and good-bye.*"

He stared at Wayde for a moment longer, and then turned, clasping his hands behind his back, and paced slowly out of the room with the air of a man who suddenly doubted his wisdom. He left Wayde staring.

Wayde remembered that conversation very vividly to-night, and how he watched for and waylaid Manningtree to hear more of this remarkable medicine. Manningtree pooh-poohed it next day, declared the thing was after-dinner garrulousness, that the alkaloid was quite unprocurable. It had been prepared by a *Salpêtriere* man who died suddenly. It *might*, by good luck turn up. He was looking for it. Certainly it had done *him* a world of good. In that tantalising interview Wayde seemed to himself more helpless and futile than ever. And then Manningtree began to offer half-hints of success, Wayde became franker in his advances; Manningtree smiled and rebuffed him. At last Wayde got to entreaties. To begin with, he had half doubted the possibility of drugging away diffidence, but he forgot all that in the ardour of pursuit. In the end he begged Manningtree to name his own terms — for he felt that this essence was really the essence of his life. It was rather a curious wooing.

"For you," said Manningtree, "it would certainly be the Water of Happiness. Out of a hanger-on, a dumb man in the gallery, it will make you a capable actor in the drama of public life —"

"Anything," said Wayde.

"You will consult me, then, in all the vital turnings of your career? — supposing I can get the stuff — and I fancy I can now."

"Willingly."

"You will give me your note of hand for £7,000, payable when you become a Cabinet Minister?"

"A Cabinet Minister!"

"Of course. You're not such a genius as all that. You'll get it safe enough." And that was all he demanded. It seemed trivial enough, balanced against the other prospect.

Wayde had been put off so much that he had expected some dishonourable condition, some appalling impossibility. He closed at once with Manningtree, and in the course of a week had swallowed his first dose.

So it came about that, seventeen years ago he had tasted of success for the first time, had for the first time in his life gone straight at his goal without doubt of himself or his success, and had won, and had continued to win. His character seemed absolutely inverted. He became prompt and skilful, gained a reputation for exceptional strength of will. Assurance had been his one thing needful. And here he was, in the smoking-room of his creator, a man of weight, a man publicly praised, and blamed, and hated, the centre of a thousand interests, a leading character, a most interesting character in the incessant novel of political life.

"I wonder," said Manningtree, breaking a lengthy meditation.

"What?" said Wayde.

"If you are fit to run alone." His eye fell on the little phial.

"No, thank you!" said Wayde, smiling.

"It's wonderful stuff."

"It is, indeed."

"It's made another man of you. Or rather, to do you justice, it's pushed aside a wrapping, and showed the man you might always have been. It's given you heart— pluck— confidence."

"It has," said Wayde.

"Well . . ."

"Yes?"

"I think I will. That physic, Wayde, that Elixir of Success, is — distilled water."

"*What?*"

"Distilled water, ingeniously tinted to give it a respectable air."

"You mean to say that this drug, this alkaloid that has made me all that I am, this —"

"Distilled water — once or twice at least common drinking-water . . . from the New River."

"You mean to say —"

"I've said it," said Manningtree, repentance dawning upon him as he flicked a dangerously long ash from his cigar into the fire.

Wayde gasped and stared at him. There was an awkward pause. Manningtree's bright eyes watched his patient askance. Then the old doctor said a certain word to himself, with infinite emphasis.

Wayde stood up, and thrust his elbow upon the mantel-shelf. A look of terror was in his eyes. "I say!" he said, "I don't understand this. Do you really mean, Manningtree, that you have been *fooling* me all these years?"

With an impatient gesture Manningtree flung his cigar into the fire. He knew now that he had made an irrevocable mistake. There was a silence.

"For seventeen years," said Wayde, slowly, and staring at him, "I have been dancing on the edge of an abyss."

"If I were not an infernal fool," said Manningtree, "if I had not suffered from this momentary smoking-room incontinence, you would have danced at the end of the chapter. I forgot what you used to be for a moment, you looked so ruddy and prosperous."

"Pure water!"

"And colouring matter. Look here, Wayde, don't stand and stare at me. Sit down and listen calmly. Look the thing squarely in the face. You are, I tell you, a man of exceptional capacity, but you were born diffident; you had a kind of congenital fixed idea. 'I can't,' running through your mind. You were really constitutionally mesmerised — like so many 'weak' people. I have seen hypnotised men told they could not step across a chalked line upon the floor, and forthwith they couldn't — merely the result of a suggestion skilfully made. I dare say you have seen the same. Well — You had a predisposition to modesty, and a few of the inevitable failures of youth had practically done for you, made a mere piece of social driftwood of you — when I became interested in you."

"Well?"

"I hypnotised you. Practically. Wayde, you have been hypnotised seventeen years. For it is really hypnotism. I planted a suggestion in your mind — I flatter myself I did it skilfully — that a certain drug I should presently exhibit would change your 'I cannot' into 'I can.' You took a lot of angling. If I had given you the stuff when first I told you — it was in

Murché's billiard-room, I remember — you would have doubted about it, taken it, shaken your head, and gone on as you were going. So I made it inaccessible, made you anxious to get it, seemed disinclined to let you have it. You remember that time? You only got it when I was satisfied your suspicion of it had been completely forgotten in the worry and exasperation of a prolonged pursuit. You clutched it at last."

"You might almost say I gorged the hook," said Wayde.

"If you take it that way you are finished, Wayde. Anyhow, you went at things and did them. Confound you! You have had a good time. Unless you are a spiritless cur you will have a good time still. And don't you see you have really only realised your own ability? You can go on doing things —"

"If I can keep my faith in myself," said Wayde, staring down into the fire. "If only . . . I can keep my faith in myself." He knitted his brows. "What the devil did you tell me for?"

Manningtree watched him narrowly.

"Faith," said Wayde, "do you know, I was just indulging in a retrospect. By Faith I have moved mountains. . . . And the thing was a mere amulet, as silly a contrivance as one of King Louis' lead Virgins, or some Monte Carlo charm. By Faith . . ."

"The trouble is," he said, presently, smiling greyly at Manningtree, "that some of the mountains are still in transit. The weight of them falls upon me suddenly. Can I . . .?"

"My dear fellow, you are just the man you were fifteen minutes ago. You are just as capable . . ."

"You forget that one little idea is knocked askew," said Wayde; "the keystone, perhaps."

A long silence. Deep thought, keen watchfulness.

"God forgive you, man!" Wayde burst out passionately, speaking loudly, with a catch in his voice. "*Why* did you tell me? Pure water! There suddenly opens below me all those gulfs I felt secure from. How you must have laughed at my self-assurance! My tongue, I see now, may lose its cunning at any moment. I have only been kept from stumbling by the belief that I could not stumble. And now you have cut that away. I feel like a somnambulist suddenly awakened while he stands upon the highest pinnacle of some monstrous building."

He put his hand to his forehead.

"Bah!" cried Manningtree, dryly. "It's only funk — this. Of course, I ought to have held my tongue. But you will forget yourself to-morrow in the House . . ."

"Only funk! My dear man, you have done the mischief. Don't try to undo it by such clumsy devices. Was ever anything the matter with me in those old days except funk? Water! Of course I shall doubt — of course! You have swung me over the precipice, and now you have cut the string. Damnation! That infernal speech to-morrow and Thursday! Oh, Manningtree!" He was crying.

In a paroxysm of feeble rage he caught up the little bottle and flung it furiously into the fire, smashing it to atoms. Then he turned towards the door. Manningtree sprang to his feet.

"Wayde!" he cried. "Stop! I have been joking! That drug is really . . ."

Wayde looked over his shoulder into the doctor's eyes and his trembling lips smiled wanly. "Too late, Manningtree," he said. "I know that joke now," and with that he went on out of the room. The last the doctor saw of him was a gesture of impotent despair.

Old Manningtree stood — one hand on the mantel-board — staring at the baize door as it oscillated back to quiet again. Then he sat down with a grunt, and looked into the fire, amidst which the splinters of glass glowed redly. "What devil possessed me to prick that bladder?" he said, presently. "How infernally casual all our graver actions are!"

"It was my gas inflated him, anyhow," he remarked to himself, in the middle of his next cigar. "And anyhow he has had a very good time for seventeen years. But he is done for."

"What a howling smash he will make of it now! . . . We must call it influenza. Or overwork. And he looked so solid and strong, too, as he sat there, thinking! . . . What an arrant coward! Simply because he felt sure he would win. . . . Heaven save me from these cankering fears!"

4
The Queer Story of
Brownlow's Newspaper

I CALL this a Queer Story because it is a story without an explanation. When I first heard it, in scraps, from Brownlow I found it queer and incredible. But — it refuses to remain incredible. After resisting and then questioning and scrutinizing and falling back before the evidence, after rejecting all his evidence as an elaborate mystification and refusing to hear any more about it, and then being drawn to reconsider it by an irresistible curiosity and so going through it all again, I have been forced to the conclusion that Brownlow, so far as he can tell the truth, has been telling the truth. But it remains queer truth, queer and exciting to the imagination. The more credible his story becomes the queerer it is. It troubles my mind. I am fevered by it, infected not with germs but with notes of interrogation and unsatisfied curiosity.

Brownlow, is, I admit, a cheerful spirit. I have known him tell lies. But I have never known him do anything so elaborate and sustained as this affair, if it is a mystification, would have to be. He is incapable of anything so elaborate and sustained. He is too lazy and easy-going for anything of the sort. And he would have laughed. At some stage he would have laughed and given the whole thing away. He has nothing to gain by keeping it up. His honour is not in the case either way. And after all there is his bit of newspaper in evidence — and the scrap of an addressed wrapper. . . .

I realize it will damage this story for many readers that it opens with Brownlow in a state very definitely on the gayer side of sobriety. He was not in a mood for cool and calculated observation, much less for accurate record. He was seeing things in an exhilarated manner. He was disposed to see them and greet them cheerfully and let them slip by out of attention. The limitations of time and space lay lightly upon him. It was after midnight. He had been dining with friends.

I have inquired what friends — and satisfied myself upon one or two obvious possibilities of that dinner party. They were, he said to me, "just friends. They hadn't anything to do with it." I don't usually push past an assurance of this sort, but I made an exception in this case. I watched my man and took a chance of repeating the question. There was nothing out of the ordinary about that dinner party, unless it was the fact than it was an unusually good dinner party. The host was Redpath Baynes, the solicitor, and the dinner was in his house in St. John's Wood. Gifford, of the *Evening Telegraph*, whom I know slightly, was, I found, present, and from him I got all I wanted to know. There was much bright and discursive talk and Brownlow had been inspired to give an imitation of his aunt, Lady Clitherholme, reproving an inconsiderate plumber during some re-building operations at Clitherholme. This early memory had been received with considerable merriment — he was always very good about his aunt, Lady Clitherholme — and Brownlow had departed obviously elated by this little social success and the general geniality of the occasion. Had they talked, I asked, about the Future, or Einstein, or J.W. Dunne, or any such high and serious topic at that party? They had not. Had they discussed the modern newspaper? No. There had been nobody whom one could call a practical joker at this party, and Brownlow had gone off alone in a taxi. That is what I was most desirous of knowing. He had been duly delivered by his taxi at the main entrance to Sussex Court.

Nothing untoward is to be recorded of his journey in the lift to the fifth floor of Sussex Court. The liftman on duty noted nothing exceptional. I asked if Brownlow said, "Good night." The liftman does not remember. "Usually he says Night O," reflected the liftman — manifestly doing his best and with nothing particular to recall. And there the fruits of my inquiries about the condition of Brownlow on this particular evening conclude. The rest of the story comes directly from him. My investigations arrive only at this: he was certainly not drunk. But he was lifted a little out of our normal harsh and grinding contact with the immediate realities of existence. Life was glowing softly and warmly in him, and the unexpected could happen brightly, easily, and acceptably.

He went down the long passage with its red carpet, its clear light, and its occasional oaken doors, each with its artistic brass number. I have been down that passage with him on several occasions. It was his custom to enliven that corridor by raising his hat gravely as he passed each entrance, saluting his unknown and invisible neighbours, addressing them softly but distinctly by playful if sometimes slightly indecorous names of his own devising, expressing good wishes or paying them little compliments.

He came at last to his own door, number 49, and let himself in without serious difficulty. He switched on his hall light. Scattered on the polished oak floor and invading his Chinese carpet were a number of letters and circulars, the evening's mail. His parlourmaid-housekeeper, who slept in a room in another part of the building, had been taking her evening out, or these letters would have been gathered up and put on the desk in his bureau. As it was, they lay on the floor. He closed his door behind him or it closed of its own accord; he took off his coat and wrap, placed his hat on the head of the Greek charioteer whose bust adorns his hall, and set himself to pick up his letters.

This also he succeeded in doing without misadventure. He was a little annoyed to miss the *Evening Standard*. It is his custom, he says, to subscribe for the afternoon edition of the *Star* to read at tea-time and also for the final edition of the *Evening Standard* to turn over the last thing at night, if only on account of Low's cartoon. He gathered up all these envelopes and packets and took them with him into his little sitting-room. There he turned on the electric heater, mixed himself a weak whisky-and-soda, went to his bedroom to put on soft slippers and replace his smoking jacket by a frogged jacket of llama wool, returned to his sitting-room, lit a cigarette, and sat down in his arm-chair by the reading lamp to examine his correspondence. He recalls all these details very exactly. They were routines he had repeated scores of times.

Brownlow's is not a preoccupied mind; it goes out to things. He is one of those buoyant extroverts who open and read all their letters and circulars whenever they can get hold of them. In the daytime his secretary intercepts and deals with most of them, but at night he escapes from her control and does what he pleases, that is to say, he opens everything.

He ripped up various envelopes. There was a formal acknowledgment of a business letter he had dictated the day before, there was a letter from his solicitor asking for some details about a settlement he was making, there was an offer from some unknown gentleman with an aristocratic name to lend him money on his note of hand alone, and there was a notice about a proposed new wing to his club. "Same old stuff," he sighed. "Same old stuff. What bores they all are!" He was always hoping, like every man who is proceeding across the plains of middle-age, that his correspondence would contain agreeable surprises — and it never did. Then, as he put it to me, *inter alia*, he picked up the remarkable newspaper.

2

It was different in appearance from an ordinary newspaper, but not so different as not to be recognizable as a newspaper, and he was surprised, he says, not to have observed it before. It was enclosed in a wrapper of pale green, but it was unstamped; apparently it had been delivered not by the postman, but by some other hand. (This wrapper still exists; I have seen it.) He had already torn it off before he noted that he was not the addressee.

For a moment or so he remained looking at this address, which struck him as just a little odd. It was printed in rather unusual type: "Evan O'Hara, Mr., Sussex Court 49."

"Wrong name," said Mr. Brownlow; "Right address. Rummy. Sussex Court 49. . . . 'Spose he's got *my Evening Standard.* . . . 'Change no robbery."

He put the torn wrapper with his unanswered letters and opened out the newspaper.

The title of the paper was printed in large slightly ornamental black-green letters that might have come from a kindred fount to that responsible for the address. But, as he read it, it was the *Evening Standard!* Or, at least, it was the "Even Standrd." "Silly," said Brownlow. "It's some damn Irish paper. Can't spell — anything — these Irish. . . ."

He had, I think, a passing idea, suggested perhaps by the green wrapper and the green ink, that it was a lottery stunt from Dublin.

Still, if there was anything to read he meant to read it. He surveyed the front page. Across this ran a streamer headline: "WILTON BORING REACHES SEVEN MILES: SUCCES ASSURED."

"No," said Brownlow. "It must be oil. . . . Illiterate lot these oil chaps — leave out the 's' in 'success.' "

He held the paper down on his knee for a moment, reinforced himself by a drink, took and lit a second cigarette, and then leant back in his chair to take a dispassionate view of any oil-share pushing that might be afoot.

But it wasn't an affair of oil. It was, it began to dawn upon him, something stranger than oil. He found himself surveying a real evening newspaper, which was dealing, so far as he could see at the first onset, with the affairs of another world.

He had for a moment a feeling as though he and his arm-chair and his little sitting-room were afloat in a vast space and then it all seemed to become firm and solid again.

This thing in his hands was plainly and indisputably a printed newspaper. It was a little odd in its letterpress, and it didn't feel or rustle like ordinary paper, but newspaper it was. It was printed in either three or four columns — for the life of him he cannot remember which — and there were column headlines under the page streamer. It had a sort of art-nouveau affair at the bottom of one column that might be an advertisement (it showed a woman in an impossibly big hat), and in the upper left-hand corner was an unmistakable weather chart of Western Europe, with *coloured* isobars, or isotherms, or whatever they are, and the inscription: "To-morrow's Weather."

And then he remarked the date. The date was November 10th, 1971!

"Steady on," said Brownlow. "Damitall! Steady on."

He held the paper sideways, and then straight again. The date remained November 10th, 1971.

He got up in a state of immense perplexity and put the paper down. For a moment he felt a little afraid of it. He rubbed his forehead. "Haven't been doing a Rip Van Winkle, by any chance, Brownlow, my boy?" he said. He picked up the paper again, walked out into his hall and looked at himself in the hall mirror. He was reassured to see no signs of advancing age, but the expression of mingled consternation and amazement upon his flushed face struck him suddenly as being undignified and unwarrantable. He laughed at himself, but not uncontrollably. Then he stared blankly at that familiar countenance. "I must be half-way *tordu*," he said, that being his habitual facetious translation of "screwed." On the console table was a little respectable-looking adjustable calendar bearing witness that the date was November 10th, 1931.

"D'you see?" he said, shaking the queer newspaper at it reproachfully. "I ought to have spotted you for a hoax ten minutes ago. 'Moosing trick, to say the least of it. I suppose they've made Low editor for a night, and he's had this idea. Eh?"

He felt he had been taken in, but that the joke was a good one. And, with quite unusual anticipations of entertainment, he returned to his arm-chair. A good idea it was, a paper forty years ahead. Good fun if it was well done. For a time nothing but the sounds of a newspaper being turned over and Brownlow's breathing can have broken the silence of the flat.

3

Regarded as an imaginative creation, he found the thing almost too well done. Every time he turned a page he expected the sheet to break out into laughter and give the whole thing away. But it did nothing of the kind. From being a mere quip, it became an immense and amusing, if perhaps a little over-elaborate, lark. And then, as a lark, it passed from stage to stage of incredibility until, as any thing but the thing it professed to be, it was incredible altogether. It must have cost far more than an ordinary number. All sorts of colours were used, and suddenly he came upon illustrations that went beyond amazement; they were in the colours of reality. Never in all his life had he seen such colour printing — and the buildings and scenery and costumes in the pictures were strange. Strange and yet credible. They were colour photographs of actuality forty years from now. He could not believe anything else of them. Doubt could not exist in their presence.

His mind had swung back, away from the stunt-number idea altogether. This paper in his hand would not simply be costly beyond dreaming to produce. At any price it could not be produced. All this present world could not produce such an object as this paper he held in his hand. He was quite capable of realizing that.

He sat turning the sheet over and — quite mechanically — drinking whisky. His sceptical faculties were largely in suspense; the barriers of criticism were down. His mind could now accept the idea that he was reading a newspaper of forty years ahead without any further protest.

It had been addressed to Mr. Evan O'Hara, and it had come to him. Well and good. This Evan O'Hara evidently knew how to get ahead of things. . . .

I doubt if at that time Brownlow found anything very

30

wonderful in the situation.

Yet it was, it continues to be, a very wonderful situation. The wonder of it mounts to my head as I write. Only gradually have I been able to build up this picture of Brownlow turning over that miraculous sheet, so that I can believe it myself. And you will understand how, as the thing flickered between credibility and incredibility in my mind, I asked him, partly to justify or confute what he told me, and partly to satisfy a vast expanding and, at last, devouring curiosity: "What was there in it? What did it have to say?" At the same time, I found myself trying to catch him out in his story, and also asking him for every particular he could give me.

What was there in it? In other words, What will the world be doing forty years from now? That was the stupendous scale of the vision, of which Brownlow was afforded a glimpse. The world forty years from now! I lie awake at nights thinking of all that paper might have revealed to us. Much it did reveal, but there is hardly a thing it reveals that does not change at once into a constellation of riddles. When first he told me about the thing I was — it is, I admit, an enormous pity — intensely sceptical. I asked him questions in what people call a "nasty" manner. I was ready — as my manner made plain to him — to jump down his throat with "But that's preposterous!" at the very first slip. And I had an engagement that carried me off at the end of half an hour. But the thing had already got hold of my imagination, and I rang up Brownlow before tea-time, and was biting at this "queer story" of his again. That afternoon he was sulking because of my morning's disbelief, and he told me very little. "I was drunk and dreaming, I suppose," he said. "I'm beginning to doubt it all myself." In the night it occurred to me for the first time that, if he was not allowed to tell and put on record what he had seen, he might become both confused and sceptical about it himself. Fancies might mix up with it. He might hedge and alter to get it more credible. Next day, there-fore, I lunched and spent the afternoon with him, and arranged to go down into Surrey for the week-end. I managed to dispel his huffiness with me. My growing keenness restored his. There we set ourselves in earnest, first of all to recover everything he could remember about his newspaper and then to form some coherent idea of the world about which it was telling.

It is perhaps a little banal to say we were not trained men for the job. For who could be considered trained for such a job as we were attempting? What facts was he to pick out as important and how were they to be arranged? We wanted to know everything we could about 1971; and the little facts and the big facts crowded on one another and offended against each other.

The streamer headline across the page about that seven-mile Wilton boring, is, to my mind, one of the most significant items in the story. About that we are fairly clear. It referred, says Brownlow, to a series of attempts to tap the supply of heat beneath the surface of the earth. I asked various questions. "It was *explained*, y'know," said Brownlow, and smiled and held out a hand with twiddling fingers. "It was explained all right. Old system, they said, was to go down from a few hundred feet to a mile or so and bring up coal and burn it. Go down a bit deeper, and there's no need to bring up and burn anything. Just get heat itself straightaway. Comes up of its own accord — under its own steam. See? Simple.

"They were making a big fuss about it," he added. "It wasn't only the streamer headline; there was a leading article in big type. What was it headed? Ah! The Age of Combustion has Ended!"

Now that is plainly a very big event for mankind, caught in mid-happening, November 10th, 1971. And the way in which Brownlow describes it as being handled, shows clearly a world much more preoccupied by economic essentials than the world of to-day, and dealing with them on a larger scale and in a bolder spirit.

That excitement about tapping the central reservoirs of heat, Brownlow was very definite, was not the only symptom of an increase in practical economic interest and intelligence. There was much more space given to scientific work and to inventions than is given in any contemporary paper. There were diagrams and mathematical symbols, he says, but he did not look into them very closely because he could not get the hang of them. "*Frightfully* highbrow, some of it," he said.

A more intelligent world for our grandchildren evidently, and also, as the pictures testified, a healthier and happier world.

"The fashions kept you looking," said Brownlow, going off at a tangent, "all coloured up as they were."

"Were they elaborate?" I asked.

"Anything *but*," he said.

His description of these costumes is vague. The people depicted in the social illustrations and in the advertisements

32

seemed to have reduced body clothing — I mean things like vests, pants, socks and so forth — to a minimum. Breast and chest went bare. There seem to have been tremendously exaggerated wristlets, mostly on the left arm and going as far up as the elbow, provided with gadgets which served the purpose of pockets. Most of these armlets seem to have been very decorative, almost like little shields. And then, usually, there was an immense hat, often rolled up and carried in the hand, and long cloaks of the loveliest colours and evidently also of the most beautiful soft material, which either trailed from a sort of gorget or were gathered up and wrapped about the naked body, or were belted up and thrown over the shoulders.

There were a number of pictures of crowds from various parts of the world. "The people looked fine," said Brownlow. "Prosperous, you know, and upstanding. Some of the women — just lovely."

My mind went off to India. What was happening in India?

Brownlow could not remember anything very much about India. "Ankor," said Brownlow. "That's not India, is it?" There had been some sort of Carnival going on amidst "perfectly lovely" buildings in the sunshine of Ankor.

The people there were brownish people but they were dressed very much like the people in other parts of the world.

I found the politician stirring in me. Was there really nothing about India? Was he sure of that? There was certainly nothing that had left any impression in Brownlow's mind. And Soviet Russia? "Not as Soviet Russia," said Brownlow. All that trouble had ceased to be a matter of daily interest. "And how was France getting on with Germany?" Brownlow could not recall a mention of either of these two great powers. Nor of the British Empire as such, nor of the U.S.A. There was no mention of any interchanges, communications, ambassadors, conferences, competitions, comparisons, stresses, in which these governments figured, so far as he could remember. He racked his brains. I thought perhaps all that had been going on so entirely like it goes on to-day — and has been going on for the last hundred years — that he had run his eyes over the passages in question and that they had left no distinctive impression on his mind. But he is positive that it was not like that. "All that stuff was washed out," he said. He is unshaken in his assertion that there were no elections in progress, no notice of Parliament or politicians, no mention of Geneva or anything about

33

armaments or war. All those main interests of a contemporary journal seem to have been among the "washed out" stuff. It isn't that Brownlow didn't notice them very much; he is positive they were not there.

Now to me this is a very wonderful thing indeed. It means, I take it, that in only forty years from now the great game of sovereign states will be over. It looks also as if the parliamentary game will be over, and as if some quite new method of handling human affairs will have been adopted. Not a word of patriotism or nationalism; not a word of party, not an allusion. But in only forty years! While half the human beings already alive in the world will still be living! You cannot believe it for a moment. Nor could I, if it wasn't for two little torn scraps of paper. These, as I will make clear, leave me in a state of— how can I put it?— incredulous belief.

4

After all, in 1831 very few people thought of railway or steamship travel, and in 1871 you could already go round the world in eighty days by steam, and send a telegram in a few minutes to nearly every part of the earth. Who would have thought of that in 1831? Revolutions in human life, when they begin to come, can come very fast. Our ideas and methods change faster than we know.

But just forty years!

It was not only that there was this absence of national politics from that evening paper, but there was something else still more fundamental. Business, we both think, finance that is, was not in evidence, at least upon anything like contemporary lines. We are not quite sure of that, but that is our impression. There was no list of Stock Exchange prices, for example, no City page, and nothing in its place. I have suggested already that Brownlow just turned that page over, and that it was sufficiently like what it is to-day that he passed and forgot it. I have put that suggestion to him. But he is quite sure that that was not the case. Like most of us nowadays, he is watching a number of his investments rather nervously, and he is convinced he looked for the City article.

November 10th, 1971, may have been Monday — there seems to have been some readjustment of the months and the days of the week; that is a detail into which I will not enter now

34

— but that will not account for the absence of any City news at all. That also, it seems, will be washed out forty years from now.

Is there some tremendous revolutionary smash-up ahead, then? Which will put an end to investment and speculation? Is the world going Bolshevik? In the paper, anyhow, there was no sign of, or reference to, anything of that kind. Yet against this idea of some stupendous economic revolution we have the fact that here forty years ahead is a familiar London evening paper still tumbling into a private individual's letter-box in the most uninterrupted manner. Not much suggestion of a social smash-up there. Much stronger is the effect of immense changes which have come about bit by bit, day by day, and hour by hour, without any sort of revolutionary jolt, as morning or springtime comes to the world.

These futile speculations are irresistible. The reader must forgive me them. Let me return to our story.

There had been a picture of a landslide near Ventimiglia and one of some new chemical works at Salzburg, and there had been a picture of fighting going on near Irkutsk. (Of that picture, as I will tell presently, a fading scrap survives.) "Now that was called—" Brownlow made an effort, and snapped his fingers triumphantly. "— 'Round-up of Brigands by Federal Police.' "

"*What* Federal Police?" I asked.

"There you have me," said Brownlow. "The fellows on both sides looked mostly Chinese, but there were one or two taller fellows, who might have been Americans or British or Scandinavians.

"What filled a lot of the paper," said Brownlow, suddenly, "was gorillas. There was no end of a fuss about gorillas. Not so much as about that boring, but still a lot of fuss. Photographs. A map. A special article and some paragraphs."

The paper, had, in fact, announced the death of the last gorilla. Considerable resentment was displayed at the tragedy that had happened in the African gorilla reserve. The gorilla population of the world had been dwindling for many years. In 1931 it had been estimated at nine hundred. When the Federal Board took over it had shrunken to three hundred.

"*What* Federal Board?" I asked.

Brownlow knew no more than I did. When he read the phrase, it had seemed all right somehow. Apparently this Board had had too much to do all at once, and insufficient resources. I

had the impression at first that it must be some sort of con-
servation board, improvised under panic conditions, to save the
rare creatures of the world threatened with extinction. The
gorillas had not been sufficiently observed and guarded, and
they had been swept out of existence suddenly by a new and
malignant form of influenza. The thing had happened practically before it was remarked. The paper was clamouring for
inquiry and drastic changes of reorganization.

This Federal Board, whatever it might be, seemed to be
something of very considerable importance in the year 1971. Its
name turned up again in an article of afforestation. This interested Brownlow considerably because he has large holdings in
lumber companies. This Federal Board was apparently not
only responsible for the maladies of wild gorillas but also for the
plantation of trees in — just note these names! — Canada, New
York State, Siberia, Algiers, and the East Coast of England, and
it was arraigned for various negligences in combating insect
pests and various fungoid plant diseases. It jumped all our
contemporary boundaries in the most astounding way. Its
range was world-wide. "In spite of the recent additional
restrictions put upon the use of big timber in building and
furnishing, there is a plain possibility of a shortage of shelter
timber and of rainfall in nearly all the threatened regions for
1985 onwards. Admittedly the Federal Board has come late to
its task, from the beginning its work has been urgency work; but
in view of the lucid report prepared by the James Commission,
there is little or no excuse for the inaggressiveness and over-
confidence it has displayed."

I am able to quote this particular article because as a matter
of fact it lies before me as I write. It is indeed, as I will explain,
all that remains of this remarkable newspaper. The rest has
been destroyed and all we can ever know of it now is through
Brownlow's sound but not absolutely trustworthy memory.

5

My mind, as the days pass, hangs on to that Federal Board.
Does that phrase mean, as just possibly it may mean, a world
federation, a scientific control of all human life only forty years
from now? I find that idea — staggering. I have always believed
that the world was destined to unify — "Parliament of Mankind
and Confederation of the World," as Tennyson put it — but I

have always supposed that the process would take centuries. But then my time sense is poor. My disposition has always been to under-estimate the pace of change. I wrote in 1900 that there would be aeroplanes "in fifty years' time." And the confounded things were buzzing about everywhere and carrying passengers before 1920.

Let me tell very briefly of the rest of that evening paper. There seemed to be a lot of sport and fashion; much about something called "Spectacle" — with pictures — a lot of illustrated criticism of decorative art and particularly of architecture. The architecture in the pictures he saw was "towering — kind of magnificent. Great blocks of building. New York, but more so and all run together" . . . Unfortunately he cannot sketch. There were sections devoted to something he couldn't understand, but which he thinks was some sort of "radio programme stuff."

All that suggests a sort of advanced human life very much like the life we lead to-day, possibly rather brighter and better.

But here is something — different.

"The birth-rate," said Brownlow, searching his mind, "was seven in the thousand."

I exclaimed. The lowest birth-rates in Europe now are sixteen or more per thousand. The Russian birth-rate is forty per thousand, and falling slowly.

"It was seven," said Brownlow. "Exactly seven. I noticed it. In a paragraph."

But what birth-rate, I asked. The British? The European?

"It said the birth-rate," said Brownlow. "Just that."

That I think is the most tantalizing item in all this strange glimpse of the world of our grandchildren. A birth-rate of seven in the thousand does not mean a fixed world population; it means a population that is being reduced at a very rapid rate — unless the death-rate has gone still lower. Quite possibly people will not be dying so much then, but living very much longer. On that Brownlow could throw no light. The people in the pictures did not look to him an "old lot." There were plenty of children and young or young-looking people about.

"But Brownlow," I said, "wasn't there any crime?"

"Rather," said Brownlow. "They had a big poisoning case on, but it was jolly hard to follow. You know how it is with these crimes. Unless you've read about it from the beginning, it's hard to get the hang of the situation. No newspaper has found out that for every crime it ought to give a summary up-to-date every day— and forty years ahead, they hadn't. Or they aren't going to. Whichever way you like to put it.

"There were several crimes and what newspaper men call stories," he resumed; "personal stories. What struck me about it was that they seemed to be more sympathetic than our reporters, more concerned with the motives and less with just finding someone out. What you might call psychological— so to speak."

"Was there anything much about books?" I asked him.

"I don't remember anything about books," he said. . . .

And that is all. Except for a few trifling details such as a possible thirteenth month inserted in the year, that is all. It is intolerably tantalizing. That is the substance of Brownlow's account of his newspaper. He read it— as one might read any newspaper. He was just in that state of alcoholic comfort when nothing is incredible and so nothing is really wonderful. He knew he was reading an evening newspaper of forty years ahead and he sat in front of his fire, and smoked and sipped his drink and was no more perturbed than he would have been if he had been reading an imaginative book about the future.

Suddenly his little brass clock pinged Two.

He got up and yawned. He put that astounding, that miraculous newspaper down as he was wont to put any old newspaper down; he carried off his correspondence to the desk in his bureau, and with the swift laziness of a very tired man he dropped his clothes about his room anyhow and went to bed.

But somewhen in the night he woke up feeling thirsty and grey-minded. He lay awake and it came to him that something very strange had occurred to him. His mind went back to the idea that he had been taken in by a very ingenious fabrication. He got up for a drink of Vichy water and a liver tabloid, he put his head in cold water and found himself sitting on his bed towelling his hair and doubting whether he had really seen those photographs in the very colours of reality itself, or whether he had imagined them. Also running through his mind was the thought that the approach of a world timber famine for 1985 was something likely to affect his investments and particularly a trust he was setting up on behalf of an infant in whom he was interested. It might be wise, he thought, to put more into timber.

He went back down the corridor to his sitting-room. He sat

there in his dressing-gown, turning over the marvellous sheets. There it was in his hands complete in every page, not a corner torn. Some sort of auto-hypnosis, he thought, might be at work, but certainly the pictures seemed as real as looking out of a window. After he had stared at them some time he went back to the timber paragraph. He felt he must keep that. I don't know if you will understand how his mind worked — for my own part I can see at once how perfectly irrational and entirely natural it was — but he took this marvellous paper, creased the page in question, tore off this particular article and left the rest. He returned very drowsily to his bedroom, put the scrap of paper on his dressing-table, got into bed and dropped off to sleep at once.

6

When he awoke it was nine o'clock; his morning tea was untasted by his bedside and the room was full of sunshine. His parlourmaid-housekeeper had just re-entered the room.

"You were sleeping so peacefully," she said; "I couldn't bear to wake you. Shall I get you a fresh cup of tea?"

Brownlow did not answer. He was trying to think of something strange that had happened.

She repeated her question.

"No. I'll come and have breakfast in my dressing-gown before my bath," he said, and she went out of the room.

Then he saw the scrap of paper.

In a moment he was running down the corridor to the sitting-room. "I left a newspaper," he said. "I left a newspaper."

She came in response to the commotion he made.

"A newspaper?" she said. "It's been gone this two hours, down the chute, with the dust and things."

Brownlow had a moment of extreme consternation.

He invoked his God. "I wanted it *kept!*" he shouted. "I wanted it *kept.*"

"But how was *I* to know you wanted it kept?"

"But didn't you notice it was a very extraordinary-looking newspaper?"

"I've got none too much time to dust out this flat to be looking at newspapers," she said. "I thought I saw some coloured photographs of bathing ladies and chorus girls in it, but that's no concern of mine. It didn't seem a proper newspaper to me. How was I to know you'd be wanting to look at them again this morning?"

"I must get that newspaper back," said Brownlow. "It's — it's vitally important. . . . If all Sussex Court has to be held up I want that newspaper back."

"I've never known a thing come up that chute again," said his housekeeper, "that's once gone down it. But I'll telephone down, sir, and see what can be done. Most of that stuff goes right into the hot-water furnace, they say. . . ."

It does. The newspaper had gone.

Brownlow came near raving. By a vast effort of self-control he sat down and consumed his cooling breakfast. He kept on saying "Oh, my God!" as he did so. In the midst of it he got up to recover the scrap of paper from his bedroom, and then found the wrapper addressed to Evan O'Hara among the overnight letters on his bureau. That seemed an almost maddening confirmation. The thing *had* happened.

Presently after he had breakfasted, he rang me up to aid his baffled mind.

I found him at his bureau with the two bits of paper before him. He did not speak. He made a solemn gesture.

"What is it?" I asked, standing before him.

"Tell me," he said. "Tell me. What are these objects? It's serious. Either —" He left the sentence unfinished.

I picked up the torn wrapper first and felt its texture. "Evan O'Hara, Mr.," I read.

"Yes. Sussex Court, 49. Eh?"

"Right," I agreed and stared at him.

"*That's* not hallucination, eh?"

I shook my head.

"And now this?" His hand trembled as he held out the cutting. I took it.

"Odd," I said. I stared at the black-green ink, the unfamiliar type, the little novelties in spelling. Then I turned the thing over. On the back was a piece of one of the illustrations; it was, I suppose, about a quarter of the photograph of that "Round-up of Brigands by Federal Police" I have already mentioned.

When I saw it that morning it had not even begun to fade. It represented a mass of broken masonry in a sandy waste with bare-looking mountains in the distance. The cold, clear atmosphere, the glare of a cloudless afternoon were rendered perfectly. In the foreground were four masked men in a brown

40

service uniform intent on working some little machine on wheels with a tube and a nozzle projecting a jet that went out to the left, where the fragment was torn off. I cannot imagine what the jet was doing. Brownlow says he thinks they were gassing some men in a hut. Never have I seen such realistic colour printing.

"What on earth is this?" I asked.

"It's *that*," said Brownlow. "I'm not mad, am I? It's really *that*."

"But what the devil is it?"

"It's a piece of newspaper for November 10th, 1971."

"You had better explain," I said, and sat down, with the scrap of paper in my hand, to hear his story. And, with as much elimination of questions and digressions and repetitions as possible, that is the story I have written here.

I said at the beginning that it was a queer story and queer to my mind it remains, fantastically queer. I return to it at intervals, and it refuses to settle down in my mind as anything but an incongruity with all my experience and beliefs. If it were not for the two little bits of paper, one might dispose of it quite easily. One might say that Brownlow had had a vision, a dream of unparalleled vividness and consistency. Or that he had been hoaxed and his head turned by some elaborate mystification. Or, again, one might suppose he had really seen into the future with a sort of exaggeration of those previsions cited by Mr. J.W. Dunne in his remarkable "Experiment with Time." But nothing Mr. Dunne has to advance can account for an actual evening paper being slapped through a letter-slit forty years in advance of its date.

The wrapper has not altered in the least since I first saw it. But the scrap of paper with the article about afforestation is dissolving into a fine powder and the fragment of picture at the back of it is fading out; most of the colour has gone and the outlines have lost their sharpness. Some of the powder I have taken to my friend Ryder at the Royal College, whose work in micro-chemistry is so well known. He says the stuff is not paper at all, properly speaking. It is mostly aluminium fortified by admixture with some artificial resinous substance.

7

Though I offer no explanation whatever of this affair I think I

41

will venture on one little prophesy. I have an obstinate persuasion that on November 10th, 1971, the name of the tenant of
49, Sussex Court, will be Mr. Evan O'Hara. (There is no tenant
of that name now in Sussex Court and I find no evidence in the
Telephone Directory, or the London Directory, that such a
person exists anywhere in London.) And on that particular
evening forty years ahead, he will not get his usual copy of the
Even Standrd: instead he will get a copy of the *Evening Standard* of
1931. I have an incurable fancy that this will be so.

There I may be right or wrong, but that Brownlow really got
and for two remarkable hours, read, a real newspaper forty
years ahead of time I am as convinced as I am convinced that
my own name is Hubert G. Wells. Can I say anything stronger
than that?

5
Walcote

It was Christmas Eve at Walcote. Most of the long saloon was in deep shadow, only here and there faint glimmers of reflected light showed where tables and vases and chairs and lounges were placed. A low screen stood before the wide fireplace. Ever and again the ruddy flicker from the spitting logs would leap and beckon over this, calling into visible existence a spectral faint room, the tall white caryatides of the great entrance, the bronze Satan that stood by the grand piano. As the unsteady shadows moved it seemed as if this latter figure stirred, waving its upraised arm, and as if the satyr caryatides smiled. A clock that ticked invisible in the dense obscurity above the mantel struck, in deep insistent tones, eleven. As the chime died away, the flickering flames sank behind the screen, a swift darkness swallowed the indistinct red room, the stirring Satan, the leering portals vanished in the black.

There was a stirring in a distant corner, a rustling noise, a sharp click, a faint clinking like the moving of a chain. Then all was silent, save the hissing and bubbling of the sap in the fire. One of the logs began a thin singing that speedily died away like the whistling of a frightened lad before the ominous stillness of the dark.

"Sss," suddenly sounded in the corner — an echo of the fire. "Sss." "Oh Edwin!"

The red tongues of fire leaped nervously up again. Dim and indistinct in one corner was a bird-like form on a perch, a gilt chain glittering faintly. The bronze nodded, the colossal distortion of its shadow on the wall crouched and leaped, the satyrs leered and blinked. The clock snapped up the seconds with grim destructive emphasis. Then unsteady footsteps could be heard without.

The thinnest golden line shone under the great door. The door swung open wide; two footmen appearing bearing silver candlesticks, other figures showing behind them.

As the light poured into the room and revealed all its elegances of silk and velvet and white and gold, it was as if the satyrs, ceasing to leer, grew breathless and motionless, as though the raised hand of Satan halted in anticipation. The beating of the clock was no longer audible, it seemed to be hushed in expectation. A figure of old Time, swaying his scythe, a remorseless, deliberate, a dreadful representation of the inevitable became visible above it. Everything was now real, distinct, and brilliant. On a fantastic perch in the corner a grey parrot blinked in the brightness.

The footmen advanced together, deposited the candles on a small round table, removed the screen, and drew the polished table nearer the fire. Three richly-dressed gentlemen followed.

"This is ever so much the best room, Edwin," said one of these sauntering in with his hands in his pockets. He was a fair complexion, ruddy-faced youth, splendidly attired in cherry-coloured satin and noble lace. He addressed his remark to one older, taller, darker, but as resplendent as himself. "I don't see, cousin, why you should object to come here," he continued, "I think ——"

"It doesn't matter now, Claude," said the one he had addressed as cousin, recent annoyance and present discomfort very evident in his voice. "A passing fancy struck me. It's all right now —— all right now we are here. Vitzelley, where will you sit?"

"Vitzelley," exclaimed the younger at the same moment, "have you noticed our parrot before? — curious bird — dumb with grief ever since the — the apotheosis of cousin Harry."

Vitzelley hesitated between them and answered both. "There. No." He was a small-eyed, keen-faced man, much older and far more soberly clad than his two companions.

"Yes," repeated Claude, "dumb with grief. Polly! pretty Polly," approaching it. "No answer, you see, Vitzelley."

The parrot raised one claw and stretched its fleshy digits, clicked its beak, and inclined its head to his finger.

"Poll, scratchy Poll. I suppose, Vitzelley, you have heard some hundred and fifty variations of our family mystery. All sorts of lies are flying about."

"The cards are ready, Claude," said Edwin in a warning voice, as the footmen, completing their arrangements, quietly vanished: "Come and sit down."

Vitzelley glanced from one to the other. He took the first pack in his hand and ran his fingers over the edges. "The old game, of course," he said to Edwin.

Claude came and sat down, thrusting his chair back to

44

display the embroidery of his vest. "Pass that decanter, Vitzelley," he said. "My cards these? Ah! Fortuna, Fortuna!"

"Vitzelley is too polite to get interested about Sir Harry," he went on presently, pouring from the decanter as he spoke: "before us — that is."

"I wish you would cut," said his cousin.

Vitzelley took the cards to deal. Then with a quiet glance at Edwin, "I have heard very little of your affair. Sir Harry thought fit to disappear because— because he had been playing cards?"

Edwin bowed his head assentingly. "It is the only explanation possibly suggesting itself. We are waiting, Claude," he said, nervously, as if desirous of changing the subject.

"That's stuff," ejaculated Claude, playing. "*I* know more than that. You *know* more than that. Sir Harry never played."

This flat contradiction caused Edwin to turn white, and glance with sharp malevolence at his cousin. It seemed to nettle him excessively. "You know very little about it, Claude," he retorted.

"I know Sir Harry never played cards."

"To my knowledge he did. Confound it!" — he had played the wrong card. "Well, well! I wish, Claude, you could avoid trying to begin a wrangle at cards."

"Who wants to wrangle?— not me! Sir Harry never played."

An uncomfortable silence followed. The game going on without a monosyllable being spoken. Then Claude drank, sucked his lips and turned to Vitzelley. "No, Vitzelley, the disappearance of Sir Harry was no bolt from his debts of honour. We are an honourable family still. I believe ——." The young man's face assumed an exceedingly sapient and confidential expression. An anxious look came into Edwin's eyes — "there was a lady in the case."

A crimson flush swept over Edwin's forehead, but he looked relieved. "Another pack, Vitzelley. Filthy luck, then, for me. It's the port. My head is as muddled and crowded as — as —"

"As a rotting corpse," supplied Claude, compensating himself for the recent passage of arms.

Another grim pause supervened, Edwin manifesting much disturbance.

"I never rightly heard the particulars of this affair," said Vitzelley, sweeping in the stakes he had just won, and seeing out of his narrow eyes, with considerable approval, the increasing distraction of one cousin and the intoxication of the other. "Was there anything odd?"

"No, delightfully simple, all of it," answered Claude. "Just pass the decanter. Thanks. Two significant facts; one Sir Harry was; two he is not. Incidentally, the day he vanished that parrot was struck dumb. That is all. You saw your brother last, by-the-bye, Edwin. Tell us all about it."

Edwin was white, and he was now playing wildly. "The cards are bewitched to-night," he said, between his teeth. He ignored Claude's words entirely.

"By Jove, Edwin!" burst out the irrepressible Claude; "why, it must be just a year to-night! Vitzelley, this is the twenty-fourth of December. Christmas Eve? of course, yes. This is the anniversary of that last appearance. Vitzelley, don't ghosts—"

"I wish you would stop this sort of thing, Claude. It distracts one from the play." Edwin certainly looked most strangely uncomfortable.

"My dear fellow! most valuable thought of mine— to you— this anniversary idea. When the year is up, you can take out— what is it? — letters of administration."

Edwin was drumming with his strong white hand on the table, and pretending to examine the lace at his wrist. "You are stopping the game, Claude."

"This, Edwin," presently resumed Claude, assuming great confidence with Vitzelley, "is a sly old dog, Vitz. You, you're a sly old dog, too, to pull in like you *are* doing. That's by the way. Well, this Edwin always pretends to get huffy, get his feelings hurt, when we fall a talking about this disappearance. Really he profits up to the hilt. You must know Sir Harry was going to marry; happy girl, happy day, all fixed. If he had married and got a little boy, poor old Eddy— out in the cold for ever. *Now*, he's as good as baronet— will be baronet I suppose after awhile. Eigh?"

"Did you really see him last?" asked Vitzelley, with a penetrating look at Edwin.

Edwin moistened his dry lips and looked straight into his face. He seemed watching his words as he spoke. "On Christmas Eve, last year, I left my brother here in this room, sitting before this fire, about eleven. About— about this time— it must have been —" His eye fell instinctively on the clock. "The footman who sleeps in the pantry below heard a bumping above and the parrot chattering. I — I was already in bed, and

46

heard nothing at all. The next morning Sir Harry had vanished. Everything had been put straight — in fact, I mean, nothing had been disturbed apparently in this room or anywhere. Since then ——"

"Viz, my lad, pass the bottle. It must have been the devil," said Claude. "Apotheosis."

"The thing has been no joke to me," complained Edwin, breathing more freely, as Vitzelley turned his attention to the cards again. "The disappearance" ——

"Four minutes to twelve," interrupted Claude, "and Saturday. Vitzelley, if we play till Sunday we see the devil, don't we? I wonder if he's like our Satan here. Perhaps he'll bring Sir Harry back."

"*Do*, in heaven's name, stop that," cried Edwin, nervous now to savageness. "You know how his disappearance has weighed on my mind; how I would give my soul to have Sir Harry, or Sir Harry's body, discovered ——"

"*Oh, Edwin!*"

Edwin became livid. "What was that? Did you speak, Vitzelley? Did you hear anything?"

Vitzelley was looking a little startled. "*I* did not speak. I thought I heard something."

"I didn't," said Claude. "Vitzelley, it's two to twelve. What happens at midnight if we keep on playing cards?"

"The red cards turn black, and the black blood red," said Vitzelley, drily; "and the picture cards make faces at you. That is all. Nothing very dreadful. What's the matter with you, Walcote; why don't you deal?"

"What are you glowering at in the candle flame?" cried Claude. "One would think it was burning blue. Don't be alarmed. It wants one minute to midnight yet."

Edwin answered with a peculiar quiver and gasping. "I — It's nothing, nothing. Fancy. I am always fancying ——. *You* can't see anything, can you? Pah, how the thing jumps and struggles! not dead yet. Will it ever be quiet? The flame, I mean."

His face was ghastly, a sickly dew was glistening on his forehead. He made a peculiar clutching motion at the candle, then looked with startled fearful scrutiny at Vitzelley, put his hand to his forehead and then on the cards.

"The candle only flickers because it wants snuffing. There is a purple glow at the neck — wick I mean — and ——"

One. Two. Three. Four. Five. Six. Slowly and solemnly the deep-voiced clock struck *Twelve*.

As the vibration of the last stroke died away, Edwin with a loud expression of disgust flung down his cards. "The face," he said. "the face — with the black tongue out! The cards, the Knaves and Kings, white faces and purple necks. What a maniac I was to come here — this room — to-night! Bah! You fools! It's a joke! What are you fools staring at?"

Neither answered a word. Vitzelley had suddenly folded his arms and leaned over the table towards him. Claude had swiftly snatched up his cards, glanced at them fearfully, and then with a slightly relieved face turned to Edwin.

A stillness, and then a low, unearthly, pervading voice sounding through it, going searchingly through all the space around them, an agonised choking voice.

"Oh, Edwin! oh, my mother! spare me, spare me! oh!" — ending in a prolonged sobbing groan.

Claude's hair rose on end. Vitzelley moved not, spoke never a word. With fingers crushing the cards in his hand, with head bowed down, distorted mouth and blinking eyes, Edwin sat, as though awaiting the stroke of doom.

The clock ticked on exultantly in the horrible stillness. The bronze Satan stood expectant behind them, the satyrs stared across the room on suppressed excitement. The shadow of Satan's uplifted arm hung terrible above the crouching shadow of Edwin. The parrot shifted on his perch and clanked its chain. A card fell audibly on the floor. Then they heard an aerial voice, that made them involuntarily glance at his cadaverous face.

"Ah! . . . the priest's hole in the turret!"

It was Edwin's voice, but he had not spoken.

Another terrible hiatus in sound, a minute — or an hour. Then a dawning light of comprehension shone in Edwin's eyes. He started up furious, his chair reeling over with a crash, and made three strides towards the parrot. The bird gave an eldritch shriek and flapped open its wide grey wings. Then Vitzelley had gripped Edwin's arm and they stood confronting.

"Fate," said Vitzelley. "You must submit. We know — enough."

A pause and then an intense whisper. "Yes, I killed him — here — last Christmas Eve. Fool that I was to come here, this night of all! We drank and quarrelled. He had stood in my way to wealth, and his wealth had won my Annie from me. He

48

taunted me. How I hated him then! I struck him suddenly with the poker, felled him, leaped on him, strangled him. There is a secret chamber in the disused turret where once the priests were hidden. Only he and I knew. He is there, rat eaten, mummified . . .

"Vitzelley, leave my arm for a moment."

He turned and faced them both.

Suddenly his rapier glittered in the light. It flashed, and the parrot toppled over and hung headless by its chain, flashed again and he was staggering, falling forward, to roll over and sigh, and lie motionless before them — to love, hate, and sin nevermore. At his feet lay the head of the parrot, the fleshy tongue still faintly quivering.

The candles flickered as if with a passing breath, the shadowy Satan moved strangely on the wall. Over the marble mantel old Time swayed his scythe grim and restless, hewing out irrevocable things.

6

The Devotee of Art

ALEC had heard his wife playing, and had thrown down his brushes and come to the chair beside the old-fashioned square piano. It was a wide, velvet-covered arm-chair, in which he had perforce to clasp his hands behind his head and lounge luxuriously if he meant to sit in it at all— a chair not easily to be sat in without perfect easiness, a chair with the embrace of Morpheus and the inspiration of the herb Papaver.

Isabel was playing very sweetly; she played by feeling as well as touch; something of Wagner's it was, something as uncertain and variable, and as invariably attractive as life itself. To listen — in that arm-chair — was like hearing the Sirens; existence became — "spiritualized," the word is — suddenly emancipated from all necessary cares and courses.

Alec had been tormenting his brain all day with the expression of a curiously obdurate face, feeling an idea growing frayed and colourless, like a captured butterfly, as he attempted to fix what beauty it had for the common eye; and the escape from technique was delicious. He slipped away from realities gladly, and wandered — no longer mortal man, but immortal soul again— in the realms of the imagination, dealing with realities boldly as became a deathless spirit. He had been working all day to develop his conception of a knightly vigil; and as Isabel played andante, the vision the music inspired him with was full of violet shadows in mysterious temples, solitary pink flames before ghostly altars, tenebrous gleamings, white robed figures faintly seen, prayer and awe — all very vague indeed, but all exceedingly beautiful. Presently, however, her white hands passed into swift allegro and his fancies grew insensibly more animated. Into his shadowy dim aisles processions came marching, torchlight banished the dimness and blazed paler into day, figures flowed in more and more, more and more the scene grew crowded, dignified priests and warriors grew more numerous, younger, more active, swarming and overflowing until temples, altars, processions, all order and stability vanished in a mazy dance of exultant figures, knights and dames, shepherds and shepherdesses, clowns, grotesques, Punchinellos, corphyrées, humanity, finally danced under by a whirl of ideal creations, imps, gnomes, fairies, satyrs, hamadryads, harpies, and oreads. Faster and faster they danced in intricate kaleidoscopic figures. Suddenly through them all, like the news of a death in a ball room, passed a shudder, a jar, — blackness rapt them away! — the music had stopped.

"Alec," said Isabel, "you are going to sleep; you distinctly snored."

"My dear girl! nothing could have been further from my thoughts. I was just shutting my eyes to enjoy the music, and thinking over a little problem in composition." He felt quite hurt.

Isabel turned back to the piano, and Alec, to avoid a repetition of this unjust misconception — she was always thinking him sleepy or unwell when reverie engaged him — opened his eyes as wide as possible and fixed them unblinkingly on her face.

"My dear, Alec, don't look like that! Are you ill? Or is there anything wrong with my hair?"

Isabel had curly dark brown hair, that dark brown which gleams golden in a slanting light. It was a little out (so Isabel called it) that night, and there were ever so many little misty gold curves and wreaths fading away round her head — the amber-shaded lamp beside her gave her quite a halo of them.

"Only Sylphs, dear Belinda," said Alec, lazily, suppressing some annoyance. "Does my look disturb you?"

Isabel considered as she went on playing. "I don't want you to stare like a hairdresser's wig block," she said judicially; "but you may *look* at me if you like."

So Alec went on looking, with greatly subdued violence, however, at the glory-surrounded head and the shadowed face.

"It was a sweet face," Alec meditated, "soft lined, tender-looking; one of those pale faces with dark eyes that are not perhaps beautiful but infinitely capable of beautiful expressions, a face never wearisome while there is life, and yet——." Alec loved his wife very greatly — more by far than he loved himself or any other loveable being, and yet—. There was this little "and yet—," this one fatal objection, very much present in Alec's mind just then, suggested by the slight vulgarity of those few words of his wife to begin with, and fostered perhaps by the

51

subdued discontent of the air that now prevailed in the music: Isabel, he thought, was a force in life antagonistic to art.

Alec was an artist not only by choice of *metir*, but of spiritual compulsion. So he fancied, and just then was thinking that his supreme love was not to be found in that warmly illuminated room, but in the dim-lit studio beyond; that for one wedded to eternal Art, marriage was a sad mistake, even, indeed, a sort of bigamy. He had been reading, as the omniscient reader will observe, that child of fancy, Algernon Swinburne; and that and Isabel's pathetic transitions from phantasies to snores, and from sylph-surrounded heads to hairdressers' wig blocks, and the melancholy music — it was really melancholy now — all worked together. It was, in fact, one of those painful moments of domestic dissatisfaction not uncommon to recently-married young men who are moderately clever and immoderately ambitious— especially after days passed in badly arranged and unsuccessful work. The theory of the wife being an earthly clog is so soothing to self love. *Ars longa vita brevis*, he thought, not a new or original idea, but one remembered from copybook learning; and here he, the artist, was actually making his *vita brevior* by becoming domesticated! Among other equally poignant reminders, Milton's words, "and that one talent which is death to hide," came into his mind. Death! the loss of immortality! were the appointed moments of probation indeed gliding inevitably by? Perish the thought! At that moment he seemed to himself— the music and the easy chair inspiring another Merlin in the spell of another Vivien; he, the potential creator of spell-beautiful paintings, spending his moments, his hours, pleasing and being pleased by a wife who compared *him* to a hairdresser's wigblock.

It was his duty to his supreme mistress, Art, not to permit this a moment longer. He would return to his proper sphere. His act was swifter than his resolution, although that supervened very suddenly on his wandering discontents.

He did not venture to look round at Isabel as he rose and walked straight into his studio, but as he closed the door he heard that the music ceased abruptly and that her dress rustled.

He lit the white-burning Solar lamp and turned it towards his picture.

Just then he heard the door behind him creak, and turning, saw it pushed open very softly, and Isabel, her face full of solicitude, appear looking in. Probably she fancied he was ill.

52

When, however, his sudden asperity of expression became evident, she disappeared, the door closing noiselessly.

It was an Italian model he had been troubled about. The fellow had fine white features, mobile lips, and liquid eyes; he was to be the knight keeping vigil. When Alec had first seen him he had been struck merely by the possibilities of looking impassioned which this young man possessed. He was fit to go into a picture quite unmodified, "Kneel. Look devout," he would have to say, paint him forthwith, and the thing would be done. But that day as he had worked at his knight's features he had been surprised and annoyed to find a curious phenomenon appearing through his efforts. Try as he would, copy with never so much painful accuracy the adolescent countenance before him, a curious sinister expression *would* come somehow upon the canvas, a look of age, and instead of devotion, furtive ridicule. He could not understand it — had been glad to leave patching it to hear his wife's playing. Now, this evening, disregarding subtleties of tint, he would have another try, wrestle with and overcome this difficulty.

"Some little inaccuracy does it," he said; "eyebrows probably too oblique," — therewith turning the white light full upon his work and taking up palette and brushes.

The face on the canvas certainly seemed animated by a spirit of its own. Where the expression of diablerie came in he found impossible to discover. Experiment was necessary. The eyebrows — it could scarcely be the eyebrows? But he altered them. No, that was no better; in fact, if anything, a trifle more satanic. The corner of the mouth? Pah! more than ever a Mephistophilesian leer — and now, re-touched, it is ominously grim. The eye then? Catastrophe! he had filled his brush with vermilion instead of brown, and yet he had felt sure it was brown! The eye seemed now to have rolled in its socket, glowing on him an eye of fire. In a flash of passion he struck the brush full of bright red athwart the picture; and then a very curious thing, a very strange thing indeed, occurred — if it *did* occur.

The diabolified Italian before him shut both his eyes, pursed his mouth, and wiped the colour off his face with his hand!

Then the *red eye* opened again and the face smiled. "That was rather hasty of you," it said.

Curiously enough, Alec did not feel frightened or very much astonished. Perhaps he was too much exasperated. "Why do you keep moving about then," he said, "making faces and all

53

that, sneering and squinting while I am painting you?"

"I don't," said the picture.

"You *do*," said Alec.

"It's yourself," said the picture.

"It's *not* myself," said Alec.

"It *is* yourself," said the picture. "No! don't go hitting me with paint again, because it's true. You have been trying to *fluke* an expression on my face all day. Really you haven't an idea what your picture ought to look like."

"I have," said Alec.

"You have *not*," contradicted the picture; "you *never* have with your pictures. You always start with the vaguest presentiment of what you are going to do; it is to be something beautiful — you are sure of that — and devout, perhaps, or tragic; but beyond that it is all experiment and chance. My dear fellow! you don't surely think you can paint a picture like that?"

Alec felt there was a lot of truth in all this. "What am I to do then?"

"Get an inspiration."

"But I thought this was an inspiration."

"Inspiration," sneered the sardonic figure; "a fancy that came from your seeing an organ-grinder looking up at a window! Vigil! ha, ha!"

Alec groaned. "Too true! I am married. The days of inspiration are past. Oh, to undo it! I would give anything in life for a return of inspiration, for a release from the humdrum life of small domesticities that is beginning. I — who would have given my soul to art!"

"As you wish," said the figure, and then everything was still.

"Eigh!" cried Alec, suddenly startled out of his cool acceptance of this phenomenon by a swift, uncomfortable realisation.

"Did you speak?" he said, after a pause.

"I say — Vezetti – *or* — whoever you are, did you say anything?"

In the stillness he could hear his own heart beating. The picture was motionless and voiceless, but the *red eye* glowed like a coal.

Very slowly he approached, and passed his hand over the paint. Paint, sure enough — unsophisticated paint. He must have been dreaming; he had read plenty of scientific matter about hallucinations and so forth, and so he was not too

54

horribly frightened; still —. He felt the red eye, but that was perfectly cool.

"Do you want to say anything more?" asked Alec, deliberately jumbling together all the colours on his palette; "because, if not —"

Dab, dab, dab, he proceeded to paint out this disagreeably outspoken creation as quickly as he could. He had some difficulty in getting out the red eye; it seemed to glow through the coatings he laid over it. At last, however, with what seemed like a quietly ironical wink, it disappeared.

Smear, smudge, wriggle, every stroke of the obnoxious figure was presently hidden. With a feeling of relief Alec drew back from the canvas. "I am a superstitious fellow," he was thinking dubiously, as he surveyed the wreck, when suddenly some lines in his aimless smearing caught his eye. "By Jove!" he exclaimed, "there's an idea there!" He framed his eyes with his hands.

He heard a light tapping at the door. It was his wife. Presently the door opened, but he did not turn towards her. "Alec," she said, "do you know the time?" She received no answer. "It is nearly midnight, Alec." Still no answer. "Are you going to paint all night, Alec?"

"Oh! yes! yes!" he answered, without turning, in a tone that made it almost a curse; and when with a faint twinge of compunction he looked round, she had gone away.

It was really a splendid idea; splendid idea is not enough; it was almost as if a divine revelation had come to Alec. The curves above suggested the intersecting arching of the roof; that smear below, the knight keeping vigil; and between, that white space, what he had been feeling for all along, a group, the watching spirits of Chivalry, Generosity, Purity, and Religion. Beautiful in form and colour, definite as bodily sight, the conception had come to him. In another minute he was frantically preparing colours. Morning should see the work under way.

He was working feverishly in the dead of night when his wife's finger-nails tapped at his studio door again. As he stepped back to get a view of his work he saw her standing in her white nightdress in the doorway. "Alec," she said, "it is four o'clock. You will make yourself ill."

"Go away," Alec answered roughly, and as her footsteps slipped along the passage he went to the door and, slamming, locked it. He thought he heard her cry, but just then his eye caught the growing picture and he forgot everything else.

When the pale daylight came streaming into the room to show the yellow in his Solar lamp, Alec was still working in frantic haste. The great masses of the picture were blocked in; already it was beautiful.

What was that? A rapping at the door. "Come in." The door is locked however. With his eyes on his picture he opens it, and hears the voice of Lizzie, the little serving maid.

"Oh, if you please, sir, missus sent me to say as she's ill, and will you come to see her."

"Ill?" said Alec, walking up to the picture and touching in some purple.

"She slipped upon the stairs, sir, last night, and her side and back are just dreffle painful this morning, sir."

"This moonlit window is supreme," said Alec, absently painting. "Ah — Lizzie!"

"Yessir."

"Fetch me some coffee and bread and butter;" and quite forgetful of his wife's illness— news, indeed, that he imperfectly heard — he goes on with his great idea of expressing the profound stillness round the watching knight by metameric vertical praying figures in the windows and on the monuments. It was a real, an undeniable inspiration which had come to him at last. Previously he thought his idea had been as spiritless almost as that extraordinary painting of the same subject saved up for an ill-starred posterity in the Chantrey Room, South Kensington. Now, in richness of accessories and colour it was worthy of Titian; in harmony of line, of Leighton or Raphael. This idea was the morning star of his fame. Work, work, work, a fortnight, perhaps, or three weeks, and then — the dawn of immortality!

The hours seemed to fly by as the masterpiece grew slowly into beauty. As it grew, all possibilities of fatigue seemed to pass away from him— he felt neither hunger nor thirst. As it grew, it entranced him more and more; fainter and fainter outward impressions came to him. Some indistinct memories of various people interrupting him, saying stupid irrelevant things about his wife being ill and what not, of the lamp being lit again, and presently going out amid a stream of red sparks up the chimney, of his having to rave the house down to get it refilled, various people trying insanely to quiet him, of the clock having stopped, and of sleeping by snatches in his clothes at the foot of the easel.

56

But all these impressions were faint and intermingled, more like the swift imperfections of a dream than real occurrences. The one consequent idea, the one grand organic growth, was the Great Picture. Ever more beautiful, nearer and nearer to perfection it grew.

It was sublime, this flawless creating under his inspired fingers. Days slipped by unheeded; thrice the Solar lamp had flickered out. Alec's life would have been altogether supreme had it not been for the faint but persistent intimations of evil to his wife, and for the reminiscences of the figure with the *red eye* that came to disturb his snatches of slumber. These things imported a vague uneasiness into the ecstatic dream of pure art he was living.

"Your wife is dangerously ill; her fall has injured her internally. She may be dying."

"Eigh! What! Is it you?"

It was his wife's mother, and behind her the doctor. They were looking at him with a peculiar dread in their eyes. But he did not mind that. Everyone had been odd these last few days.

"She is dying," the Doctor said, solemnly.

"Dying is she? Who did you say?" He went up to the picture again, touching it fondly.

"Your wife."

"My wife — Doctor! what's the day of the month?"

"The Vigil. Don't go away, Doctor, without seeing my picture. What did you say the date?"

"Eigh! Then there's — yes, just time for the Academy!"

Presently he was standing on the landing bawling, "Lizzie!"

"In the name of heaven, man, be quiet! Do you want to commit murder?"

"Murder! Nonsense! I want a cab. The Vigil is finished!"

The precious picture! He must carry the canvas down in his own arms. How hushed the house was. The two servants stood in the background in the hall with a look of profound awe on their faces. The triumph of accomplishment is already beginning. Evidently they know *now* that he is a genius. All the world will know that soon.

As he enters the cab the Doctor appears at the door with a white face, comes down the steps and clutches his arm, saying something.

"You idiot! Leave go my arm, will you?"

Then the cab is rumbling on its way to Burlington House.

Alec, with the picture on his knees, regards it lovingly.

It is very beautiful, but the light is dim. Presently it seems as if — yes, the light is shimmering through; the oiled canvas is growing transparent. It is really very strange; indeed, it is disagreeable. The work he has painted over shows; all the elemental smears and smudges are there. Then beneath that, the *thing* that those smears and smudges were to hide, *that* begins to grow perceptible. First, a red glimmer, then a faint outline. The sinister face, the ardent eye, become every moment more emphatic, seeming to have burnt out all the beauty he has worked for. Yes! it is the diabolical figure with the *red eye*, grinning exultantly; then, with a laugh, speaking:

"You see I am still here."

"Who — what?" gasps Alec, and then, with lower jaw dropping, is silent.

"You are consecrated to art now. My friend, did you catch what the Doctor said to you?"

Smash!

All is indistinct for a little while after this; there is even a slight confusion about his identity. He sees himself lying with a crushed hand among the wreck of the cab, which has collided with a timber wagon. He can feel the pain and tingling of the wound, notices the great picture smashed hopelessly beside him, a gaping hole knocked through it, simulating curiously the shape of that weird red-eyed figure, and then the thought comes into his mind, *where is he?*

Then it is a hospital ward. The transition is abrupt; probably he has fainted. "His hand is to be amputated," one hard-featured nurse tells another in his hearing.

Hand and work gone together — the *ignis fatuus* of immortality has vanished. Bitterness and sorrow come upon him, and the need of refuge and comfort. With a great yearning, his thoughts rush back to his wife, her gentle touch, her tender eyes, her soothing voice. A frightful pang goes through him — the Doctor's words come to his mind "In the name of decency come back — she is dead." The nympholept is disenchanted. What has he cast away for the phantasm of praise? Then the full comprehension of his acts appears in all its hideousness. Oh, the vileness, the folly, the mad ingratitude of it! What could have impelled him, what demon possessed him?

"You were inspired."

He turns his head. Beside the bed with folded arms and

grimly smiling face, stands his creation, the red-eyed man.

He would scream, but he can find no voice; would spring away out of the bed, but motion is denied him.

"You wished to be inspired. Art and the domestic virtues jarred together. Your wife is dead; she had to die when you gave your soul to art."

"Gave my soul to art?"

"Yes. Ha, hah! It is a pity your hand is smashed."

And suddenly the red-eyed man had sat down on Alec's body and was glaring with his one fiery orb into his fce. "What did you make *me* for?" His breath was sulphurous, it made Alec's nostrils and mouth burn; and the arm too grew terribly painful again, as though a thousand red-hot needles were probing it.

"Oh, my wife! I am dying."

"Don't call your wife; you are mine," hissed the fiend close to his face.

"Listen!" he continued, with cruel deliberation. "When a painter paints a form without a soul to it, without, that is, a clear intention expressed by it; when he paints aimlessly and reck-lessly in the hope of some spirit coming into it by accident — *sometimes a spirit comes*. I came so to yours, and you know the bargain I struck with you."

It was horrible. The demon was as heavy as lead, and his breath burnt Alec's nostrils. But the most bitter of all the terrible things he was suffering, more bitter even than his fear and agony for himself, was his remorse for his wife. Sacrificed for art — what was art compared with her loving, protean sweetness? His short married life with her, a thousand things that he had forgotten, came rushing back to his memory with the bitter hopelessness of the Peri's glimpse of heaven.

"My wife," he cried, "my wife!"

The demon bent closely over him, hoarsely whispering, "Gone, gone." Then he stretched out something black over his eyes — a cloak, or was it a wing?

All was as black as futurity. A sense then of sinking swiftly down through a black, bottomless void. Could he be dying — or dead? It seemed as if he was being sucked down an infinite black funnel, an eternal mäelstrom. Was there no hope? Suddenly through the awful silent space sounded his wife's voice —

"Alec!"

He looked up. She stood a measureless distance above, clothed in radiant light, looking down with infinite compassion and forgiveness upon him. He stretched out his arms, and would have cried to her, but his voice would not come to him. Then into his mind came the thought of that great gulf which separates those who have despised love from joy and beauty for ever.

Down, down, down.

"Alec!"

"Alec, wake up!"

He was sitting in the old velvet-covered armchair beside the piano, and his wife was bending over him. He blinked like an owl. Then he realised that he had pins and needles in his left arm. "Have I been to sleep?" he asked.

"Yes, of course. When I saw you going to sleep again, I knew it was no good trying to prevent you, so I left off playing and went away. I should have thought, though, that Lizzie, dropping the tray downstairs, would have been sufficient to wake you."

"That," said Alec, rubbing his eyes as he rose from the old armchair's embrace; "why, that must have been the cab accident!"

"You are very affectionate to-night," his wife said presently, as they went downstairs together.

"I am repenting, dearest, of a sin against you, of letting an idle dream come between us."

And thereupon he was "very affectionate" again.

7
A Misunderstood Artist

THE gentleman with the Jovian coiffure began to speak as the train moved. " 'Tis the utmost degradation of art," he said. He had apparently fallen into conversation with his companion upon the platform.

"I don't see it," said this companion, a prosperous-looking gentleman with a gold watch-chain. "This art for art's sake— I don't believe in it, I tell you. Art should have an aim. If it don't do you good, if it ain't moral, I'd as soon not have it. What good is it? I believe in Ruskin. I tell you —"

"*Bah!*" said the gentleman in the corner, with almost explosive violence. He fired it like a big gun across the path of the incipient argument, and slew the prosperous-looking gentleman at once. He met our eyes, as we turned to him, with a complacent smile on his large white, clean-shaven face. He was a corpulent person, dressed in black, and with something of the quality of a second-hand bishop in his appearance. The demolished owner of the watch-chain made some beginnings of a posthumous speech.

"*Bah!*" said the gentleman in the corner, with even more force than before, and so finished him.

"These people will never understand," he said, after a momentary pause, addressing the gentleman with the Jovian coiffure, and indicating the remains of the prosperous gentleman by a wave of a large white hand. "Why do you argue? Art is ever for the few."

"I did not argue," said the gentleman with the hair. "I was interrupted."

The owner of the watch-chain, who had been sitting struggling with his breath, now began to sob out his indignation. "What do you *mean*, sir? Saying *Bah!* sir, when I am talking—"

The gentleman with the large face held up a soothing hand. "Peace, peace," he said. "I did not interrupt you. I annihilated you. Why did you presume to talk to artists about art? Go away, or I shall have to say Bah! again. Go and have a fit. Leave us — two rare souls who may not meet again — to our talking."

"Did you ever see such abominable *rudeness*, sir?" said the gentleman with the watch-chain, appealing to me. There were tears in his eyes. At the same time the young man with the aureole made some remark to the corpulent gentleman that I failed to catch.

"These artists," said I, "are unaccountable, irresponsible. You must ——"

"Take it from whence it comes," said the insulted one, very loudly, and bitterly glaring at his opponent. But the two artists were conversing serenely. I felt the undignified quality of our conversation. "Have you seen *Punch*?" said I, thrusting it into his hand.

He looked at the paper for a moment in a puzzled way; then understood, thanked me, and began to read with a thunderous scowl, every now and then shooting murderous glances at his antagonist in the opposite corner, or coughing in an aggressive manner.

"You do your best," the gentleman with the long hair was saying; "and they say, 'What is it for?' 'It is for itself,' you say. Like the stars."

"But these people," said the stout gentleman, "think the stars were made to set their clocks by. They lack the magnanimity to drop the personal reference. A friend, a *confrère*, saw a party of these horrible Extension people at Rome before that exquisite Venus of Titian. 'And now, Mr Something-or-other,' said one of the young ladies, addressing the pedagogue in command, 'what is *this* to teach us?' "

"I have had the same experience," said the young gentleman with the hair. "A man sent to me only a week ago to ask what my sonnet 'The Scarlet Thread' *meant?*"

The stout person shook his head as though such things passed all belief.

"Gur-r-r-r," said the gentleman with *Punch*, and scraped with his foot on the floor of the carriage.

"I gave him answer," said the poet, " 'Twas a sonnet, not a symbol."

"Precisely," said the stout gentleman.

" 'Tis the fate of all art to be misunderstood. I am always grossly misunderstood — by every one. They call me fantastic, whereas I am but inevitably new; indecent, because I am unfettered by mere trivial personal restrictions; unwholesome."

"It is what they say to me. They are always trying to pull me to earth. 'Is it wholesome?' they say; 'nutritious?' I say to them, 'I do not know. I am an artist. I do not care. It is beautiful.' "

"You rhyme?" said the poet.

"No. My work is — more plastic. I cook."

For a moment, perhaps, the poet was disconcerted. "A noble art," he said, recovering.

"The noblest," said the cook. "But sorely misunderstood; degraded to utilitarian ends; tested by impossible standards. I have been seriously asked to render oily food palatable to a delicate patient. Seriously!"

"He said, 'Bah! Bah! to *me!*" mumbled the defunct gentleman with *Punch*, apparently addressing the cartoon. "A cook! Good *Lord!*"

"I resigned. 'Cookery,' I said, 'is an art. I am not a fattener of human cattle. Think: Is it Art to write a book with an object, to paint a picture for strategy?' 'Are we,' I said, 'in the sixties or the nineties? Here, in your kitchen, I am inspired with beautiful dinners, and I produce them. It is your place to gather together, from this place one, and from that, one, the few precious souls who can appreciate that rare and wonderful thing, a dinner, graceful, harmonious, exquisite, perfect.' And he argued I must study his guests!"

"No artist is of any worth," said the poet, "who primarily studies what the public needs."

"As I told him. But the next man was worse — hygienic. While with this creature I read Poe for the first time, and I was singularly fascinated by some of his grotesques. I tried — it was an altogether new development, I believe, in culinary art — the Bizarre. I made some curious arrangements in pork and strawberries, with a sauce containing beer. Quite by accident I mentioned my design to him on the evening of the festival. All the Philistine was aroused in him. 'It will ruin my digestion.' 'My friend,' I said, 'I am not your doctor; I have nothing to do with your digestion. Only here is a beautiful Japanese thing, a quaint, queer, almost eerie dinner, that is in my humble opinion worth many digestions. You may take it or leave it, but 'tis the last dinner I cook for you.' . . . I knew I was wasted upon him.

"Then I produced some Nocturnes in imitation of Mr Whistler, with mushrooms, truffles, grilled meat, pickled walnuts, black pudding, French plums, porter — a dinner in soft velvety black, eaten in a starlight of small scattered candles. That, too, led to a resignation: Art will ever demand its martyrs."

The poet made sympathetic noises.

"Always. The awful many will never understand. Their conception of my skill is altogether on a level with their conceptions of music, of literature, of painting. For wall decorations they love autotypes; for literature, harmless volumes of twaddle that leave no vivid impressions on the mind; for dinners, harmless dishes that are forgotten as they are eaten. *My* dinners stick in the memory. I cannot study these people — my genius is all too imperative. If I needed a flavour of almonds and had nothing else to hand, I would use prussic acid. Do right, I say, as your art instinct commands, and take no heed of the consequences. Our function is to make the beautiful gastronomic thing, not to pander to gluttony, not to be the Jesuits of hygiene. My friend, you should see some of my compositions. At home I have books and books in manuscript, Symphonies, Picnics, Fantasies, *Etudes* . . ."

The train was now entering Clapham Junction. The gentleman with the gold watch-chain returned my *Punch*. "A cook," he said in a whisper; "just a common cook!" He lifted his eyebrows and shook his head at me, and proceeded to extricate himself and his umbrella from the carriage. "Out of a situation too!" he said — a little louder — as I prepared to follow him.

"Mere dripping!" said the artist in cookery, with a regal wave of the hand.

Had I felt sure I was included, I should of course have resented the phrase.

8

Le Mari Terrible

"You are always so sympathetic," she said; and added, reflectively, "and one can talk of one's troubles to you without any nonsense."

I wondered dimly if she meant that as a challenge. I helped myself to a biscuit thing that looked neither poisonous nor sandy. "You are one of the most puzzling human beings I ever met," I said, — a perfectly safe remark to any woman under any circumstances.

"Do you find me so hard to understand?" she said.

"You are dreadfully complex." I bit at the biscuit thing, and found it full of a kind of creamy bird-lime. (I wonder why women *will* arrange these unpleasant surprises for me — I sickened of sweets twenty years ago.)

"How so?" she was saying, and smiling her most brilliant smile.

I have no doubt she thought we were talking rather nicely. "Oh!" said I, and waved the cream biscuit thing. "You challenge me to dissect you."

"Well?"

"And that is precisely what I cannot do."

"I'm afraid you are very satirical," she said, with a touch of disappointment. She is always saying that when our conversation has become absolutely idiotic — as it invariably does. I felt an inevitable desire to quote bogus Latin to her. It seemed the very language for her.

"Malorum fiducia pars quosque libet," I said, in a low voice, looking meaningly into her eyes.

"Ah!" she said, colouring a little, and turned to pour hot water into the teapot, looking very prettily at me over her arm as she did so.

"That is one of the truest things that has ever been said of sympathy," I remarked. "Don't you think so?"

"Sympathy," she said, "is a very wonderful thing, and a very precious thing."

"You speak," said I (with a cough behind my hand), "as

though you knew what it was to be lonely."

"There is solitude even in a crowd," she said, and looked round at the six other people— three discreet pairs— who were in the room.

"I, too," I was beginning, but Hopdangle came with a teacup, and seemed inclined to linger. He belongs to the "Nice Boy" class, and gives himself ridiculous airs of familiarity with grown-up people. Then the Giffens went.

"Do you know, I always take such an interest in your work," she was saying to me, when her husband (confound him!) came into the room.

He was a violent discord. He wore a short brown jacket and carpet slippers, and three of his waistcoat buttons were (as usual) undone. "Got any tea left, Millie?" he said, and came and sat down in the arm-chair beside the table.

"How do, Delalune?" he said to the man in the corner. "Damned hot, Bellows," he remarked to me, subsiding creakily.

She poured some more hot water into the teapot. (Why must charming married women always have these husbands?)

"It *is* very hot," I said.

There was a perceptible pause. He is one of those rather adipose people, who are not disconcerted by conversational gaps. "Are *you*, too, working at Argon?" I said. He is some kind of chemical investigator, I know.

He began at once to explain the most horribly complex things about elements to me. She gave him his tea, and rose and went and talked to the other people about autotypes. "Yes," I said, not hearing what he was saying.

" 'No' would be more appropriate," he said. "You are absent-minded, Bellows. Not in love, I hope — at your age?"

Really, I am not thirty, but a certain perceptible thinness in my hair may account for his invariably regarding me as a contemporary. But he should understand that nowadays the beginnings of baldness merely mark the virile epoch. "I say, Millie," he said, out loud and across the room, "you haven't been collecting Bellows here — have you?"

She looked round startled, and I saw a pained look come into her eyes. "For the bazaar?" she said. "Not yet, dear." It seemed to me that she shot a glance of entreaty at him. Then she turned to the others again.

"My wife," he said, "has two distinctive traits. She is a born

66

poetess and a born collector. I ought to warn you."

"I did not know," said I, "that she rhymed."

"I was speaking more of the imaginative quality, the temperament that finds a splendour in the grass, a glory in the flower, that clothes the whole world in a vestiture of interpretation."

"Indeed!" I said. I felt she was watching us anxiously. He could not, of course, suspect. But I was relieved to fancy he was simply talking nonsense.

"The magnificent figures of heroic, worshipful, and mysterious womanhood naturally appeal to her — Cleopatra, Messalina, Beatrice, the Madonna, and so forth."

"And she is writing —"

"No, she is acting. That is the real poetry of women and children. A platonic Cleopatra of infinite variety, spotless reputation, and a large following. Her make-believe is wonderful. She would use Falstaff for Romeo without a twinge, if no one else was at hand. She could exert herself to break the heart of a soldier. I assure you, Bellows —"

I heard her dress rustle behind me.

"I want some more tea," he said to her. "You misunderstood me about the collecting, Millie."

"What were you saying about Cleopatra?" she said, trying, I think, to look sternly at him.

"Scandal," he said. "But about the collecting, Bellows —"

"You must come to this bazaar," she interrupted.

"I shall be delighted," I said, boldly. "Where is it, and when?"

"About this collecting," he began.

"It is in aid of that delightful orphanage at Wimblingham," she explained, and gave me an animated account of the charity. He emptied his second cup of tea. "May I have a third cup?" he said.

The two girls signalled departure, and her attention was distracted. "She collects — and I will confess she does it with extraordinary skill — the surreptitious addresses —"

"John," she said over her shoulder, "I wish you would tell Miss Smithers all those interesting things about Argon." He gulped down his third cup, and rose with the easy obedience of the trained husband. Presently she returned to the tea-things. "Cannot I fill your cup?" she asked. "I really hope John was not telling you his queer notions about me. He says the most remarkable things. Quite lately he has got it into his head that he has a formula for my character."

"I wish *I* had," I said, with a sigh.

"And he goes about explaining me to people, as though I was a mechanism. 'Scalp collector,' I think is his favourite phrase. Did he tell you? Don't you think it perfectly horrid of him?"

"But he doesn't understand you," I said, not grasping his meaning quite at the minute.

She sighed.

"You have," I said, with infinite meaning, "my sincere sympathy —" I hesitated — "my whole sympathy."

"Thank you *so much*," she said, quite as meaningly. I rose forthwith, and we clasped hands, like souls who strike a compact.

Yet, thinking over what he said afterwards, I was troubled by a fancy that there was the faintest suggestion of a smile of triumph about her lips and mouth. Possibly it was only an honourable pride. I suppose he has poisoned my mind a little. Of course, I should not like to think of myself as one of a fortuitously selected multitude strung neatly together (if one may use the vulgarism) on a piece of string, — a stringful like a boy's string of chestnuts, — nice old gentlemen, nice boys, sympathetic and humorous men of thirty, kind fellows, gifted dreamers, and dashing blades, all trailing after her. It is confoundedly bad form of him, anyhow, to guy her visitors. She certainly took it like a saint. Of course, I shall see her again soon, and we shall talk to one another about one another. Something or other cropped up and prevented my going there on her last Tuesday.

9

The Rajah's Treasure

BETWEEN Jehun and Bimabur on the Himalayan slopes, and between the jungles and the higher country where the pines and deodars are gathered together, ruled the Rajah, of whose wonderful treasure I am telling. Hundreds of thousands of people between Peshawur and Calcutta heard of that treasure in its time. And the curious thing about it was that the Rajah kept it not buried inaccessibly, but in a patent safe, securely placed in a little room below the hall of audience.

Very great was the treasure, people said, for the Rajah had prospered all his days. He had found Mindapore a village, and behold! it was a city. Below his fort of unhewn stone the flat-roofed huts of mud had multiplied; and now there sprang up houses with upstairs rooms, and the place which had once boasted no more than one buniah man, engendered a bazaar in the midst of it, as a fat oyster secretes a pearl. And the Rajah had walled his city about.

Moreover, the Holy Place up the river prospered, and the road up the passes was made safe. Merchants and fakirs multiplied about the wells, men came and went, twice even white men from the plain on missions to the people over beyond the deodars, and the streets of the town were ever denser with poultry and children, and little dogs dyed yellow, and with all the multitudinous rich odours of human increase.

The Rajah pushed his boundaries east and west, the *Pax Britannica* consenting, and made his fort ever larger and stronger, and built himself a palace at last, and a harem, and made gardens, so that he could live magnificently and dispense justice to all that owned his sway. And indisputably he did dispense justice— in the name of Allah! upholding the teaching of His prophet, in a purely Oriental manner of course, throughout all his land. Such were the splendid proportions of the Rajah's rule.

The Rajah was a portly, yellow-faced man, with a long black beard, now steadily growing grey, thick lips, and shifty eyes. He was pious, very pious in his daily routine, and swift and unaccountable in his actions. None dared withstand him to his face, even in little things, and not a woman in the harem dared, by any device, try and wheedle him from his will. He kept his own thoughts and went his own way without counsel from any man; he was a lonesome man, and he seemed even jealous of himself.

Golam Shah, his vizier, was but a servant, a carrier of orders; and Samud Singh, his master of horse, but a driller of soldiers. They were tools, he would tell them outright in his pride of power, staves in his hand that he could break at his will. He went rarely to the harem, taking no delight in the society of women or singers, or in nautches; and he was childless. And his cousin, the youth Azim Khan, loved and feared him, and only in the remotest recesses of his heart dared to wish the Rajah would presently die and make a way to the throne. And Azim grew in years and knowledge, and Golam Shah and Samud Singh sought his friendship with an eye to the milder days that would come. But the Rajah did not die; he grew a little plumper and a little more grey, and that was all; until the days came when the talk of the treasure spread through the land.

It would be hard to say when first the rumour spread about the bazaars of the plain that the Rajah of Mindapore was making a hoard. None knew how it began or where. Perhaps from merchants of whom he had bought. It began long before the days of the safe. It was said that rubies had been bought and hidden away; and then not only rubies, but ornaments of gold, and then pearls, and diamonds from Golconda, and all manner of precious stones. Even the deputy commissioner at Allapore heard of it. At last the story re-entered the palace at Mindapore itself, and Azim Khan, who was the Rajah's cousin and his heir, and nominally his commander-in-chief, and Golam Shah, the chief minister, talked it over one with another in a tentative way.

"He has something new," said Golam Shah querulously; "he has something new, and he is keeping it all from me."

Azim Khan watched him cunningly. "I have told you what I have heard," he said. "For my own part I know nothing."

"He goes to and fro musing and humming to himself," said Golam meditatively, "as one who thinks of a pleasure."

Azim Khan was inclined in an open-minded way *chercher la femme*.

"No," said Golam; "it is not that. He was never like that. He

70

is near three score, and besides, these three months or more it has been, and it still keeps on. His eyes are bright, his cheeks flush. And something he hides, hides ever, and will not let me know or suspect ——"

"More rubies, they are saying," said Azim dreamily, and repeated, as if for his own pleasure, "Rubies." For Azim was the heir.

"Especially is it since that Englishman came," said Golam, "three months ago. A big old man, not wrinkled as an old man should be, but red, and with red hair streaking his grey, and with a tight skin and a big body sticking out before. So. A hippopotamus of a man, a great quivering mud-bank of a man, who laughed mightily, so that the people stopped and listened in the street. He came, he laughed, and as he went away we heard them laugh together ——"

"Well?" said Azim.

"He was a diamond merchant, perhaps — or a dealer in rubies. Do Englishmen deal in such things?"

"Would I had seen him!" said Azim.

"He took gold away," said Golam.

Both were silent for a space, and the purring noise of the wheel of the upper well, and the chatter of voices about it rising and falling, made a pleasant sound in the air. "Since the Englishman went," said Golam, "he has been different. He hides something from me — something in his robe. Rubies! What else can it be?"

"He has not buried it?" said Azim.

"He will. Then he will want to dig it up again and look at it," said Golam, for he was a man of experience. "I go softly. Sometimes almost I come upon him. Then he starts ——"

"He grows old and nervous," said Azim, and there was a pause.

"Before the English came," said Golam, looking at the rings upon his fingers, as he recurred to his constant preoccupation; "there were no Rajahs nervous and old."

"The English are for a time," said Azim philosophically, watching a speck of a vulture in the air, over the walnut trees that hid the palace.

That, I say, was even before the coming of the safe. It came in a packing case. Such a case it was as had never been seen before on all the slopes of the Himalayan mountains, it was an elephant's burden. It was days drawing nearer and nearer tediously. At Allapore the news preceded it, and crowds went to see it pass upon the railway. Afterwards elephants and then a great multitude of men dragged it up the hills. And this great case being opened in the Hall of Audience revealed within itself a monstrous iron box, like no other box that had ever come to the city. It had been made, so the story went, by necromancers in England, expressly to the order of the Rajah, that he might keep his treasure therein and sleep in peace. It was so hard that the hardest files powdered upon its corners, and so strong that cannon fired point blank at it would have produced no effect upon it. And it locked with a magic lock. There was a word, and none knew the word but the Rajah. With that word, and a little key that hung about his neck, one could open the lock; but without it none could do so.

So the story whispered its wonderful self about the city. The Rajah caused this safe to be built into the wall of his palace in a little room beyond the Hall of Audience. He superintended the building up of it with jealous eyes. And thereafter he would go thither day by day, once at least every day, coming back with brighter eyes. "He goes to count his treasure," said Golam Shah, standing beside the empty daïs.

And in those days it was that the Rajah began to change. He who had been cunning and subtle became choleric and outspoken. His judgment grew harsh, and a taint that seemed to all about him to be assuredly the taint of avarice crept into his acts. He seized the goods of Lal Dûm, the metal worker, because, forsooth, he had stabbed his wife; and he put a new tax upon the people's cattle, and sweated the bribes of those who stood about him in the Hall of Audience. Also a touch of suspicion of those about him replaced his old fearlessness. He accused Golam Shah to his face of spying upon him, and uttered threats. Moreover, which inclined Golam Shah to hopefulness, he seemed to take a dislike to Azim Khan. Once indeed he made a kind of speech in the Hall of Audience. Therein he declared many times over in a peculiarly husky voice, husky yet full of conviction, that Azim Khan was not worth a half anna, not worth a half anna to any human soul.

In these latter days of the Rajah's decline, moreover, when merchants came, he would go aside with them secretly into the little room, and speak low, so that those in the Hall of Audience, howsoever they strained their ears, could hear nothing of his speech. These things Golam Shah and Azim Khan, and Samud

Singh, who had joined their councils, treasured in their hearts.

"It is true about the treasure," said Azim; "they talked of it round the well of the travellers, even the merchants from Tibet had heard the tale, and had come this way with jewels of price, and afterwards they went secretly telling no one." And ever and again, it was said, came a negro mute from the plains, with secret parcels for the Rajah. "Another stone," was the rumour that went the round of the city.

"The bee makes hoards," said Azim Khan, the Rajah's heir, sitting in the upper chamber of Golam Shah. "Therefore, we will wait awhile." For Azim was more coward than traitor.

Golam Shah heard him with a touch of impatience, notwithstanding that the feebleness of Azim was Golam's chief hope in the happy future that was coming.

Such were the last days of the reign of the Rajah of Mindapore, in the days when the story of the making of his hoard had spread abroad from Peshawur to Calcutta. "Here am I," said the wife of the deputy-commissioner at Allapore, enlarging on the topic, "wearing paste, while the ground is positively lumpy with buried treasures."

"But isn't it maddening that that horrid old man should have so much?"

"He has —" . . . And here would follow a catalogue.

At last there were men in the Deccan even who could tell you particulars of the rubies and precious stones that the Rajah had gathered together. But so circumspect was the Rajah that Azim Khan and Golam Shah had never even set eyes on the glittering heaps that they knew were accumulating in the safe.

The Rajah always went into the little room alone, and even then he locked the door of the little room — it had a couple of locks — before he went to the safe and used the magic word. How all the ministers and officers and guards listened and looked at one another as the door of the room behind the curtain closed!

The Rajah changed indeed, in these days, not only in the particulars of his rule, but in his appearance. "He is growing old. How fast he grows old! The time is almost ripe," whispered Samud Singh. The Rajah's hand became tremulous, his step was now sometimes unsteady, and his memory curiously defective. He would come back out from the treasure room, and his hand would tighten fiercely on the curtain, and he would stumble on the steps of the daïs. "His eyesight fails," said

Golam. "See! — his turban is askew. He is sleepy even in the forenoon, before the heat of the day. His judgments are those of a child."

It was a painful sight to see a man so suddenly old and enfeebled still ruling men. That alone would have given a properly constituted heir-apparent a revolutionary turn of mind. But the treasure was certainly the chief cause that set the idle, garrulous, pleasure-loving Azim plotting against his cousin. A throne was a thing one might wait for, in his opinion — a throne and its cares; but the thought of those heaps of shining stones and intricate golden jewels was a different matter. Azim had had a year of college education, and was so far an enlightened man. He understood investments, and credit, and the folly of hoarding. Moreover, the thought of so much latent wealth set him thinking of the pleasure of life and his well nigh lost youth.

"He may go on yet, a score of years," said Golam Shah.

Azim became a greedy hearer of rumours.

It was through Azim and Golam, who was humiliated and pained by his master's want of confidence, that the leprosy of discontent came into the State. The Land Tax, the Salt Tax, the Cattle Tax became burthens; the immemorial custom of leaving the troops unpaid became a grievance; the Commissioner at Allapore heard tales, and was surprised to find growing evidence of mismanagement in what he had long thought a passably well governed native state. Also the chief mollahs were sounded, and there was talk of gifts and the honour of the shrine. And the two eunuchs, and the women of Rajah's harem became factors of the greatest moment in the State. Coffee was tried, but the Rajah was wary — and sweetmeats he had shunned from his youth.

"Should a ruler hoard riches," said Shere Ali, in the guard-room, "and leave his soldiers unpaid?" That was the beginning of the end.

It was the thought of the treasure won over the soldiers, even as it did the mollahs and the eunuchs. Why had the Rajah not buried it in some unthinkable place, as his father had done before him, and killed the diggers with his hand? Surely India is not what it was. "He has hoarded," said Samud with a chuckle — for the old Rajah had once pulled his beard — "only to pay for his own undoing." And in order to insure confidence, Golam Shah went beyond the truth perhaps, and gave a sketchy account of the treasures to this man and that, even as a casual eye witness might do.

Then, suddenly and swiftly, the palace revolution was accomplished. When the lonely old Rajah was killed, a shot was to be fired from the harem lattice, bugles were to be blown, and the sepoys were to run out in the square before the palace, and fire a volley in the air. The murder was done in the dark save for a little red lamp that burnt in the corner. Azim knelt on the body and held up the wet beard, and cut the throat wide and deep to make sure. It was so easy! Why had he waited so long? And then, with his hands covered with warm blood, he sprang up eagerly — Rajah at last! and followed Golam and Samud and the eunuchs down the long, faintly moonlit passage, towards the Hall of Audience.

As they did so, the crack of a rifle sounded far away, and after a pause came the first awakening noises of the town. One of the eunuchs had an iron bar, and Samud carried a pistol in his hand. He fired into the locks of the treasure room and wrecked them, and the eunuch smashed the door in. Then they all rushed in together, none standing aside for Azim. It was dark, and the second eunuch went reluctantly to get a torch, in fear lest his fellow murderers should open the safe in his absence.

But he need have had no fear. The cardinal event of that night is the triumphant vindication of the advertised merits of Chobbs' unrivalled safes. The tumult that occurred between the Mindapore sepoys and the people need not concern us. The people loved not the new Rajah — let that suffice. The conspirators got the key from round the dead Rajah's neck, and tried a multitude of the magic words of the English that Samud Singh knew, even such words as "Kemup" and "Gorblimey"— in vain.

In the morning, the safe in the treasure room remained intact and defiant, the woodwork about it smashed to splinters, and great chunks of stone knocked out of the wall, dents abundantly scattered over its impregnable door, and dust of files below. And the shifty Golam had to explain the matter to the soldiers and mollahs as best he could. This was an extremely difficult thing to do, because in no kind of business is prompt cash so necessary as in the revolutionary line.

The state of affairs for the next few days in Mindapore was exceedingly strained. One fact stands out prominently, that Azim Khan was hopelessly feeble. The soldiers would not at

75

first believe in the exemplary integrity of the safe, and a deputation insisted in the most occidental manner in verifying the new Rajah's statements. Moreover, the populace clamoured, and then by a naked man running, came the alarming intelligence that the new Deputy Commissioner at Allapore was coming headlong and with soldiers to verify the account of the revolution Golam Shah and Samud Singh had sent him in the name of Azim.

The new Deputy-Commissioner was a raw young man, partly obscured by a pith helmet, and chock full of zeal and the desire for distinction; and he had heard of the treasure. He was going, he said, to sift the matter thoroughly. On the arrival of this distressing intelligence there was a hasty and informal council of state (at which Azim was not present), a counter revolution was arranged, and all that Azim ever learnt of it was the sound of a footfall behind him, and the cold touch of a pistol barrel on the neck.

When the Commissioner arrived, that dexterous statesman, Golam Shah, and that honest soldier, Samud Singh, were ready to receive him, and they had two corpses, several witnesses, and a neat little story. In addition to Azim they had shot an unpopular officer of the Mindapore sepoys. They told the Commissioner how Azim had plotted against the Rajah and raised a military revolt, and how the people, who loved the old Rajah, even as Golam Shah and Samud Singh loved him, had quelled the revolt, and how peace was restored again. And Golam explained how Azim had fought for life even in the Hall of Audience, and how he, Golam, had been wounded in the struggle, and how Samud had shot Azim with his own hand.

And the Deputy Commissioner, being weak in his dialect, had swallowed it all. All round the Deputy Commissioner, in the minds of the people, the palace, and the city, hung the true story of the case, as it seemed to Golam Shah, like an avalanche ready to fall; and yet the Deputy-Commissioner did not learn of it for four days. And Golam and Samud went to and fro, whispering and pacifying, promising to get at the treasure as soon as the Deputy Commissioner could be got out of the way. And as they went to and fro so also the report went to and fro—that Golam and Samud had opened the safe and hidden the treasure, and closed and locked it again; and bright eyes watched them curiously and hungrily even as they had watched the Rajah in the days that were gone.

"This city is no longer an abiding place for you and me," said Golam Shah, in a moment of clear insight. "They are mad about this treasure. Golconda would not satisfy them."

The Deputy Commissioner, when he heard their story, did indeed make knowing inquiries (as knowing as the knowingness of the English goes) in order to show himself not too credulous; but he elicited nothing. He had heard tales of treasure, had the Commissioner, and of a great box? So had Golam and Samud, but where it was they could not tell. They too had certainly heard tales of treasure — many tales indeed. Perhaps there *was* treasure.

Had the Deputy Commissioner had the scientific turn of mind, he would have observed that a strong smell of gunpowder still hung about the Audience Chamber, more than was explained by the narrative told him; and had he explored the adjacent apartments, he would presently have discovered the small treasure-room with its smashed locks, and the ceiling now dependent ruins, and amid the ruins the safe, bulging perilously from the partly collapsed walls, but still unconquered, and with its treasures unexplored. Also it is a fact that Golam Shah's bandaged hand was not the consequence of heroism in combat, but of certain private blasting operations too amateurishly prosecuted.

So you have the situation: Deputy Commissioner installed in the palace, sending incorrect information to headquarters and awaiting instructions, the safe as safe as ever; assistant conspirators grumbling louder and louder; and Golam and Samud getting more and more desperate lest this voice should reach the Deputy's ears.

Then came the night when the Commissioner heard a filing and a tapping, and being a brave man, rose and went forthwith, alone and very quietly, across the Hall of Audience, pistol in hand, in search of the sound. Across the Hall a light came from an open door that had been hidden in the day by a curtain. Stopping silently in the darkness of the outer apartment, he looked into the treasure room. And there stood Golam with his arm in a sling, holding a lantern, while Samud fumbled with pieces of wire and some little keys. They were without boots, but otherwise they were dressed ready for a journey.

The Deputy Commissioner was, for a Government official, an exceedingly quick-witted man. He slipped back in the darkness again, and within five minutes, Golam and Samud, still fumbling, heard footsteps hurrying across the Hall of Audience, and saw a flicker of light. In another moment Lieutenant Earl, in pyjamas and boots, but with a brace of revolvers and couple of rifles behind him, stood in the doorway of the treasure-room, and Golam and Samud were caught. Samud clicked his pistol and then threw it down, for it was three to one — Golam being not only a bandaged man, but fundamentally a man of peace.

When the intelligence of this treachery filtered from the palace into the town, there was an outbreak of popular feeling, and a dozen officious persons set out to tell the Deputy Commissioner the true connection between Golam, Samud, and the death of the Rajah. The first to penetrate to the Deputy Commissioner's presence was an angry fakir, from the colony that dwelt about the Holy place. And after a patient hearing the Deputy Commissioner extracted the thread of the narrative from the fabric of curses in which the holy man presented it.

"This is most singular," said the Deputy Commissioner to the Lieutenant, standing in the treasure room (which looked as though the palace had been bombarded), and regarding the battered but still inviolable safe. "Here we seem to have the key of the whole position."

"Key!" said the Lieutenant. "It's the key they haven't got."

"Curious mingling of the new and the old," said the Deputy Commissioner. "Patent safe — and a hoard."

"Send to Allapore and wire Chobbs, I suppose?" said the Lieutenant.

The Deputy Commissioner signified that was his intention, and they set guards before and behind and all about the treasure room, until the proper instructions about the lock should come.

So it was that the *Pax Britannica* solemnly took possession of the Rajah's hoard, and men in Simla heard the news, and envied that Deputy Commissioner his adventure with all their hearts. For his promptitude and decision was a matter of praise, and they said that Mindapore would certainly be annexed and added to the district over which he ruled. Only a fat old man named MacTurk, living in Allapore, a big man with a noisy quivering laugh, and a secret trade with certain native potentates, did not hear the news, excepting only the news of the murder of the Rajah and the departure of the Deputy Commissioner, for several days. He heard nothing of the disposition of the treasure — an unfortunate thing, since, among other things, he had sold the Rajah his safe, and may even have known the word by which the lock was opened.

The Deputy Commissioner had theatrical tastes. These he gratified under the excuse that display was above all things necessary in dealing with Orientals. He imprisoned his four malefactors theatrically, and when the instructions came from Chobbs he had the safe lugged into the Hall of Audience, in order to open it with more effect. The Commissioner sat on the daïs, while the engineer worked at the safe on the crimson steps.

In the central space was stretched a large white cloth. It reminded the Deputy Commissioner of a picture he had seen of Alexander at Damascus receiving the treasures of Darius.

"It is gold," said one bystander to another. "There was a sound of chinking as they brought the safe in. My brother was among those who hauled."

The engineer clicked the lock. Every eye in the Hall of Audience grew brighter and keener, excepting the eyes of the Deputy-Commissioner. He felt the dignity of his responsibilities, and sat upon the daïs looking as much like the *Pax Britannica* as possible.

"Holy Smoke!" said the engineer, and slammed the safe again. A murmur of exclamations ran round the hall. Everyone was asking everyone else what they had seen.

"An asp!" said someone.

The Deputy Commissioner lost his imperturbability. "What is it?" he said, springing to his feet. The engineer leant across the safe and whispered two words, something indistinct and with a blasphemous adjective in front.

"*What?*" said the Deputy Commissioner sharply.

"Glass!" said the engineer in a bitter whisper. "Broken bottles. 'Undreds!"

"Let me see!" said the Deputy Commissioner, losing all his dignity.

"Scotch, if I'm not mistaken," said the engineer, sniffing curiously.

"Curse it!" said the Deputy Commissioner, and looking up to meet a multitude of ironical eyes. "Er ——"

"The assembly is dismissed," said the Deputy Commissioner.

*   *   *

"What a *fool* he must have looked!" wheezed MacTurk, who did not like the Deputy Commissioner. "What a *fool* he must have looked!"

"Simple enough," said MacTurk, "when you know how it came about."

"But how did it come about?" asked the station-master.

"Secret drinking," said MacTurk. "Bourbon whiskey. I taught him how to take it myself. But he didn't dare let on that he was doing it, poor old chap! Mindapore's one of the most fanatically Mahometan states in the hills you see. And he always was a secretive kind of chap, and given to doing things by himself. So he got that safe to hide it in, and keep the bottles. Broke 'em up to pack, I s'pose, when it got too full. Lord! I might ha' known. When people spoke of his treasure ——. I never thought of putting that and the safe and the Bourbon together! But how plain it is! And *what* a sell for Parkinson. Pounded glass! The accumulation of years! Lord! — I'd 'a given a couple of stone off my weight to see him open that safe!"

10
The Presence by the Fire

It never occurred to Reid that his wife lay dying until the very last day of her illness. He was a man of singularly healthy disposition, averse on principle to painful thoughts, and I doubt if in the whole of his married life his mind had dwelt for five minutes together on the possibility of his losing her.

They were both young, and intimate companions — such companions as many desire to be and few become. And perhaps it was her sense of the value of this rare companionship that made her, when first her health declined, run many an avoidable risk rather than leave him to go his way alone.

He was sorry that she was ill, sorry she should suffer, and he missed her, as she lay upstairs, in a thousand ways; but though the doctor was mindful to say all the "preparatory" phrases of his profession, and though her sister spoke, as she conceived, quite plainly, it was as hard for him to understand that this was more than a temporary interruption of their life, as it would have been to believe that the sun would not rise again after to-morrow morning.

The day before she died he was restless, and after wandering about the house and taking a short walk, he occupied himself in planting out her evening primroses — a thing she had made a point of doing now for ten springs in succession. The garden she had always tended, he said, should not seem neglected when she came down again. He had rather his own work got in arrears than that this should happen.

The first realisation, when the doctor, finding all conventional euphemisms useless, told him the fact at last in stark, plain words, stunned him. Even then it is doubtful if he believed. He said not a word in answer, but the colour left his face, and the lines about his mouth hardened. And he walked softly and with white, expressionless features into her room.

He stood at the door-way, and looked for a minute at her thin little features, with the eyes closed and two little lines between the brows, then went and knelt by the bed and looked closely into her face. She did not move until he touched her hair and very softly whispered her name.

Then her eyes opened for a moment, and he saw that she knew him. Her lips moved, and it seemed that she whispered one of those foolish, tender little names that happy married folk delight in inventing for one another, and then she gathered her strength as if with an effort to speak distinctly. He bent mechanically and heard the last syllables of *au revoir*.

For a moment he did not clearly understand what the words were. That was all she said, and as for him, he answered not a word. He put his hand in hers, and she pressed it faintly and then more faintly. He kissed her forehead with dry lips, and the little lines of pain there faded slowly into peace.

For an hour they let him kneel, until the end had come; and all that time he never stirred. Then they had to tap his shoulder to rouse him from his rigour. He got up slowly, bent over her for a moment, looking down into her tranquil face, and then allowed them to lead him away.

That was how Reid parted from his wife, and for days after he behaved as a man who had been suddenly deprived of all initiative. He did no work; he went nowhere outside the house; he ate, drank and slept mechanically; and he did not even seem to suffer actively. For the most part, he sat stupidly at his desk or wandered about the big garden, looking with dull eyes at the little green buds that were now swiftly opening all about him. Not a soul ventured to speak to him of his loss, albeit those who did not know him might have judged his mood one of absolute apathy.

But nearly a week after the funeral the floodgates of his sorrow were opened. Quite suddenly the thing came upon him. Her sister heard him walk into the study and throw himself into a chair. Everything was still for a space, and then he sprang up again and she heard him wailing, "Mary! Mary!" and then he ran, sobbing violently and stumbling, along the passage to his room. It was grotesquely like a little child that had suddenly been hurt.

He locked his door; and her sister, fearing what might happen, went along the passage. She thought of rapping at the door, but on second thoughts she refrained. After listening awhile she went away.

It was long after the first violence of his grief had passed that Reid first spoke of his feelings. He who had been a matter-of-fact materialist was converted, I found, to a belief in immortality by the pitiless logic of her uncompleted life. But I think it was an imperfect, a doubting, belief even at the best. And to strengthen it, perhaps, he began to show a growing interest in the inquiries of those who were sifting whatever evidence there may be of the return of those who are dead.

"For I want my wife now," said he. "I want her in this life. I want her about me — her comfort, her presence. What does it matter that I shall meet her again when I am changed, and she is changed? It was the dear trivialities, the little moments, the touch of her hand, the sound of her voice in the room with me, her distant singing in the garden, and her footfall on the stairs. If I could believe that," he said, "if I could believe ——"

And in that spirit it was that he kept to the old home, and would scarcely bear that a thing within or without should be altered in any way. The white curtains that had been there the last autumn hung dirty in the windows, and the little desk that had been her own in the study stood there still, with the pen thrown down as he fancied she had left it.

"Here, if anywhere," he said, "she is at home. Here, if anywhere, her presence lives."

Her sister left him when a housekeeper was obtained, and he went on living there alone, working little and communicating for the most part with these dead memories. After a time he loved nothing so much as to talk to her, and I think in those days that I was of service to him. He would take me about the house, pointing to this trivial thing and that; and telling me some little act of hers that he linked therewith. And he always spoke of her as one who still lived.

"She does" so and so, he would say; "she likes" so and so. We would pace up and down the rich lawn of his house. "My wife is particularly fond of those big white lilies," he would say, "and this year they are finer than ever." So the summer passed and the autumn came.

And one day late in the evening he came to me, walking round the house and tapping at the French window of my study, and as he came in out of the night I noticed how deadly white and sunken his face was and how bright his eyes.

"I have seen her," he said to me, in a low, clear voice. "She has visited me. I knew she was watching me and near me. I have felt her presence for weeks and weeks. And now she has come."

He was intensely excited, and it was some time before I could get any clear story from him.

He had been sitting by the fire in his study, musing, no doubt going over for the hundredth time, day by day and almost hour by hour as he was wont to do, one of the summer holidays they had spent together. He was staring, he said, into the glowing coals, and almost imperceptibly it was that there grew upon him the persuasion that he was not alone. The thought took shape slowly in his mind, but with a strange quality of absolute conviction, that she was sitting in the armchair in front of him, as she had done so often in the old days, and watching him a-dreaming. For a moment he did not dare to look up, lest he should find this a mere delusion.

Then slowly he raised his eyes. He was dimly aware of footsteps advancing along the passage as he did so. A wave of bitter disappointment swept over him as he saw the chair was empty, and this incontinently gave place to a tumult of surprise and joyful emotion. For he saw her — saw her distinctly. She was standing behind the chair, leaning over the back of it, and smiling the tender smile he knew so well. So in her life she had stood many a time and listened to him, smiling gently. The firelight played upon her face.

"I saw her as plainly as I see you," he said. "I saw the smile in her eyes, and my heart leapt out to her."

For a moment he was motionless, entranced, and with an instantaneous appreciation of the transitoriness of this appearance. Then suddenly the door opened, the shadows in the room rushed headlong, and the housemaid came in with his lamp lit and without the shade — a dazzling glare of naked flame. The yellow light splashed over the room and brought out everything clear and vivid.

By mere reflex action he turned his head at the sound of the door-handle, and forthwith turned it back again. But the face he had longed for so patiently had vanished with the shadows before the light. Everything was abruptly plain and material. The girl replenished the fire, moved the armchair on one side, and took away the scuttle lining to refill it with coals. A curious bashfulness made Reid pretend to make notes at his table until these offices were accomplished. Then he looked across the fireplace again, and the room was empty. The sense of her presence, too, had gone. He called upon her name again and again, rubbed his eyes, and tried to force her return by concentrating his mind upon her. But nothing availed. He could see her no more.

84

He allowed me to cross-examine him in the most detailed way upon this story. His manner was so sane, so convincing, and his honesty so indisputable, that I went to bed that night with my beliefs and disbeliefs greatly shaken. Hitherto I had doubted every ghost story I had heard; but here at last was one of a different quality. Indeed, I went to bed that night an unwilling convert to the belief in the phantasms of those who are dead and all that that belief implies.

My faith in Reid was confirmed by the fact that from late August, when this happened, until December he did not see the apparition again. Had it been an hallucination begotten of his own intense brooding it must inevitably have recurred. But it was presently to be proved beyond all question that the thing he saw was an exterior presence. Night after night he sat in his study, longing for the repetition of that strange experience; and at last, after many nights, he saw her for the second time.

It was earlier in the evening, but with the shorter winter days the room was already dark. Once more he looked into his study fire, and once more that fire glowed redly. Then there came the same sense of her presence, the same hesitation before he raised his eyes. But this time he looked over the chair at once and saw her without any flash of disappointment.

At the instant he felt not the faintest suspicion that his senses deceived him. For a moment he was dumb. He was seized with an intense longing to touch her hand. Then came into his head some half-forgotten story that one must speak first to a spirit. He leant forward.

"Mary!" he said very softly. But she neither moved nor spoke. And then suddenly it seemed that she grew less distinct.

"Mary!" he whispered, with a sudden pang of doubt. Her features grew unfamiliar.

Then suddenly he rose to his feet, and as he did so the making of the illusion was demonstrated. The high light on a vase that had been her cheek moved to the right; the shadow that had been her arm moved to the left.

Few people realise how little we actually see of what is before our eyes: a patch of light, a patch of shadow, and all the rest our memory and our imagination supply. A chance grouping of dim forms in the dusky firelit study had furnished all the suggestion his longing senses had required. His eyes and his heart and the humour of chance had cheated him.

He stood there staring. For a moment the disintegration of

the figure filled him with a sense of grotesque horror and dismay. For a moment it seemed beyond the sanity of things. Then, as he realised the deception his senses had contrived, he sat down again, put his elbows on the table and buried his face in his hands.

About ten he came and told me. He told me in a clear hard voice, without a touch of emotion, recording a remarkable fact. "As I told you the other thing, it is only right that I should tell you this," he said.

Then he sat silently for a space. "She will come no more," he said at last. "She will come no more."

And suddenly he rose, and without a greeting, passed out into the night.

11

Mr. Marshall's Doppelganger

I

AMONG the curious cases which I, as a once active member of the Society for the Rehabilitation of Abnormal Phenomena, have been called upon to investigate, that of Mr. Marshall's apparition to the Rev. George Burwash, of Sussexville, and to the Rev. Philip Wendover, his curate, is certainly by no means the least curious. It was communicated to the Society by the Rev. George Burwash himself, with a mass of authenticating evidence quite in excess of the ordinary case of this description.

The Rev. George Burwash is one of that little army of honest and worthy amateur investigators scattered throughout the country — clergymen, retired officers, professors keeping holiday, and ladies of every description — who, in spite of a certain inexperience in the handling of human evidence, are doing such excellent work in reviving the erst decadent belief in spiritual entities.

The apparition occurred on Christmas Eve, 1895, and his communication was read before the Society in the subsequent January. My inquiries in Sussexville were prosecuted during the April and May following.

A doppelganger is a phantasm of a living person. Such phantasms are believed by many quite reputable people nowadays to be of frequent occurrence and, as in the case I had to examine, are often curiously purposeless. Here we had Mr. Marshall appearing suddenly and with a disturbed countenance before Mr. Burwash and his curate, uttering horrible imprecations, threatening him, and then suddenly disappearing. He cursed and threatened without rhyme or reason; his procedure was totally without symbolic value. But so vivid and so sonorous was the phantasm that at the time it did not enter into the head of Mr. Burwash to regard him as anything but a real person, albeit the figure moved with a curious gliding motion, markedly different from walking. Until it vanished, indeed, the thought of ghosts did not occur to him. The manner of disappearance and the subsequent silence, as the reverend gentleman described them, were, however, quite sufficiently ghost-like for any reasonable person.

My first proceeding in elucidating this interesting case was, of course, to visit the scene of the appearance, and, courteously but exhaustively, to cross-examine Mr. Burwash and Mr. Wendover.

Mr. Burwash occupies a house on the hillside above the church, and in consequence of the growth of his family he has, for the sake of quiet, built himself a small but convenient study of pine up the hill. A path crosses over the crest of the hill, and descends steeply from a little gate near the study between the vicarage hedge and the churchyard wall to the lych gate in the main road below.

On Christmas Eve Mr. Burwash had been writing late at his Christmas sermon, having been delayed during the day by a parcel of spookical literature, and it was after midnight that he finished. His curate, with whom he is, for a vicar, on exceptionally friendly terms, came into the study and sat smoking, while the vicar alternately talked to him and punctuated his discourse for the morrow. It adds to the interest of the case that this curate, Mr. Wendover, was a declared sceptic.

When the punctuation was completed the vicar got up, stretched, and opened his study door to look out at the weather. He saw by the glare from the door that a few flakes of snow were falling, and he was preparing to turn and remark upon this to the curate when suddenly, and abruptly, Mr. Marshall appeared outside the gate, and stood for a moment, swaying exactly like a drunken man, and apparently struggling with violent internal emotions. Then finding his voice, he poured forth with dramatic unexpectedness, a volley of curses, so gross and personal that I had the greatest difficulty in persuading Mr. Burwash, in the interests of science, to repeat them.

The curate became aware of Mr. Marshall's presence for the first time when he heard this outbreak. He sprang to his feet, and saw Marshall distinctly over his superior's shoulder. Then, as abruptly, the man staggered and vanished into the night. As he did so, a gust of wind whirled the snowflakes about, and the study door behind Mr. Burwash slammed violently. Mr. Burwash was shut out and the curate in.

As soon as he had recovered from his surprise, Mr. Burwash went to the gate, expecting to find Marshall lying there — but up the hill and down, the pathway was deserted.

That, substantially, was the story of the vision of Mr. Burwash, and by itself it would, of course, have had little or no interest. As I immediately pointed out, Marshall himself may have passed that way in an intoxicated condition, and his sudden and gliding disappearance may have been due to his feet slipping on the frozen snow that veneered the pathway. The closing door, too, by cutting off the light, may have aided that effect. And the path is so steep that one can reasonably imagine a man who had lost his footing going down the entire slope of the hill in a second or so; in the time, that is, that it took Mr. Burwash to reopen his door. That, indeed, was the view Mr. Burwash himself at first took of the matter.

Mr. Wendover, of course, agreed with him. But having a scarcely explicable doubt about the business lurking in his mind, the vicar took the very first opportunity of taxing Marshall, who is usually a sober and steady man, with the almost unpardonable insults he had uttered overnight. In any case, and without the faintest suspicion that anything psychic had happened, the vicar would have done so.

This opportunity of reproof he made in the afternoon of Christmas Day. He found Mr. and Mrs. Marshall drinking strong tea together, and it carried out the common-sense theory of the affair that Marshall should have a headache still, and have been quite unable to participate with any enjoyment in their simple but of course extremely bilious Christmas meal. And he freely and contritely admitted he had been drunk overnight.

But when Mr. Burwash proceeded with some heat to charge him with the filthy blasphemies of the previous evening, Mrs. Marshall fired up indignantly. And then it was that the extraordinary side of this incident came to light. There was the clearest evidence — evidence strong enough to hang a man, indeed, if need had been — that Marshall had never been near the vicar's study at all on Christmas Eve; that the thing was an absolute impossibility; that, in fact, about half-past eleven, half an hour before the apparition that is, he had been picked up helplessly drunk by some charitable neighbours about a couple of hundred yards from the Seven Thorns, carried the whole mile and a half to his own home, taken into his own kitchen, and dumped down there at the very moment when his almost equally inebriated doppelganger was insulting the vicar three-quarters of a mile away.

I tested every link in the chain of evidence, as I thought, and not a link failed. Mrs. Marshall told me how she had gone to bed, being tired, and how when the good man failed to appear after half-past ten she had grown anxious, and at last, hearing voices outside, had shivered out of bed and gone to the window. A Mr. Ted Apps, two brothers named Durgan, one a blacksmith and the other a watchmaker, and a Mr. Hetherington, a baker, were walking in a leisurely and voluminous manner along the road, singing as they walked. She knew Mr. Apps, and opened the window and called to him. She asked him whether he had seen Marshall.

At that the little party stopped and interrogated one another. They all distinctly remembered Marshall being at the Seven Thorns, and until she had called their attention to the matter had had a vague impression that he was still, convivially, with them. Her wifely anxiety being only too evident, and they full of that feeling of mutual helpfulness that still, thank Heaven, distinguishes our homely country Christmastide, it was natural they should offer to return for him.

"Aw ri', Miz Marshall," they cried one after the other, in a reassuring voice, and turned, and making the night cheerful with Marshall's name, returned round the long winding road towards the Seven Thorns. All were seasonably inebriated, and no doubt they were now scattered distantly and not in an amiable knot together as they reeled along calling after Marshall; but all distinctly remember what was happening at the time.

I have elaborately verified the story from all four of them. Everything was as explicit as evidence could be. " 'Twarn't nart hun' yards orf Se'n Thorns," said the blacksmith Durgan, "that us found en. There 'e was with 'is 'ed agenst th' old fence and his blessed owd white legs" — it was Mr. Marshall's weakness invariably to wear a peculiarly light variety of corduroy trousers— "stickin' art—jes' 'elpless 'e was. 'Ad t' carry en every blessed yard, us did. 'E wuz bad, I tell 'ee."

The others corroborated exactly. Marshall's speech they agreed was incoherent— shapeless in fact. Had he been able to surmount one impossibility and get up to the vicar's study, it would have been equally impossible for him to have articulated a curse. Of that they were all convinced. And I imagine that the process of carrying him home along the dark road must have been a pretty severe test of insensibility.

"Didn't you drop him?" I asked of the elder Durgan.

"Oh, we dropped 'e," said Durgan reassuringly. "We dropped en right 'nough. And lord! what a job we did 'ave, a picking of en up, to be sure——" And he proceeded to give me a detailed narrative, as he remembered it, of the entire journey.

Consequent upon Mr. Marshall's incapacity to walk, Mrs. Marshall had to come down and open the door in order that they might carry him in. But being in a déshabille that she considered unbecoming, she stipulated that they should not enter until she had time to retire upstairs again. As they came in, she held a candle over the banisters and directed them where to deposit their burden. Mr. Apps, being in a festive mood, then demanded drinks round, but the others being soberer, over-ruled him, and after they had retired she descended and locked the front door. Afterwards it would seem that Mr. Apps returned, hammered at the door and demanded drinks again. Twice or three times she said she was alarmed in this way and then Mr. Apps apparently abandoned his quest.

She laid great stress on the aggressive behaviour of Mr. Apps, on account of the trouble about the missing sausages and mince pie to which I shall presently allude. As Marshall rarely drank, and as Mrs. Marshall was a person of refined tastes with a womanly horror of an intoxicated man, she did not go down to him in the kitchen until the early morning, and then she found him, still in a drink-sodden sleep, upon the hearthrug, with a pool of melted snow about him. And there, what one may call the case of the alibi, ends.

Now here we have an extraordinary contradiction between two perfectly credible stories. On the one hand two clergymen, and one a sceptic and even a scoffer at psychic experts, witness that Marshall was in one place, and on the other, four indisputably honest villagers and the man's own wife testify as emphatically that he was in quite another place. I sifted and weighed every scrap of evidence, and could see no way to reconcile the two except by taking the view Mr. Burwash took, and admitting a belief in doppelgangers. To that effect I finally reported to the Society. Altogether I gave the business a clear seven days.

Only one alternative to that acquiescence seemed possible to me, and that was that the vicar and his curate, in spite of the almost vehement assurance of Mr. Burwash, had not seen

Marshall at all. I spent three days seeking a colourable substitute for Marshall, a person who seen casually might have been mistaken for him, and not one could I find. He had a noticeably long nose, a fresh complexion, and a large mouth. Even in his dress he was distinctive. In view of the fact that the light of the vicar's study fell fully on the face of the apparition, the mistaken identity notion failed hopelessly as an explanation. It was doppelganger or nothing. Doppelganger, to my mind, seemed the more credible climax. In the whole course of my career as a psychic inquirer, I had certainly never come upon any occult phenomenon so absolutely a tried and proven thing.

I ask the reader to stop at this stage to recapitulate the case as I have stated it, and to consider whether the proof does not seem to be practically complete. No one at all familiar with modern psychical research will find any discredit to the story in the absolute carelessness and purposelessness of the appearance.

II

Mention has already been made of the Rev. Philip Wendover in connexion with this story. Mr. Wendover belonged to that large, and, I fear I must write prejudiced, class, who will not have psychic phenomena at any price. He was a fair, athletic young man; and he had formerly been an assistant master at Dinchester. To that I must ascribe his extraordinary facility with slang, which occasionally even affected his pulpit deliverances. From first to last, while I was unravelling this story, he had nothing but derision for me, in spite of his being my most important witness. Indeed I quite sickened of his pet phrase of "tommy-rot."

"What tommy-rot it all is!" he would say in his riotous amiable way. "A grown man, presumably sane and educated, spending days and days hunting the ghost of a dead superstition for a lot of piffling old fools in London. Why the deuce don't you dig, man? — do something useful? You're strong enough."

"Well," I would say, "here are my facts ——"

"Oh! facts be jiggered!" he would say. "Facts that prove doppelganging are facts I have no respect for."

"But I have," I would say.

"What beastly rot! You've got a flaw somewhere. You know you have. If facts prove arrant nonsense, it shows that there's something wrong."

Then I would begin to state my case. "Show me the flaw," I would say.

And directly I began to marshal my evidence, he would lose his brief temper and begin to shout me down. Did I think he had the time to go over every leaky tinpot ghost story in the country before he had a right to disbelieve? And I would raise my voice to avoid being shouted down.

"If Marshall has a doppelganger let him bring him up here in the daylight," he would say, and similar illogical nonsense; offering to board and clothe the two of them for a year out of his own meagre income, shouting extravagant promissory notes at the doppelganger, and so forth. And then, suddenly at the height of our shouting, he would leave off quite abruptly, stare savagely at his pipe, and ask me for a match.

"Have you a match?" he used to say, as though that was the thing that had driven him to revolt, that, by a tacit understanding, suspended the quarrel. I would hand him a match to relight his pipe. He would make some indifferent remark at a tangent, and we would go on talking and smoking together like a pair of brothers. The row, when it must have seemed to an eavesdropper on the point of blows, would vanish before one could snap one's fingers. For his choleric outbreaks, like my own, were as brief as they were violent, like tropical thunderstorms more than anything else in the world.

Now after I had returned to my chambers in Museum Street, I was surprised one afternoon in May by a visit from Wendover. I was collecting some new and interesting evidence upon crystal-gazing that had recently come to hand, when I heard him noisily ascend the stairs.

He came in with all the tumultuous violence of triumphant common-sense, shouting and blowing, flung his umbrella on a haunted sofa I had on loan under observation, slapped down his hat on the planchette, and sat in my easy chair.

"Give me some tea, my good man," he bawled.

"And then I'll tell you an eye-opener. Your doppelganger! He's hoist!"

I tried to be as cool and acrid as possible though this irruption was certainly something of a shock, and I begged him to let me know how the hoisting was accomplished. And waving his bread and butter at me to accentuate his story, and ever and anon drinking his tea noisily and eagerly, he told me the true story of the Marshall doppelganger.

93

"You know there was a thundering row blowing up about Mrs. Marshall's sausages and mince pie?" he said. "Libel actions and all that?"

I remembered the trouble quite distinctly — too distinctly, indeed, for it was a side issue into which Mrs. Marshall was always running, and which made Apps suspicious and reluctant under examination. The disappearance of these dainties on Christmas Eve from her kitchen I had always regarded as a troublesome irrelevance.

So far as I had formed a judgment in that matter at all I had gone with the general sentiment of the village, and suspected Apps and his friends. For clownish thieving of that kind was just the sort of thing that would commend itself to the rustic mind as a very good Christmas joke indeed.

"What has the mince pie got to do with the story?" I said.

"Everything," said Wendover, and he drank, winking at me over his teacup.

"Old Franks!" said Wendover, putting his cup aside and leaning forward as he spoke to touch my knee.

"What of Franks?" I said, for I had never suspected that elderly sinner had any connexion with the case.

"Drunk!" said Wendover. "Drowsy tipsy in the Seven Thorns, a week ago; discussion running high on the great mince-pie and sausage question. Did Apps take 'em, or didn't he? Friend of Apps indignant, tried running down Mrs. Marshall. 'Everybody knows Mrs. Marshall's mince pies are worse than her sausages, not worth stealing; wouldn't have 'em at a gift.' 'Ain't they?' says old Franks, hiccoughing and winking. 'That's all you know,' said old Franks."

Wendover paused, looked at me, took up two slices of bread and butter, laid them face to face, bit them enormously, and looked at me again.

"My good man," I said, "have you come all this way from Sussexville to tell me that?"

"That and some other things," said Wendover, disposing of the bread and butter.

" 'How do you know?' says Apps' friend. 'Never you mind,' said old Franks, appearing to realise he'd made a slip; and there, in spite of a few leading questions to the old man, his criticism on Mrs. Marshall's mincemeat came to an end."

"Well," I began.

"Wait a bit," said Wendover. "When old Franks had gone, as he did rather quickly after that, the peculiar way in which he had spoken was remarked upon. Could it be that he had stolen the mince pie in question? Occasionally he did odd jobs for Marshall, as everyone knew, and it might be that sometime on Christmas Eve he had ventured ——"

"Really, this pothouse gossip ——"

"You wait. It wasn't long before this little suspicion came to my ears, and I must confess I didn't think very much of it at the time, nor did I connect it with your well-authenticated case. Who would? But going past Marshall's, who should I see, as I thought, but Marshall himself planting beans. He was stooping down with his back to me, so that his nether garments formed most of the view."

"I went to the wall and shouted, intending to have a quiet word with him about this missing pie and sausage. He looked up and then I saw the mistake I'd made at once. It wasn't Marshall at all, but the excellent Franks, doing a bit of a job in a pair of Marshall's cast-off breeks. Ah! — now you sit up! No men could be less alike about the head and face and complexion, I'll admit, but seen — that way — well, there was really an astonishing resemblance. Easily be mistaken."

"But the vicar — you both of you said you saw his face!"

"So we did, and heard his voice. But the other gents in the case — drunk — dark night ——"

That staggered me for a moment. I'd never thought of a mistake in identity creeping into the case on that side. I could quite imagine four drunken men making such a mistake, but the point was that even if Mrs. Marshall didn't see her husband's face overnight, she did the next morning.

"Now, don't you think that I've come up here with a story half told," said Wendover, replying to this objection, "because I haven't. I've simply settled the whole blessed question. It's a concession to your weakness, I know, but directly the possible resemblance of old Franks to Marshall dawned on me I determined I would clear up the muddle from end to end. I went to Franks and began to talk parochialism to him, and suddenly I hit him on the knee.

" 'I know all about it, Franks, my man,' I said. 'Own up!' He knew me pretty well, and he looked at me for half a minute over those old glasses of his. 'I won't tell a soul in Sussexville,' I said. 'I promise on my honour. But how the deuce did you get out of

Marshall's kitchen and him in?' I suppose he saw the twinkle in my eye.

" 'He was in the little tool-shed hard by the waterbutt, Muster Wendover,' he said, 'an' his boots took off an' put under the currant bushes as tidy as cud be. Couldn't wake him nohow. And the snow a-fallin'— it wuzn't common charity not to leave en.' "

"You see?" said Wendover.

I saw only too plainly. "They carried home old Franks thinking it was Marshall ——"

"While Marshall was swearing and cursing his way home by the footpath over the hill."

"And when Marshall did get home ——"

"Mrs. Marshall, firm in her faith that he was already safely, if swinishly, deposited in the kitchen, let him hammer and swear at his own sweet will, putting it down to Apps.

"Franks, when he came to in the small hours," he added, "thought at first that he was in Heaven — it shows what a conscience void of offence will do for you — his last thought before losing consciousness having been that he was dying (such being the effect of the cheaper spirits at the Seven Thorns), and his first on resuming consciousness was that he was dead. The moonlight was shining in through the frosty window, and it was cold and spacious and clean, as he'd been led to expect Heaven would be. And close to hand, as he fumbled about, were sausages and a mince pie.

"It was only when old Franks had felt about and got the back door open, and came upon Marshall, that his muddled brain began to grasp the realities of the case."

"Humph!" I said, trying to find a flaw in his explanation. It was atrociously exasperating, after I'd published that report, and when the society was just making so much of me. He sat watching my conflict, so far as my face revealed it. "Doppelgangers!" he remarked unendurably.

I rose from my seat. I caught his hat and flung it violently across the room, among the spirit photographs. Possibly I said this and that. I turned and found the curate had his pipe out. "Have you a match, old chap?" he said, with the utmost tranquillity.

12

The Thing in No. 7

AFTER the regatta there was a firework display on Southsea Common. I turned out after dinner with Bailey — this was before he broke his legs — and Wilderspin and another man, a tall man whose name I forget. The day had been hot and close, and the night was overcast. But this was all the better for the fireworks.

The fun had already begun. A big rocket went hissing up, and burst into a cloud of pink and green sparks that vanished as they drifted down. We heard the people hum. The crimson flare of a Bengal light followed, and the frameworks upon which the transparencies were to appear came suddenly out of the darkness, and we saw the face and hands of a man in a blouse behind the fixtures, blood-red in the glare. There were crowds of people. I should think all Portsmouth and Southsea, and the greater part of Landport and Portsea must have turned out of doors; I never saw so many people on the Common before.

We pushed across to get into the noise and the fun of it. Away to the right the big pier with the pavilion was outlined in a cool white light, but it seemed almost deserted, and to the left, a black squat mass, was Southsea Castle. Against the sea-front of this one could see the sea washing up what looked like the ghosts of breakers, so pale and unsubstantial they were compared with the red glare. Then suddenly the Bengal light went out, and for a minute one had to feel one's way in the dark.

We soon got among the people. There was plenty of noise and stir, of course; everyone seemed moving and talking. In this country people seem to get quite courageous and talkative after dark. There were lots of girls about in light dresses, looking very pretty and mysterious in the dim — so we had to keep an eye on Bailey. There was scarcely any wind, and the smoke hung about close to the ground. It gave one a metallic taste in the mouth, and now and then set one coughing. It was all part of the fun. Every now and then a rocket would go up with a shuddering rush, then perhaps a writhing and hissing flight of golden serpents; crackers were banging; they certainly kept things brisk enough. I remember it was just before they set the transparencies going that I looked up at a big red rocket and saw the clouds all red above it, and driving fast across the sky. I recalled that afterwards when the storm began.

The transparencies were not altogether a success. The middle one went off fitfully, and we got the back of the head and one ear of the Prince of Wales before any of the rest. The profile simply would not catch on. The big transparency to the right took on well, but the ship to the left fizzled about the mainmast. Somehow all this struck the sense of humour of the crowd, and they began cheering wildly. We could dimly see a chap dabbing at the figure's nose with a pole carrying a match.

It was then the storm broke. The thunder seemed to fall right down upon us out of the dim sky. It began at the same time as the lightning, and sounded like a big gun fired close to my ears. And never before or since have I seen such lightning. It was brighter than day. It must have been instantaneous, for not a soul on the Common stirred while it lasted, but it seemed to last an age. I shall never forget all that huge crowd of people agape in that ghastly light, and motionless.

I suppose the thunder reverberated, but I heard nothing but the first report. I stood stunned for a minute in the blank darkness that succeeded. I became aware again of the head and shoulders of the Prince of Wales dotted out in yellow lights, and of people moving and talking round me and looking up at the sky. And then, like a lash, came the hail.

There was a stir. People began to fumble with umbrellas — those who had the forethought to bring them — and then, "I'm off home," said Bailey, and we began running, and everyone round us too, towards the distant houses at the back of the Common.

I shall never forget the storm, even for its own sake. Every moment the lightning winked and flashed and there seemed no end to the thunder. One clap trod on the tail of another. By the flashes one could see all that great flat Common alive with people — little black people — thousands of them — running. They were whooping and screaming, and some of the ladies reefed up their dresses scandalously for better speed. The hail was pouring down upon them out of the height of the sky in ragged grey streamers. And the lightning, blinding white it was, with a blue edge! Here and there short stretches of fence had been put across footpaths to let the grass grow again, and against these the people ran in the dark and formed knots and eddies in the flood, for all the world like water against a rock in a rapid. Far behind us were the transparencies still fizzing away yellow and dim. The profile of the big figure had caught on at last, but his back was burnt out. The Solent, boiling under the hail, and the forts in the distance were livid under the storm.

We were soon drenched, though we ran hard. Somehow we had kept together. Bailey had led us at first, howling cheerfully, and with his jacket pulled over his head, until he collided with one of those beastly little foot-high railings they put along the edge of their turf. That gave Wilderspin the lead, and made Bailey an indifferent fourth. Presently we got out of the rout of the people. The place where we lodged was No. 6 Cholmondeley Parade, facing the sea. Of course, most of the folks made for the throat of one or other of the three great roadways that open upon the Common. The Cricketers' Inn was simply gorged with people, and a crowd struggling outside.

Now, as I say, Wilderspin had got the lead, and he evidently meant to keep it. For my own part, I was out of breath and inclined to slacken my pace, but he spurted as we got near the house. The third man — I forget his name, but I think it was Pryor or Preyer — was running close behind me. I could hear the squash of his boots — for there was now half an inch of water on the ground — and a kind of whooping as he panted.

Then in the dim light of the street lamp I saw Wilderspin tear up the steps to the portico of a house. The lightning blazed livid, and I saw the whole house distinct and brilliant. It was the wrong house!

It was an empty house, as one could see by the black blankness of its windows, and I was aware, without clearly distinguishing what it was, that something black hung over the stuccoed parapet above. Then I saw with a slight feeling of surprise that the door was beginning to open in front of Wilderspin, and then came the darkness again. I heard the door slam.

I gasped out something incoherent about my getting in first after all, and keeping in my chuckle at Wilderspin's mistake against a better opportunity, rushed up the steps to the door of No. 6 and hammered at the knocker. The other man was hard on my heels, and then came Bailey panting.

"What a sell for old Wilderspin!" said Bailey.

"I suppose," said I, "he's groping about in the passage,

wondering why the deuce the hall-lamp is not lit."

We stood panting, and expecting every moment to see Wilderspin emerge crestfallen upon the portico next to us. We were too breathless to talk. A couple of minutes passed, and our own door opened.

"He's humbugging," said the tall man; "let's go in and leave him to follow."

"Come along, Wilderspin," I shouted.

The tall man went in and stood dripping on the oil-cloth in the hall. "Come along in and change," he said. "Never mind Wilderspin."

We heard the door of No. 7 click and slam again.

"I'm going after him," said Bailey. "He's such a queer chap."

He spoke my thought. Wilderspin was one of those odd, excitable fellows who will start at a shadow. I remember I nearly scared him into a fit once by quietly putting a head of barley in his ear in the course of a country walk. Somehow, I could not imagine him willingly hiding in an empty house after dark.

Bailey made no more ado, but clambered over into the portico of No. 7. The houses, I may mention, are part of a long terrace. There are steps up to each house, and the doors come together in pairs.

"You will ring, sir, when you are coming in," said the servant, a girl inclined to be impertiment, as they often are in boarding-houses. With that she closed the door.

I followed Bailey.

The door of No. 7 was opening slowly and very quietly. Behind it the gradually widening strip of passage was black and silent, except where the corner of the window lighting the staircase downstairs could be seen, clear and pale. We hesitated. The door became stationary, and then slowly closed again.

We looked at one another.

The thing affected me somehow like a trap. I hesitated. "Confound it!" said I. "What *is* there to be afraid of?" and flung the door open. A flash of lightning lit the hall for an instant.

Now, one can see distinctly by the flash of lightning only when one has something approaching a definite conception of the thing to be seen. I saw the empty hall very clearly, even to the darker patch on the oilcloth where the hat-stand had been, and the window to the staircase winked black as the rest of the things were illuminated. But the black lump at the head of the staircase puzzled me for a moment.

I pulled out a loose wax vesta from my pocket and struck it. It blew out. Bailey came in and shut the door after him, and I struck another.

All this had happened in silence. But as soon as the match flared we both started at once.

"Wilderspin, man!" said I, "what on earth's the matter?"

He was in a kind of sitting position, crouched on the staircase, and jammed hard against the wall. His head was turned towards something round the bend of the staircase that we could not see. One hand was too tense, he was simply cowering away from something and staring at it.

The match suddenly flared and went out. Then I heard a kind of moan, and something blundered towards me in the dark and almost knocked me over. It gripped me convulsively by the coat. I will confess I was scared in the darkness, and then as I put up my hand to defend myself I knew it was Wilderspin.

"Oh!" he cried, "save me! save me!"

His fright infected me. Bailey was frightened too, I think. He suddenly opened the street door, and out we all blundered, Wilderspin sobbing and clutching me.

The door slammed. Then as we stood on the doorstep it began to open again in that noiseless, sinister way it had. It was too much for me, it was too much for all of us. We went down the steps in a hurry.

Wilderspin began to sob louder. Some people under umbrellas were hurrying along the Parade towards us, laughing. "Let's take him in," said Bailey; "he's been scared out of his wits." I will admit I never took my eyes off the portico of No. 7 while we were outside No. 6. I don't quite know what I expected. We helped him up stairs and sat him on his bed. It was no good asking him questions. He simply sat on his bedside and shivered and stared in front of him. The fright seemed to have altered the expression of his face for good.

At last we determined to put some spunk into him with brandy, but it only made him worse. We put him to bed and that seemed to soothe him better. Presently he began crying quietly on his pillow, for all the world like a youngster.

"I will go into No. 7," said the tall man, "if anyone else will come."

101

"Hang it!" said Bailey, "I'd rather be devoured by ghouls than by this curiosity."

I said I would come too. But we waited until Wilderspin was asleep.

I suppose it was about half-past eleven o'clock when we went out, and things were as quiet as midnight. We went up to the door of No. 7. "Give me a match or two," said the tall man.

It made me jump almost out of my shoes to hear a voice in my ear suddenly. I turned and saw a policeman grinning behind me. He had stolen up to us with those list-covered shoes of his. "What's the little game?" he said, suddenly blinding me with his lantern.

"There's something wrong in this house," said the tall man. "The door was open."

The policeman examined each of us very deliberately with his lantern. "Not *your* sort," I think he said, and then went up and lit the hall with his lantern. Then the circle of light came round to the open door. "Looks like chisels," he said. "After the gas-fittings and plumbing, I suppose."

He went into the hall and we followed quietly. The brilliant unsteady circle of his lantern preceded him. Then he gave vent to a sudden "Ugh!" He was almost exactly in the place where we found Wilderspin, and the beam of his light fell through the banisters and followed the direction of Wilderspin's stare.

"Look," he said to the tall man.

Then Bailey looked, and then I.

I don't think it is any use to describe what we saw. I suppose that the peculiar horror of the thing was the way in which the front of the face had been injured. I quite understand what it must have been to Wilderspin, jumping at him out of the dark as the lightning flashed. However, there is no reason why one should descend to details.

Even when we saw it we did not understand. But the tall man presently found an explanation.

The dead man was one of those miserable thieves who rob empty houses of their plumbing and gas-fittings. The house had no lightning conductor, but above it was a flag-staff, stupidly tipped by a gilt spearhead, and braced by zinc wires instead of ropes. It was the charred and splintered remains of this, I found next day, that I had noticed about the parapet of the house. The flash of lightning — very probably it was the first flash that had started the rush from the Common — must have struck the flag-staff, and then come streaming down through the gas-fittings, water-pipes, and whatever other conducting substances afforded it a path to the earth. Above the body, at the turn of the staircase, was a very pretty little brass bracket lighting the landing, and a brass handrail ran down the wall. No doubt the poor wretch had been in contact with these, when he was so suddenly and awfully struck out of the roll of the living.

Poor Wilderspin was in a bad way for many days, and the rest of our holiday went chiefly to comfort him. But there is less permanent injury from the shock than one might expect. He always was nervous and excitable, and so in still greater measure he remains.

13
The Thumbmark

WE three students, who had arrived early, stood at the window of the laboratory and looked at the ruins of the house opposite. It was a windy, showery morning; the roadway glistened with the wet, and the sky behind the blackened ruins showed gaps of deep blue through its drifting covering of cloud. The vivid spring-green of the young chestnuts and lilacs in front of the house contrasted strangely with the black wreck behind them. The fire had completely gutted the place; most of the roof had fallen in, and through the carbonised outlines of the windows, which retained scarcely a shred of glass, one looked upon charred walls and all the indescribable desolation that follows a conflagration. Oddly enough, though some part of the wall had collapsed over the portico, the little bedroom above it was completely uninjured, and we could see, still hanging upon the water-streaked wall-paper, a framed photograph of a soldier in uniform.

The new student, a pale man with black hair — Chabôt, I think, was his name — was especially absorbed in the contemplation of the wreck. "Was no one injured?" he asked.

"No one, fortunately," said Wilderspin.

The new man grunted.

Porch entered shouting: "Have you chaps heard? Great Anarchist outrage! London in panic! Why aren't you terror-stricken? This comes of the abominable examination system. Not one of you has had leisure to see a newspaper this morning."

We all started round.

"Listen," said Porch, striking an attitude. "Yesterday that was the home of Inspector Bulstrode — the celebrated Inspector Bulstrode — and we never knew it! Now behold it!"

"How do they know it *is* the work of an Anarchist?" asked the new student, as Askin entered the room.

"They put every accident that happens down to Anarchists, just now," said Wilderspin.

"The police," said Porch, "have very good reason to regard this outrage as the work of an Anarchist, so the papers say. But nothing has transpired. However, it's very nice of the Anarchists to pick a house right in front of our windows. It will relieve the rigours of our last week's cramming immensely."

"It has made Smith late for once," said Wilderspin, looking at his watch.

"I saw him over the way," said Askin, "as I was coming down the street."

"Jove! What was he doing over there?" asked the new man very quickly.

"Prying, I suppose," said Askin. "He was talking to one of the policemen, and he had a box in his hands with some black stuff in it. I suppose he will expect us to analyse that."

"Here he comes!" said Wilderspin.

We all turned to the window again. Mr. Somerset Smith, our excellent instructor in chemistry, had appeared at the side-door opposite, and was coming along by the side of the house towards the street gate. He carried a box labelled "Hudson's Soap," and in it was a quantity of blackened rubbish, including, among other curiosities, a broken glass jar. His queer broad face was screwed up into an inscrutable expression. He came across the roadway deep in thought, and was presently hidden from us as he approached the steps to the portico. We heard him come up to his little preparation room, next the laboratory, and slam the door.

The four or five other students who constituted the class came in one by one.

We were soon loud in an animated discussion of Anarchist outrages. Mason had heard that it was Smith himself who had discovered that the fire opposite was the work of an incendiary, and that he had found a charred scrap of an inflammatory placard. Askin made an obvious joke at this. The new man asked a great many questions in a quick nervous manner. The excitement seemed to be bringing out his conversational gifts; for hitherto he had been rather conspicuous for a reserve that most of us considered sulky in its quality. We stopped our clamour as Smith entered.

Contrary to his usual practice he did not go straight to the blackboard, but came down the middle aisle of benches towards the window. He was carrying a paper-weight of black marble in one hand, and in the other a number of slips of white paper. These he put down on Wilderspin's bench. He peered at the crowd of us from beneath his heavy eyebrows.

"Anyone absent?" he asked.

"No one, sir," said somebody.

"This fire over the way, gentlemen, is a very singular affair indeed — very singular. Possibly none of you know how it was occasioned. But you ought, I think, to know without any delay that a strong suspicion attaches here; a suspicion, that is to say, that the incendiary — for it was no accident, but deliberate arson — obtained his materials from this place. So far as I can judge, the house was fired by means of phosphorus dissolved in carbon bisulphide."

There was a simultaneous exclamation from the class.

"As you are aware, gentlemen, from the course of elementary study we pursued last autumn, when phosphorus dissolved in carbon bisulphide is exposed to evaporation, the phosphorus is precipitated in such a finely divided state that it catches fire. Well, the coal-plate, it would seem, had been taken up, a considerable amount of paper thrown down among the firewood and small coal that lay on the floor of the cellar, and then a copious supply of this solution — which must, gentlemen, have been mixed in this house — was poured upon it. Evaporation began at once, the phosphorus presently caught and set the paper going, and in half an hour a nice little fire was burning its way upstairs to wake the Inspector and his family.

"How did I ascertain this? Partly by accident and partly by research. The accident was this. About ten o'clock last night I had occasion to visit my preparation room, and I smelt the very distinctive smell of carbon bisulphide vapour. I traced this to the store-room next door, and, entering, saw at once that the stores had been tampered with. A bottle of starch mucilage had been upset, and the contents were dripping from the table to the floor. Several other bottles had been taken down and not replaced. Looking round with the idea of discovering a theft, I failed to detect the absence of anything at first except the carbon bisulphide, but presently I noticed the phosphorus jar was empty. The inference was either that some student contemplated a chemical entertainment at home at my expense, or that some incendiarism was on foot. In either case I was naturally anxious to discover the culprit, and it seemed to me that no time was so favourable as the immediate moment when the room was exactly as he had left it. You know we scientific people are rather fond of problems of evidence."

He looked keenly round the group of us. So did I. Unless he

was a far better physiognomist than I, nothing was to be detected. To me every one looked interested, and all more or less disconcerted by his suspicion. Askin, for instance, was blushing; Wilderspin, who had a nervous trick of twitching the corner of his mouth, was twitching it violently; and the lips of the new man were white.

"Now I am happy to say that when I left the laboratory I had a hint, that presently developed into evidence as absolutely conclusive of who had taken my carbon bisulphide as any evidence could be."

A dramatic pause. For my own part I was a little scared. Suppose Mr. Smith was jumping to a conclusion? It might be inconvenient for some of us.

"The gentleman, quite inadvertently, had written his signature to the theft; had left his sign-manual to his act — literally his sign-manual, gentlemen."

He smiled oddly at us. We expected him to point someone out with his finger. He looked for a moment at the little slips of paper on the bench beside him, and hesitated. We were all naturally very much excited by this time.

"You don't mean," said the new student — "you don't mean that the man who stole that carbon bisulphide was so absent-minded — so madly absent-minded — as to write his name —— ?"

Our teacher, still smiling, shook his head in negation. "Not quite that," he said. Clearly he meant to prolong the agony.

"When this fire broke out opposite," he proceeded calmly, "I had a suspicion that the things were connected. Very early this morning — before sunrise, in fact — I went over there. I traced the fire, with the help of the firemen, down to the cellar. It had been lit, as I supposed it must have been, through the coal-plate. I raked about for my carbon bisulphide bottle among the cinders and ashes in the cellar so soon as they were cool enough for the search; and I could not find it. My suspicions of our connection with that fire grew a little fainter, but I still clung to them. The cellar was extremely hot, and my investigations in consequence superficial, so that I determined to repeat the search more thoroughly later in the day. To fill the time up, after breakfast and a bath I went into the garden and hunted about there. First I found a familiar stopper, and that excited me; then, under a lilac-bush, I found the bottle — broken, I suppose by the foot of a fireman. The label, you will remember, on those store-room bottles is a large paper one, and goes almost all the way round."

He stopped and smiled benevolently at us.

"On that label there were visible the words 'Carbon Bisulphide,' and also 'Dismal Stinks,' written by some gentleman in pencil."

"Oh, but I wrote those three or four days ago!" said Askin, hotly.

"I can quite imagine you did. I say there was nothing else *visible* upon the label. But you will remember, gentlemen, that our friend had upset a bottle of starch mucilage. Now let me remind you of the properties of starch mucilage. It is colourless itself, but with iodine it gives a beautiful purple-blue colour. It is a test for iodine, even when the latter is in the smallest conceivable proportion."

"It will go blue with one part of iodine in four hundred and fifty thousand of water, Thorpe says," said Wilderspin.

"Very good. I see you are ready for your examination. Now, before I left the laboratory I had noticed that our friend had dabbled his fingers in this starch, for upon the door-handle I perceived something that might be the dim marks of them, and on testing with iodine was delighted to verify my suspicion. They were, however, too vague for my purpose. Now, I felt that if I got the bottle there would certainly be some traces of our friend's fingers on the label, since he must inevitably have held it in such a way as to print them. Accordingly I have developed that label with a very weak solution of iodine; and now, gentlemen, I am happy to say I have three blue fingermarks and a beautiful thumbprint."

He paused for our astonishment.

"You may have heard of Professor Galton," said our teacher, going on a little more rapidly, and taking the paper slips up again. "He has made a special study of the lines upon the human thumb, and has proposed it as a method of identifying criminals. He has taken thousands of impressions from inked human thumbs at the Anthropometric Laboratory at South Kensington, and in no two human beings are these impressions alike. He has published a book of his prints, and a very good book it is too. So here you see I have a little printers' ink mixed with oil smeared on this paperweight, and here are some little slips of paper, and the whole matter will be settled in a few minutes. If the miscreant is present we shall find him; if not—"

"Look out!" cried Wilderspin.

I turned round, to see the new man holding a bottle in either hand. The Anarchist had discovered himself. One bottle was poised ready to throw. It had a ground glass label, and was probably some acid. I ducked instinctively, and the missile whizzed over my head, touched Smith on the shoulder, and ricochetted with a terrific smash into a stand of boiler-tubes beyond. There was the keen smell of nitrogen oxides in the air. The second bottle happily flew wide, bowled over a Bunsen burner and two tripods, and mowed down all the small bottles of reagents on Wilderspin's bench.

I never saw men scatter so quickly. I turned with some idea of grappling with the lunatic, and saw him grip a bottle of sulphuric acid — oil of vitriol, that popular ingredient of the Parisian love-philtre. This was too much for me, and I dodged round the bench forthwith. Some of the fellows had got out of the room and stood on the staircase, whither Smith had also made good his retreat. I saw Wilderspin, his mouth twitching more than ever, behind one of the other benches. As soon as we got a chance we both followed the example of the rest and scuttled out upon the landing. A small bottle of hydrochloric acid caught Wilderspin in the neck, made him yell dismally, and turned his coat a bright red forthwith.

There was method in the Anarchist's madness. He threw nothing more so soon as he had gained possession of the laboratory, but proceeded to raid round and collect together all the bottles of acid, corrosive sublimate, lunar caustic, and so forth, upon the bench nearest the window. He clearly meant to invest his arrest with peculiar difficulty. But Smith was still equal to him. He had run into the store-room, and re-emerged with a huge jar of that most unendurable gas, sulphuretted hydrogen. "Take out the bung and fling it in," said he — "quick!" and returned for the pungent virtues of the ammonia. We followed this up with a carboy of hydrochloric acid and the ammonium sulphide, a gas only rivalled in its offensiveness by the sulphuretted hydrogen. The enemy scarcely grasped our import until these vapours spread towards him, and merely dodged behind a bench. In thirty seconds there was as unpleasant a conflict of chemical odours in that room as one can well imagine, and the air was dense with white clouds of ammonium chloride. The enemy soon discovered our aim and tried a charge. As the jar of ammonium sulphide went in and smashed on the floor, I saw a small bottle fly towards me through the reek, but it missed the doorway and knocked the blackboard over.

"Stand out of the way!" shrieked the Anarchist, looming up through the rising fog and stench, but we slammed the door and shut him and his atmosphere in together. He tugged furiously at the handle and hammered madly at the panel. I heard him yell for mercy and fall a-coughing. I thought we had beaten him, and would have opened the door had not Smith, fearing a rush, restrained me. The Anarchist's footsteps retreated and there was silence. We expected another rush at the door. Presently a bottle smashed against it, and after a minute or so another. Then there was an interval of silence. Possibly three minutes passed. Askin was attending to Wilderspin in the store-room, the rest of us were grouped about the landing. "He must have fallen down suffocated," said Porch. "The window!" exclaimed Smith, suddenly; "he must have got out by the window. I never thought of the window. Has anyone heard the window go? You three men" — he indicated myself, and Porch and Mason — "stop by the door."

The rest clattered downstairs with Smith. We heard the front-door open and their voices from the little courtyard in front of the house. Then we ventured to open the laboratory door again, and saw the end window open and the clear air beating in through the mist. The Anarchist had escaped us. Smith had been a little *too* intellectual in his treatment of the case, and scarcely vigorous enough. "After that thumbmark," said he when the class met next morning amid the débris of the laboratory — "after that thumbmark he ought to have surrendered at once. There was not a loophole left for him. Logically, at any rate, he was hopelessly cornered. For him to start throwing acids about, gentlemen! It was a thing I did not anticipate. Most unfair of him. This kind of thing robs detective work of all its intellectual charms."

14

A Family Elopement

"YOUR wife does not notice our being together?" asked Miss Hawkins.

"I think not," said Mr. Gabbitas; "she is talking to that Theosophist."

The Theosophist was a slender young man from India, but his hair might have come from the Soudan. Mrs. Gabbitas was a lady with intellectual features of a Roman type; and a shallow desire for profundity. She was clearly very much interested in what the Hindoo had to say; so Miss Hawkins turned again to Gabbitas.

"I said, I cannot go on like this," said Gabbitas.

"Speak lower," said Miss Hawkins, bending her curls towards him.

"I cannot go on like this — *dearest*," said Gabbitas, trying to put as much tender passion as possible into a hoarse whisper.

"What can we do?" said Miss Hawkins.

"So much as we dare do — flight," said Gabbitas. "Let us get out of all this into a sunnier clime. With you" ——

"Hush! They are coming to ask me to sing," said Miss Hawkins. "Presently. Wait."

Mr. Gabbitas yielded her up at this crisis with the best grace he could, and went and propped himself against a wall where he could watch her profile.

"She is awf'ly clever," said the refined young gentleman to the left of him, to his friend.

"And virtuous," said his friend. "But that's a mistake. She really ought to do something just a little — cheerful, you know. People are not going to run after singers just because they sing, you know."

"She knows that," said the refined young gentleman. "She's clever enough. There will be an exploit" ——

"Good Heavens!" said Gabbitas under his breath. "Such motives in my sweet little Minnie. I can't stand this." And he hastily sought a vacant piece of wall elsewhere.

"It is sweet to be with you again," he whispered to her

presently, with a sense of infinite relief. "And now, dearest, frankly, will you, dare you — come with me? If you know, dearest, how I have longed for you, how my soul craves—— So" (very loud) "I had a very jolly time indeed."

The latter inane sentence because somebody had loomed up just behind Miss Hawkins's chair.

"Gone now," said Gabbitas. "Tell me, dearest, quickly. Whisper. Dare you?"

[*Pause.*

"For *you*," whispered Miss Hawkins very softly, looking down.

Gabbitas took that as an affirmative. "My darling, my own! The warmth will show. I mean to say—— Do you find the room hot?"

"What disconcerts you now?"

"I caught Mrs. Gabbitas's eye just then. I think she wants to go home. That Theosophist has left her."

Now qualified observers state that a man who means to run away from his wife, even if that wife have features Roman rather than beautiful and a tendency to theosophy, suffers considerable twinges of compunction. Gabbitas certainly did. Even if one's marriage is chiefly a success from the mercenary point of view, a habit of mutual consideration grows insensibly out of the necessity of a common life. Mrs. Gabbitas was silent and pensive in the carriage, and it was unusual and became her. He tried a little conversation. Moreover, he wanted to find out if she had noticed any of his passion in his face as he talked to Minnie.

"It was a very successful affair, dear," he remarked. "They had some lovely sandwiches, I noticed."

"Yes," said Mrs. Gabbitas, turning dreamy eyes upon him. "The sandwiches were Lovely, and the decorations were Lovely too. And the music. It has been the most Lovely evening I can imagine."

"I am glad you liked it so much, dear," said Gabbitas.

She smiled mysteriously at him. She seemed to be suddenly affected with an unusual tenderness. "*Dear* husband," she said.

"What is up now?" thought Gabbitas. "She is not going to pump me." And he remarked, "Yes, dear."

"You have always been a good husband to me, dear."

"Ra-*ther*," said Gabbitas privately; and aloud, "Always."

"You may kiss me, dear."

Gabbitas did as he was bid, and that was all. After this treat Mrs. Gabbitas relapsed into her corner. She did not suspect, then, after all. Gabbitas was greatly relieved. Yet she had never spoken in quite this way before. If she meant to develop sentimentally a new inducement was added to elopement.

And again and again, and yet again, three times altogether in a fortnight, Mrs. Gabbitas returned to this same peculiar soft mood. One or two things she said startled Gabbitas extremely at the time. However, he kept on accumulating his luggage at his chambers nevertheless, for he was a hard man with his conscience.

"She cannot *know*," he said to himself, following her with his eyes, after one of these conversations. "No; if she knew she would make a shindy. She would certainly make a shindy. I know her disposition. I suppose she has got this new style from some novel. Poor old Mimsie!"

As he went by her door he paused momentarily, for she seemed to be on her knees and weeping by the bed-side. That was through looking out of the corners of his eyes. When he looked straight he saw that she was only packing a dress-basket, and he went on downstairs relieved.

Five days after the last of these remarkable conversations Gabbitas found himself on the Southampton platform of Waterloo Station with a large pile of boxes, masculine and feminine, in his care, and an exhilarating sense of wrong-doing in his heart. Miss Hawkins mingled timidity and self-possession delightfully.

"This is the end of London and respectability," said Gabbitas.

"And the beginning of life, dear," said Miss Hawkins.

"We have twenty minutes to spare. Shall we walk to Waterloo Bridge, take a last look at the dear, dismal old Embankment, the Tower, Westminster, and the rest of it? After this we shall have a glut of blue skies."

They still had five minutes to spare when they returned. They walked up the platform and down again.

"Here is *our* luggage," said Gabbitas.

By the side of their heap was a similar one. A little portmanteau in this caught his eye. It seemed familiar. "Is not that mine?" he asked the porter.

"Mrs. Da Costa," read the porter on the label; "for Lisbon."

"No, that is not mine," said Gabbitas, "And yet it seemed . . .

somehow . . . funny. We should see that our seats have not been taken, I think, now, dear."

At the door of their compartment a man was standing with his back towards them. He was evidently a foreigner; his hair formed a peculiar frizzy mat, such as no Englishman could or would exhibit. As they approached he turned.

There was a pause of mutual inquiry.

"Mr. Jamasji Ganpat!" said Gabbitas.

Mr. Ganpat, the eminent theosophist, looked at them stupidly. He seemed scared for a moment. Then his face lit up. He raised his hat. "Mr. Gabbitas — with Miss Hawkins!"

Miss Hawkins turned half round to pull a loose thread out of her travelling rug.

"We are going down to Southampton," said Mr. Gabbitas, collecting his resources. "Together. To meet Mrs. Gabbitas."

"Indeed!" said Mr. Ganpat, and his eye wandered round to the waiting-room door. He seemed nervous. "Do you know," he said, "I think I must . . . I had better . . . It is unfortunate. Excuse me." he turned his back suddenly and hurried away.

"It was better to recognize him," said Gabbitas. "How nervous he seems. I wonder if he suspects. Perhaps he is shocked. Hullo!"

Ganpat had not been able to reach the door of the waiting-room in time. It opened. Somebody appeared in a grey travelling-dress — a flaxen-haired lady, with Roman features, smiling sweetly at him.

"Mimsie!" exclaimed Gabbitas, with addenda.

"Mrs. Gabbitas!" said Miss Hawkins.

The smile of Mrs. Gabbitas died away at the sight of Ganpat's alarmed visage. She sought over his shoulder for the cause.

"Oh, my poor George!" she exclaimed faintly.

And then she saw Miss Hawkins. "*You!*"

"Take your seats!" howled the guard; "take your seats, please!"

"I suppose," said Gabbitas, finding curses *sotto voce* no comfort, "under the circumstances we had all better get in together and explain."

And in a minute four singularly depressed and silent people were travelling in a first-class compartment out of Waterloo Station. Mrs. Gabbitas sat in the middle seat, and stared hard at the opposite cushions. Gabbitas stared at her. Miss Hawkins

114

sat in one corner and tore strips with elaborate precision, off the corner of her society paper. The Hindoo looked pensively out of the window and hummed a barbaric tune of two notes.

It was one of those conversations that are difficult to begin. Mrs. Gabbitas broke the silence at Vauxhall.

"This is *perfectly* ridiculous," she said abruptly and hotly. "Idiotic! We can't do anything now."

"That, dear, is just what I feel," said Miss Hawkins very slowly and without looking up, making a new kind of sinuous strip.

"It will not be even a romantic scandal," said Mrs. Gabbitas with tears in her voice. "Nothing original. It will be just *funny*. Horrible! *Beastly!*"

The meeting lapsed into silence.

"I do not know," said Mr. Ganpat with a half-laugh. "What. It is funny."

Again meditation reigned.

Beyond Clapham Gabbitas cleared his throat.

"Yes?" said Mrs. Gabbitas.

"We have," said Gabbitas, "got into this mess, and we have to get out of it. I and Ganpat might fight" ——

"No, no," said Ganpat. "Ladies present! No fight."

"We might fight," said Gabbitas; "but I do not see exactly what we should be fighting for."

"Precisely," said Ganpat. "Nothing worth fighting for." He smiled reassuringly at Mrs. Gabbitas.

"The reputations of the ladies must not suffer," said Gabbitas.

"Again precisely," said Ganpat, becoming animated. "And now you hear *me*. Now I will tell you. What will we do? Here is Mrs. Gabbitas and Miss Hawkins. Hear me to my final end. Then we part. I and you, Mr. Gabbitas, I and you go to Paris. Is not that well? It is an excursion that we have planned. You, my — I mean Madam— you, Madam, go with Miss Hawkins. You go to — go to — where?"

"Lisbon will be far enough, as the things are labelled."

"Ye-es," said Miss Hawkins, taking her strips and tearing them transversely into squares. "It's sensible. I am sure *I* don't mind. Now."

"That is admirable. What do *you* say, Gabbitas?"

The eye of Gabbitas rested on Miss Hawkins for a moment. "This is a beastly mess," he said.

115

Miss Hawkins glanced up, and he fancied she nodded imperceptibly. He turned to Ganpat.

"Very well, that will do."

"We have all been very silly," said Mrs. Gabbitas — "idiots, in fact."

"And, as far as I can see," said her husband, "nobody can throw stones."

"Dere is no injured innocents in this carriage at all," said Mr. Jamasji Ganpat; but the remark was coldly received.

"And now," said Mrs. Gabbitas, "everything being settled, let us talk of something else."

"Ringlets," said Miss Hawkins, making her paper scraps into two heaps in her lap; "ringlets, dear, are coming into fashion after all."

15
Our Little Neighbour

OUR first encounter with our little neighbour happened when we were looking over the house preparatory to taking it. It's a peculiar little house, built into the side of the hill, so that a great bank comes on the north and east of it, faced with brick, and higher than the chimneys. There is a garden in front, with the house on one side, this high brick wall on two others, and on the fourth a privet hedge and the road, and all up the brick wall run great ropes of ivy. There is another garden behind on a level with the roof, to which one goes out of the yard by some brick steps, and by the gable and chimneys visible over the fence of this we first became aware of our neighbour's existence.

My wife liked the oddness of the place. It was a house with a character of its own. "This queer little attic garden," said she, "is delightful. I will smother it with red and white poppies next year."

"There is someone's orchard runs down to the wall and overlooks the front of our house," said I; "so that we may have people looking down our chimneys, and inspecting the dinner. That's rather a disadvantage. These are apple and plum trees."

I went to the palings, and found these were thickly studded with nails along the top. The fence was too high to see over.

We came down the steep brick steps again, and Mariana went into ecstasies about the hall. She would have a yellow paper and brown paint, and her aunt's heirlooms, two small watercolours by Birkett Foster, along the wall.

At last we drifted into the front garden again.

"In the place of the flower-beds," said I, "I would prefer turf."

"It would be easy to recast the garden," said my wife. "But we mustn't touch all that splendid ivy——" Then she stopped for a moment, and then came a queer change in her voice. "George," she said, "we are overlooked."

I glanced at her quickly, and saw she was looking at the top of the high wall that overhung house and garden, and that she had a startled expression in her eyes. Following her gaze, I had my first glimpse of our little neighbour.

He had just been looking down upon us, and was turning away, so that all I caught was his shoulder, his ears, and the top of his head as he receded. He wore a bluish coat but seemingly old and greasy — and I judged from the curve of his shoulder that he was a hunchback. There was a black skull-cap on his head, and it seemed to me that he had no hair.

I looked at Mariana. Her brows were knit. "*Horrid* little creature!" she said.

"I scarcely saw him," said I.

"He was looking down at us."

"I suppose we're interesting to him as we're going to be his neighbours."

"But did you see his face?"

To judge by Mariana's expression it was not a very pleasant face. "Apparently," said I, "he's . . . what is it? . . . Piebald? . . . No . . . Albino!"

"He's *horrid!*" said Mariana.

"But this," said I, "is a digression. We were speaking of turf here and a garden chair."

"I don't like his face," said Mariana, and looked up again. She was so much put out that for some time she would not return to the subject of our arrangements, but kept repeating that our little neighbour was an ugly little creature. I had to show signs of vacillation in the matter of the sideboard before I could get her mind away from this individual over the wall. And after Mariana had taken the fullest advantage of my weakness in that matter she returned to him immediately.

"You *will* ask the agent who he is?" she said — twice. "Somehow, I don't like the thought of him as a neighbour."

So said I to the house agent, "Who is — the gentleman in blue that we saw looking down from the wall!"

The agent started and looked at me. "That's a difficult question," he said. "It hardly comes in my province."

Then I asked him what neighbours we had above the wall. "A gentleman named Hanotaux, I fancy," said the agent; "a literary gentleman, so I understood."

"Living alone?" I asked.

"No, he lives with his brother," said the agent; and then finding I was bent upon pressing the point he did not wait for further questions. "It *may* have been the brother you saw," he said. "I've seen him dressed in blue. A shortish gentleman — and

118

bent rather — without a scrap of hair. He's . . . well, he's *afflicted*. He was born so. But he's quite harmless, I can assure you."

"He can't possibly be any annoyance," the agent insisted. "It's really very sad for the poor little creature — cooped up in the house and garden — he never comes out because the village boys exasperate him. But his brother is very good to him — really very good. And he's never done any harm to a single creature."

"All the same, I don't like him," said Mariana again, on the way to the railway station.

At that I read Mariana a lecture on charity, for in one direction at least she is hard-hearted. She cannot endure ugly misery. The intense pathos of ungainliness is lost upon her. She recoils from unwashed beggars and cripples, from any suggestion of physical suffering. Yet she can be tender enough over a rain-soaked kitten or a nice dead canary. I told her as much.

"You didn't see how he looked at me, or you'd think differently," said Mariana, and clenched the discussion abruptly with that very feminine reply.

I saw the face of the creature for the first time when we moved in. The people from the London furniture warehouse were taking in that sideboard of Mariana's as I came in at the gate. "He'll know it when he sees it again," said one of the men in green baize aprons. I wondered who "he" was, and then looked up and saw him.

He certainly had anything but a prepossessing face. I think the peculiar offence was in the irregular teeth, the dropping, everted nether lip, and the pink eyes, but, I must confess, I cannot describe his visage in detail. He was watching our move-in with a grin upon his face, a slobbering leer that was certainly not engaging.

I will admit I felt — what our little servant would doubtless call a "turn". Possibly, too, I had a flash of irritation at our affairs being spied upon. Then I was ashamed of myself for grudging the poor demented outcast creature the petty satisfaction he had in our arrival. By way of reparation for my first sensations, I turned towards him and waved my hat, as one might do to a child.

He grinned, anything but prettily, and waved his arms in reply. They were very long arms — at least, in proportion to his little body. And he began a brutal travesty of speech by way of greeting.

When I heard his inarticulate mouthings I turned and followed the sideboard into the house.

When I came out again I looked at him out of the corner of my eye, and he was still gesticulating. It occurred to me that it was rather foolish to encourage him overmuch, and I affected to be unaware of his presence.

Yet all day the thought was in my mind of the poor darkened, inarticulate creature hanging over the fence along the top of the wall and trying to express his dim thoughts to me, trying to signal something — Heaven knows what — and I felt a little sorry for having turned my back on him. To tell the truth, his grotesque appearance and the conditions under which he was living had laid hold of my imagination. I thought of him wandering about the narrow garden between the spiked palings, which constituted his world, and, reading my own feelings into him, I imagined the horrible monotony of his existence. That evening he was gone, to Mariana's great relief; but the next morning he was back at his post, and in the excess of my philanthropy I waved my hand to him.

I made the acquaintance of Morton, the village doctor, that day.

"You'll be having that Hanotaux bogle for a neighbour," said he. "Have you seen it? It's a gruesome thing to have aye peering over the wall at you, man."

He always spoke of our little neighbour as *it*. "So far as I can ascertain," said he, "the thing is twenty-three or twenty-four years old, but it looked precisely the same five or six years ago. I've attended it twice for fits. Hanotaux cannot be just right, or he would not have the thing about him. He would send it to an asylum. Something wrong up above is congenital with both of them, I'm thinking. It's got a nasty temper too, for once it bit my finger. Bit its medical attendant, man!"

"Hanotaux," continued the doctor, after a pause, "has given it a room opening out upon the garden, and the whole of the garden except a part behind the kitchen he has fenced off, for it to disport itself in. I remonstrated with him about it once, and says he, 'He's good Hanotaux blood anyhow, and I'm not going to have him imprisoned in an asylum to be tyrannised over by doctors and attendants, and to be experimented upon for the good of science'. And he began to provoke me to argue about the medical profession, and hospitals and vivisection, and so got away from the bogle."

"I suppose," said I, catching his mode of expression, "the thing's as happy where it is as it could be anywhere."

"That's not it," said Morton. "It's my belief the thing's dangerous."

"Nonsense!" said I, though his tone of conviction made me uncomfortable. "It's never done anything — in that way, has it?"

"No," said Morton, "it's pure supposition on my part. But, you see, . . . Well, it used to go out in the village, I hear, when it was younger, and the boys teased it, and it used to get into furious passions, and so came by its first fit. And after it was secluded in the house it made a dead set at one of the servants and she had to leave. It's a queer brute and there's no counting on it. Partly it's as it is because it's a malformed albino, but chiefly it's atavism; it's one of those cases where Nature tries back and fetches up the ancestral savage out of the past to trouble us. People think a creature like that just goes about gibbering; but, depend upon it, that bogle has a mind of its own that works — in its way — just as much as ours do. It has — it must have — hopes and desires of its own, though they are as crippled and repulsive as its body. They won't all be satisfied, I'm thinking, by a high fence with spikes and a garden."

"No," said I — missing his drift; "I dare say the thing — the poor little wretch — is dismal enough."

I saw the unhappy subject of our conversation on my return, at his post of observation. I waved my hat at him, but he made no response. He had his head craned out, as if he was trying to see into our drawing-room.

I found Mariana in the hall. "How do the pictures look?" said I.

She looked quite worried. "Do get him to go away," she said. "He has been up there all the morning."

"He means no harm," said I; "you're over-fanciful."

"I'm not, George. Really I can't bear him. He has been mopping and mowing up there ——"

I saw the tears standing in her eyes. At that I turned and opened the front door, with the idea of shaking my fist at him. But our little neighbour had gone.

So much happened in the first two days of our tenancy. I thought that we should get used to him, and that he would tire of watching us. I thought, too, that Mariana would find that he meant no harm, and for my own part maintained a friendly relation by means of waved hat and hand. But things became worse in the course of a fortnight rather than better, and at last I began to think that the annoyance she felt was affecting her nerves. She kept away from the windows as much as possible and seemed to dread going out, which involved going across the garden under our little neighbour's eye. And she would cross-examine me about all the bolts and window fastenings after I had locked up of a night, and I could see she dreaded even the shadows of our own house after dark. I caught the infection of her antipathy, and began at last to detest the very sight of our living gargoyle, and to rejoice over a rainy day that would drive him indoors as much as I had ever previously rejoiced over a fine.

At last it was unbearable, and I called on Hanotaux, but he was out, and after missing him a second time I wrote him a letter. He was evidently a cantankerous person, for he replied that he failed to see how we could object to his own brother using his own garden. I called upon him after that, but got nothing for my pains. Hanotaux simply would not see things from our point of view. No doubt it was rude for his brother to stare, but we must make allowance for his affliction. My wife, I urged, was very nervous. "You cannot hold me responsible for your wife's peculiarities," said Hanotaux, with a sardonic gleam. Then I offered to pay for a high fence along the top of the wall. Hanotaux shook his head. "I don't see why I should lose my view on your account," he said.

It was when I returned from this that I heard a new offence of this disagreeable little monster. Mariana had been in the upstairs garden, when the all too familiar grinning visage had appeared in the branches of an apple-tree on the other side of the fence, into which he had swung himself by his long arms. "He seemed close to me," said Mariana. "I don't know how I got down the steps again."

That evening it was that I began making hostile demonstrations at this nuisance of ours, stamping my foot, shaking my fists, and shouting "Go away!" He grinned, and made his horrible inarticulate noises at me, but presently he seemed to realise that I was not in fun this time, and at that he looked disconcerted, and suddenly disappeared. He turned in such a queer manner that I was almost inclined to think he dropped on all fours. Presently, when I was syringing the Gloire de Dijon in front of the house, it occurred to me that I might use the weapon in my hand pretty effectually if I had much more trouble with him.

Now the next thing that happened I cannot describe very exactly, for the simple reason that it has never been properly described to me. It must have been very disagreeable. I was in my study and my wife was in our dressing-room. I heard her scream, and running in to her, found her kneeling beside the bed and just at the beginning of a faint, and I noticed indistinctly that there was something like a brown bird that passed from the corner of the window. When she revived I questioned her. So far as I can understand she had suddenly seen the face of our disgusting little neighbour *upside down* outside the window. An inverted face, at any time, is not a nice thing to see suddenly — even though it be a pretty one. I suppose he had clambered along the ivy and hung down by means of his long arms.

When I had recovered her and learnt this, I will confess my charitable feelings towards this incubus vanished. I was furiously angry, and, I fancy, a little afraid of what he would do. This experience was new. Evidently, the little brute had only just discovered the climbable nature of our creeper in his queer and anything but pleasant attempts upon our company, or rather, upon my wife's company. I went off to Marvin, the solicitor, and then to Hanotaux again. The law considered I had a case, and perhaps in the course of a little time . . . At which I left the office blaspheming.

When I got home I got an axe and began to chop at the main stem of the ivy, in the corner between the house and the wall. In the midst of this I heard a chuckling, throaty sound above that I knew only too well. I went indoors and returned with the syringe.

The little beast was waving his ape-like arms at me in a threatening manner, and his face was full of diabolical malice. "So it's war," said I, and forthwith the jet from the syringe took him fairly in the face. The water sprayed out from the corners of his ugly grin, making him more suggestive of a gargoyle than ever.

This time there was no mistaking it. He dropped on all fours and vanished.

Mariana woke me in the middle of the night. She was sitting up in bed listening. At first — for I am a heavy sleeper — I was disposed to be angry at being awakened, but then I heard a steady rustling in the ivy outside.

"Don't be frightened, little one," said I, and getting out of bed I began to grope about for the matches. I think at that moment I was capable of murder.

Then came a crackling noise, and then a hissing sound, as though a lot of crumpled paper had been drawn smartly across the window. The whole queer, quick noise terminated in a thud, and this was immediately succeeded by a low moan.

As the match flared I saw Mariana in the bluish glare, ghastly with terror. I went to her at once, and she clung to me, too frightened even to sob.

"Don't leave me!" she said. "Don't leave me!"

Presently, as we sat there in the flaring light of a candle, we heard a faint whining from the garden, then it changed to a still fainter sobbing, and died down into absolute stillness.

I tried to comfort Mariana as well as I could, but until the dawn came she would not let me leave her, or even unclasp her clinging arms. For the most part, during that interminable watching, we sat holding one another in silence. At last, however, as the daylight grew strong, her grasp loosened and she fell asleep. And when I was assured of her, I went down and unchained the front door and looked out.

The first thing I saw was one great stem of ivy torn down from the wall, and then almost at my feet was the dead body of our little neighbour. There was a red stain on the gravel towards the flower-bed, and a flat red triangle stuck out between his shoulder-blades.

Overcoming my feeling of repulsion, I turned him over and found the handle of a big knife, like a bread-knife, sticking out of his chest. Evidently he had been climbing down the ivy with this in his hand, and had stabbed himself in his fall.

It was a very bright, fresh morning, and all the world lay still under the pink sunrise. I thought for a moment, and then I decided to go round and call up Hanotaux.

That ends the story of our little neighbour. When Mariana awoke, the body was gone, and the red stains had been dug into the gravel. I avoided any errors on the side of truth in the account I gave her. She knows nothing of the knife, and thinks our little tormentor broke his neck — which is, so far as the phrase goes, a death by no means horrible. But nevertheless, to save her — and perhaps myself as well — from haunting memories, I had — at some profit to the ingenious landlord — to get released from my agreement and leave the house. I had the gravest dread that the memory of this little monster would seriously affect Mariana's health, which at that time was by no means robust, but I am happy to say that my fears were not confirmed.

16

The Loyalty of Esau Common
A Fragment*

THE native land of Esau Common was Aurelia, the head and centre of that great political system, the Aurelian Empire, and he was born near the capital, in the very suburbs indeed of Brumosa, the mightiest city in many respects that the world has ever seen. And rather indiscreetly, as one is apt to do in this matter, he was born a lower middle class Aurelian of no particular family and less than no particular expectations of wealth or influence in life. He was born in a little room over a shop full of picture frames, and of lengths and samples of picture framing, and amidst a faint smell of glue, and his first cry mingled with the uproar of a traction engine that was blundering along the paved suburban High Street upon which the rattling sash windows of his birth chamber gave. Moreover, his father was a man whose trade had made him a vehement critic and contemner of artists, an avid reader, and, if possible, a purchaser of all books, excepting only novels and works upon art, that came in his way. And these two circumstances gave certain qualities with which Providence (inexplicably careless of his social position) had endowed our Esau, a rather unusual and possibly unnatural direction.

The exceptional qualities that constituted Esau's endowment resembled each other (and most other exceptional qualities) in being finally of very doubtful value to him; in most other respects they differed. One was a gift of the mind and the second was a gift of the character. The first gift was a certain uncommon quality of imagination and intelligence as indisputable as it is indefinable. In the dialect of the old schoolmaster who made a precarious living by pretending to teach the tradesmen's sons in that Brumosan suburb, he was "quick at

* This fragment was written in February, 1901, at Sta Marghrita, in Ligure, and it was intended to open a series of kindly but instructive stories about the British army. This project was abandoned. The fragment remains the picture of a point of view — H.G.W.

126

figures," he was also "quick" at drawing — though he found no other copy in the school save the schoolmaster — and, at an astonishingly early age, he grasped the fact that the practice of reading gave rewards incommensurably great. He was a "great reader," said his mother. And it was remarked by the curate who prepared him — in spite of precociously shrewd theological objections — for his first communion in the official church of the Aurelian Empire, that he was a lad of "unusual intelligence."

Now "unusual intelligence" alone in persons of the Aurelian middle-class is apt to lead to tragedies. The great Aurelian Empire does not recognise the necessity of persons of "unusual intelligence" springing up in its lower middle class. It is an empire distinctively characterised by its eminent sense of order and decorum. It goes to inordinate cost to maintain a special class of superior persons, and for "unusual intelligence" to appear outside that class displays, to say the least of it, an uncivil disregard of wise and careful arrangements — somewhere. In most instances "unusual intelligence" of such irregular origin is starved and ignored, or at most permitted to exert itself, under proper patronage, in the ineffectual field of the arts. But it chanced that the tenor of the frame dealer's discourse on art in general and his best customers in particular gave his son an early and quite incurable bias against the practice of art in any form, while the parental collection of books gave it an equally strong bent towards the graver and more spacious interests of public affairs. And this bent presently got a very definite direction to one particular public affair, the question of military methods and efficiency, by the outbreak of a small but humiliating war upon the outskirts of the Aurelian Empire and a visit that Esau paid, just at that adolescent period when undying ambitions are begotten, to an uncle who was a butler near Blundershot, the great permanent camp of military exercises in Aurelia.

Esau discovered that to think of war, to study war, to prepare for and somewhere to play that mighty game was the one supremely desirable thing in life.

He might just as well have decided that his calling in life was to play cricket with the fixed stars, so far as any prospect of realising his ambition went. In the army of the Aurelian Empire at that time there were two distinct and practically uninterchangeable sorts of soldier. There were the officers and the privates. The Aurelian private soldier was almost invariably a man of the lowest class — if he was not, that was his misfortune, for he was treated as such on all occasions. Unlike the ordinary common citizen, he was supposed to be unable to read, and such scanty instruction as was given him in the art of war — there was a strong feeling in the army against privates who "knew too much" — was bawled at him by sergeant-instructors of exceptional lung power. Under pressure from these instructors he was compelled to pursue an ideal of soldierly smartness by cutting his hair very short — except a little lock on the brow which he called his "quiff" — and greasing the roots. Popularly he was called a "swaddy" or a "Jimmy" — "our Jimmies" people would say affectionately in times of war and "bloomin' Jimmies" in times of peace — and his brightly conspicuous blue baize uniform was resented in all but the meanest drinking houses and places of public resort. The public was perpetually regaled with stories and anecdotes of the amours of "Jimmy" with the nursegirl and the cook, and that women of this sort were accustomed to pay pence to "Jimmy" for his public company was one of the dearest legends of the great Aurelian public. The practical promotion open to "Jimmy" culminated in such a position as an embezzling mess clerk or as a sergeant-instructor, from which altitude he might bawl even as he had been bawled at, and impose on fresh generations of "Jimmies" that mysterious ideal of soldierly smartness, "the quiff." To become an officer was an accident too rare, too altogether dependent upon the remote opportunity coming to meet the rare gift, to enter into his ambitions. Clearly there was no way through enlistment as a private soldier by which Esau might dream of becoming anything more than raw material in the art of war.

And the officers of the Aurelian army formed an equally inaccessible class. The general public of this great empire, in spite of its inordinate pride in its imperial ascendency, was probably as mean souled as any public has ever been. It would not even educate its own children, but cheerfully permitted them to be trained in the sectarian schools of various prose-lytising bodies "to keep down the rates," and instead of assiduously seeking through all its available resources for men of exceptional gifts and energy to shape and guide the military forces upon which its ascendency finally depended, it acquiesced and indeed rejoiced in a system which amounted practically to the conversion of each of the few score undermanned regiments it maintained into a social club. Its officers were paid a mere honorarium, its subalterns received less money than if they had been tenth-rate clerks, and on the other hand the officers' dining arrangements, their contributions to the regimental band and Kursaal, and their hospitalities were conceived in a spirit of magnificent profusion. It was the boast, the glory of the Aurelian army, that an officer — even with a code of honour that condoned unpaid tradesmen's bills — "could not live on his pay," and consequently that its officers were "Gentlemen," which in Aurelia meant richly-living men. The centre of regimental expenditure was the mess, and a regiment was more or less a "crack" regiment in just the proportion that its officers were expensive messers. This of course narrowed the choice of the Aurelian empire in the matter of officers to the limited class of the rich, and even of these the more adventurous and the more intellectual travelled or played the more exciting game of public affairs. For most of these officers service in that army was not regarded as an arduous profession, but as a way of passing the time, and with the natural disinclination of prosperous people to risk brain pressure, it was regarded as a breach of good manners among them to "talk shop." The Aurelians were very proud of the class of officers, at once showy, impressive and inexpensive, that was obtained in this way, and it was believed as firmly that "Jimmy" would not serve under a man who was not a "gentleman" as that he was tipped pennies by servant girls. And certainly only young men with a taste for bright blue baize, and servant girls' pennies, and acting as waiters in a class club, were very urgently tempted — in peaceful times at any rate — to enter the Aurelian army.

Now as Esau's father was a man of small means, Esau was no sort of "gentleman" at all, and the mere whisper of his becoming an officer in the army would have sent every friend and relation he possessed into inextinguishable laughter. They would have yelled with laughter at the idea of the profession of arms being a remunerative calling. It would have seemed to these singular people as funny as apprenticing a boy to a duke. So Esau, when his school days were over, became a clerk, and afterwards turned the fruits of his father's library to the business of journalism. And the Aurelian army did not visibly suffer in the slightest degree for the loss of that exceptional intelligence and imagination of his. The empire was at peace, and not a mess entertainment but was the brighter for the absence of Esau's no doubt vulgar manners, his not very cheerful face, and the inglorious parsimony his presence would have entailed.

But, as I said, Esau had not one exceptional gift but two, and the second was that queer set of elements in the will that make a man dogged. He could see obstacles, at times he saw them big, but he could not see impossibilities. He was interested in the art of war, he wanted to play that game, — it was not the outward show of soldiering captivated him, not the band and the uniform, not the effect of the mess glories on the feminine mind, nor the tramp, tramp, tramp, all of which elements indeed seemed to him rather boring accessories, but the Real Thing. And because he could not be a professional soldier he did not propose to bury his ambition out of sight and turn to other things. At any rate there was nothing to prevent him studying, thinking about, dreaming about and, if necessary, experimenting about, this great actuality. So the reading of his early manhood was all of campaigns and theories, his holidays led him wherever military exercises were in progress, and for a time, under the immediate command of a wholesale draper and the remote control of a superseded lieutenant-colonel of the regular army, he studied thirst and hunger, bank holiday crowds, and the thinnest sham of sham fighting as a volunteer.

In time Esau came to know quite a lot about war, to feel even that he could imagine what it might be — when the next war came.

At the very first he had come to this matter with a vague suspicion that the Aurelian army was not the supreme expression of human science and forethought. And as his knowledge grew his suspicion expanded into a conviction that, partly by reason of the base parsimony of the Aurelian taxpayer and the dodgy incapacity of the statesmen he favoured, and partly by reason of the aggressive exclusiveness of the Aurelian wealthy, who would rather see a thing not done than have it done by a low-class fellow-countryman, the Aurelian army was about as inefficient and inadequate a fighting machine as any empire in the world — except perhaps the Chinese — had ever tempted Providence by maintaining. It was undermanned, it was stupidly officered, its economy was controlled by civilian clerks who knew nothing of war and cared less, its drill was fifty years out of date, it was short of horses and devoid of transport, and he became more and more convinced that nothing but a miracle could save it from overwhelming disaster if ever it came into collision with either the army of Saltaria or that of Barbarossa, Aurelia's great rivals in the world. Not, indeed, that either of these armies struck Esau as being exceptionally efficient or incapable of disaster. But they outclassed the Aurelian force quite hopelessly for all that.

Now this realisation distressed Esau very much. Aurelia was a splendid and spacious empire, with a glorious language and literature and a gallant history — even if it lacked gallant taxpayers— and Esau's pride in his race and nationality was (to begin with) an almost religious passion. And here, marring his pride and darkening his future for him, he perceived more and more clearly this flaw upon its glories!

The thing kept him awake at night, and by day it distressed him to the pitch of perpetually wanting to "do something" and never being able to get that something done in a satisfactory manner. He wrote letters — letters to influential military people, who did not answer him or snubbed him pitilessly; he wrote letters to papers that made him seem a conceited and jealous detractor of happily-placed officials; he wrote articles that he found it very hard to get printed or that finally got themselves torn up again in a fit of unpatriotic pique. He tainted the little reputation he had made as a journalist by his attentions to this topic. His chief editor had to stipulate that when Esau wrote articles about this and that he should not "go dragging in the army grievance," and Cockshot, the humorous writer and talker, added, "Hello, Common! What's the Aurelian officer done *now?*" to his collection of daily jests. To which Esau usually answered, "Nothing."

And when his patriotic ardour began to cool under the discovery of his absolute insignificance in the Aurelian scheme of things, another passion grew to replace it, and that was the exasperation of a man who believes in his own capacity and finds it universally denied, who finds his life slipping past him with no chance, with no shadow of an opportunity to prove him more than a windy contemner of his superiors.

By three and thirty he was a bitter man. His birthday fell on the great Aurelian bank holiday, when all over the country that volunteer force which was the Aurelian excuse for avoiding conscription did what were called "manœuvres." By habit or accident he found himself walking in the pine woods near Blundershot, the great Aurelian camp of arms. He had come upon a battalion in the shape of a straggling crowd standing and firing a volley at two hundred yards preparatory to delivering a bayonet charge, and fleeing this horrid vision, he had come upon another massing, apparently to receive shrapnel at seven hundred yards. Finally his luck had brought him out upon the crest of a hill from which the final march past was to be seen dim and far away through dense clouds of dust.

He sat down upon a gate and watched the dark masses shape about and move, and every now and then the warm breeze brought the strains of their numerous excellent (and totally unnecessary) bands to his ears. There were over twenty thousand men away there— infantry— in battalions that invariably fell short of their full strength; there were a squadron or so of cavalry, half a battery, a machine gun section or so, and twenty-nine men with bicycles. The entire force had no means of supply nor transport whatever; it was fed by a Wholesale Grocery Firm that supplied its own carts, and whatever survivors a month of campaigning might leave of it were bound by every arrangement to be bootless and in rags, unless the enemy supplied them in the prisoner's enclosure.

Esau's emotions took form at last in words. He misapplied his condemnation. "You fools!" he said, addressing the collected masses.

A voice answered him, a voice with a faintly foreign accent. "Peace advocate, I presume?"

Esau turned and discovered a grey golf cap, a bronzed nose and a red moustache. The golf cap, lifted, disclosed a pair of keen grey eyes.

"Not a bit of it," said Esau.

"Well?" said the stranger argumentatively.

"They'd be about as much good in a fight," said Esau, "as a Hyde Park demonstration."

"Looks pretty stocky stuff, some of it," said the stranger.

Esau made no direct reply. "There's a point," he said, "where courage becomes lunacy. A man who seriously proposes to go into a campaign as a volunteer soldier under the Aurelian War Office is either sick of his life or an idiot."

"Studied the question?"

"A little," said Esau.

"What's wrong?"

He had opened the floodgates. "Everything," said Esau, and assumed a more comfortable position on his gate. "For example ——"

The stranger struck Esau as a person of unparalleled intelligence. He did not simply listen, he punctuated Esau's remarks with brief intelligent sentences of appreciation. In the first place, explained Esau, this volunteer army has not one tenth of the guns it ought to have, it has no cavalry, it has no transport and no stores; in a country abounding in horses there is no organisation for registering and using the national stock of horseflesh for transport, and it wears unserviceable uniforms. It is indeed a mere costly and inefficient emergency apparatus for filling up infantry battalions in the regular army that ought never to need filling. Its drill is obsolete. "Drill!" cried Esau, "they haven't begun to drill! All they can do is to march up and down in lines and files and masses, and shoot at targets. Those crowds there couldn't fight. They're only organised for processions— and a sort of deadly rioting in savage lands! We haven't such a thing as a fighting regiment in the world!"

The stranger sought explanations. Esau expanded.

"The first thing a battalion should be taught to do," he said, "is surely to fight in a battle. There's three principal things in that section — to learn to advance, to learn to stick tight and tackle an advance, and what's hardest and most necessary to learn, to move back fighting. As for the last — they haven't dreamt it's possible! The others they play at at odd times. But just imagine what a battalion might be that was trained— say as well as a second-rate football club— to play up, and stiffen, and come back and rally! Why not?"

"It isn't done — anywhere."

"I know," said Esau. "*But it might be*. It's all the fighting they want to know, you know, now, and if they learn it at the price of marching ragged on parade — what does it matter? And the next thing they want to know — every man of them and the whole lot collectively— is just how to keep their little stomachs in order and their feet clean and tidy over all sorts of ground." His voice thickened with indignation. "They shy our poor devils of Jimmies," he cried, "into wildernesses of mud, up icy mountains, into hot deserts; they send them where there is nothing but putrid water to drink and with emergency rations for three days ahead clamouring to be eaten or thrown away— and never till the war comes do they give them a ha'porth of training in judgment or self-restraint! You know the fighting in warfare is nothing to the other thing— the travelling. That's the principal thing an army does in war, it moves about. But until this army of ours is actually in a war it never moves itself a bit. It squats in barracks while its officers give entertainments and play cricket and polo, and half the men in each skeleton battalion are trotting about doing housework and washing up and all that. But you know if everyone connected with this army was not a cursed fool, it would burn its barracks and—march."

"Where?"

"Everywhere. All round the Aurelian empire, in carts, on horses or bicycles—bicycles for preference—this army should go, battalions full up, rationed, armed, guns and everything, ready to fight."

"In bad weather?"

"Always."

"Rough on it?"

"Not a bit of it! It's the barracks are hell for soldiers! It's the dread of barracks keeps decent men out of the army. It's the barracks that make one man in twelve desert! The suicides at Blundershot are proverbial. They'd learn soon enough how not to let marching be rough on them. They'd see the world. Think of the sort of recruits they'd get for a bicycle tour round the empire with the off chance of fighting like football. Eh? They'd rope in something better than the lout who wants a blazing uniform—because of the girls—and has to be trained to sight his rifle by command. Just think of it! Beautiful regiments of brown hard seasoned men, with sound feet and sound insides, and all their stuff compactly with them; all of them knowing just what to do and just how to do it. Think of 'em going off white and young south-east, and coming back hard and brown out of the west. Eh? Everlastingly."

"But there must be a reason," began the red-haired man.

"The reason is that the army is a social institution. Where'd the hunt be? Where'd the band be? How about the annual sports? No tennis for 'em! No cricket! Think, above all, of the wives of the titled officers!"

Esau expanded still further. He poured out the bitterness of his soul upon the strange ordering of things that made warfare the privilege of a particular class, the honour of soldiering a perquisite of wealth. He admitted to this stranger the tragedy of his thwarted ambitions with that freedom and intimacy that is sometimes so much more possible with strangers than it is even with our nearest friends.

The red-haired man meditated upon him.

134

"I too was born an Aurelian," he said at last.

"But now?"

"Life was too strictly defined in this country for my father. He did not like that state unto which it had pleased God to call him. And as sticking in that state is one of the fundamental articles of religion at home here, he went to Marantha, where they have a different creed. I was sixteen years old then. And now — I am a Maranthian."

Esau looked at him with a new interest, for Marantha was a curiously situated country, sunken as it were between encircling arms of the Aurelian empire, and threatened — it was openly said in both countries— by that process of expansion that seemed to be the Aurelian destiny.

"But," he said. "Don't you find that mix your sympathies a little?"

The Maranthian shook his head.

"You don't feel yourself an Aurelian?"

"Not a bit of it. Why should I?"

"You can come back to the land where you spent all the impressionable years of your life and feel a foreigner?"

The red-haired man looked at the dusty regiments away there and smiled up at Esau. "Don't you?" he asked.

"Not a bit of it!"

"Where do *you* come in?"

Esau looked interrogation.

"*They* don't want you," said the red-haired man.

"They will," said Esau, not very confidently.

"Not a bit of it. They'd rather run their Empire on the rocks and scuttle it, than take help from a common man like you. What is it they call you?"

He hesitated.

"Bounder?" suggested Esau.

"Yes. That's the word, Bounder, Outsider, Poor Man, Not in the Know."

Esau stared at the distant march past. The red-haired man pursued his advantage. "*Your* empire," he said. "Did it bother to educate you?"

"I did my learning in a National school."

"There you are! The Empire didn't want you. It handed you over to a society of pious people and let 'em bring you up on charity and cheap teachers, to their own particular brand of piety, eh? It paid the very least it could for you. It only did that

135

out of shame. It treated you as bad men treat their bastards. And afterwards?"

Esau took a higher line. "One gives to the Empire; it's a Duty, not a Charity."

"They won't *let* you give! 'Keep out of it, you low-class brute!' That's the Empire's compliments to *you!* 'Let our officer-boys of the proper class learn war with your blood and —— Take your gifts to hell!' Has it ever spoken differently to you?"

Esau straddled his gate defensively. "The day will come ——," he said.

"When you will die and be buried," said the red-haired man. "Since the Ironsides faded from the world, they've run no risks of men of *your* sort getting their hands on the machines."

They came upon a pause. "Now in Marantha," said the red-haired man, as though he spoke aloud, "a good soldier is a good soldier, wherever he was born."

Esau did not answer.

"Why should you not go to Marantha?" said the red-haired man, suddenly firing point blank.

"What does Marantha want with soldiers?" asked Esau.

"It wants 'em, anyhow," said the red-haired man, "and it sees that it gets them."

"Why?"

"To prepare for war is to avoid it."

"Not always."

"It is the best."

"What possible country could Marantha fight?"

The red-haired man shrugged his shoulders.

"I am an Aurelian," said Esau.

"The country does not admit it," said the red-haired man.

"It lets me live here."

"Like any other foreigner. You have no more to do with official Aurelia than with official Barbarossa or official Saltaria. In the language of polite Society — you don't exist. Now, in Marantha, you can exist just as much as you see proper."

Esau shook his head, and the red-haired man, being a man of tact, presently passed to other things. And when they parted he saw that they exchanged addresses, and Esau discovered that his interlocutor was Commandant Thomas Smith in that army of Marantha that never dreamt of fighting. And in the night Esau lay awake turning over many spacious issues.

At first the matter of his thoughts was intensely personal,

then it became political, and finally that specialist side of him got the upper hand. If ever that war came — if after all Marantha should fight — what possible chances could Marantha hope for?

Suddenly he began to discover chances. In the morning he found his brain had got that problem forward to a very interesting stage. He devoured his breakfast and went out and bought as good a selection of Maps of Marantha and portions of Marantha as Brumosa could afford him, and for some days his income as a journalist was in suspense as he studied this more congenial theme. "If, after all," he said, "they should try and make an army — on these lines. . . ."

"By Jove!" cried Esau, "if they do that, they will beat us."

He stood up, smitten to the heart by a vision. "If *I* had the making of this army——!" he cried. "It would be the finest war ——!"

When he had studied the country he came to the army that Aurelia would have to fight in that country, but Aurelia possessed very little information about the army of Marantha. In the current number of a high-class review, however, Esau found a curious article on Marantha by a gentleman of position whose gist was this, that the Maranthians, who had once been excellent sharpshooters, could now no longer shoot.

"Now I wonder what he and his relatives have been talking about!" said Esau, and presently found himself hunting for further information.

He discovered himself short of ready money — he was not the sort of man who keeps a big current account — so he drew on some reserves, declined some new journalistic work that offered, and set himself to pursue these unsuspected chances for the Maranthians that had dawned upon him in the middle of the night. He meditated upon Commandant Thomas Smith until that gentleman assumed something of a legendary quality in his memory.

He chanced upon a paragraph in an evening paper, a not very conspicuous paragraph, referring to certain Custom House difficulties that had arisen with Marantha.

"It's nothing," said Esau, after thrice reading the paragraph. "It's the sort of little hitch that might happen at any time."

And the next day he had a visit from Commandant Thomas Smith.

Common came through the folding doors between his bedroom and his living room, to discover Commandant Smith standing near the window, pulling his red moustache and affecting to be unaware of the maps, sketches and memoranda that littered the writing table.

"Well?" said Commandant Smith.

"Well?" said Esau.

"Have you thought it over?"

"As a problem — yes, a good deal."

"As a personal problem?"

"No, as a problem in the art of war."

"That follows later. How about yourself?"

"I'm an Aurelian," said Esau, and took down his tobacco and pipe.

Commandant Smith sat down. "Cigarette?" said Esau, and handed tobacco and papers.

Commandant Smith reopened his attack. He developed his theory of the Aurelian Empire with patient elaboration. "What I want to do," he said, "is to clear away this delusion of yours that you belong to this Empire or that it belongs to you in any sort of way whatever. This Empire is a plutocratic officialdom supported by constituencies of fools. You don't come in anywhere. You're a lodger. I don't suppose you even vote?"

"I didn't last election," admitted Esau. "The Liberals put up a Jew and the Conservatives put up a railway barrister— and I don't like either sort."

Commandant Smith claimed the point by a gesture.

"All the same," said Esau, "I'm an Aurelian."

Commandant Smith restated his case.

"I'm an Aurelian," said Esau.

"Now look here," said Smith, and meditated for a moment with his eye on the heap of maps, "you persist in thinking you are an Aurelian. Very well! I will tell you now what everyone in Marantha believes, that your upper-class people here mean to pick a quarrel with us, wholly and solely to annex us, not with any friendly desire for unity, but simply that they may give us the benefit of that same tight system of exclusive class government — supported by a sham of party elections — that keeps everything here, schools, army, trade, in a state of such amazing efficiency. Well— we don't want those Blessings. We've an old rascal as President, but anyhow we've got checks on him. On the whole we don't do so badly. We think the Republican idea is something worth fighting for. And so we are getting ready to fight. I will tell you presently in honest round figures just what we count upon in men, material and support. Of course I shall give you no proofs— I shall just tell you. At present they do not know that we are getting ready to fight, they do not know how we mean to fight, they know nothing of our resources and nothing of our temper. I don't believe that a single person in authority here has taken the trouble to mug these maps you have there for half an hour. They do not even know whom they will send against us ——" He paused.

"Well?" said Esau.

"Well," said Commandant Smith, "as you are so sure you are an Aurelian, you are one of those who are going to make war upon us. Get ready to do it. Hunt up the whole question, study the game till you know it like your hand. When you know all about it, tell 'em. Offer to help them anyhow — volunteer. I know for a fact they are going to fight us with forty thousand men ——"

Esau turned on him quickly.

"They *are*, I tell you. *You* know better. Tell 'em it can't be done."

"You can do anything with forty thousand men ——"

"Not 'Jimmies' in bright blue baize under amateurs who think they are professionals, and short of horses and guns. . . . But that's beside the mark! I give you leave to play the loyal Aurelian for a year. Get to work, try and set your country to make use of what you know and what you can do. *Give* yourself — don't ask for pay —"

"Well ——"

"And when the year is up, if Aurelia will have nothing of you ——"

"I will serve another year," said Esau Common.

Commandant Smith made a movement of impatience. He turned in his chair and his voice went up to the note of irritation. "Confound it!" he shouted; "don't you see that all this is not loyalty to Aurelia; its simply a stupid self-devotion to this privileged governing class! Do you think we should object to union, if we might come in fair and equal? Not a bit of it! But we know they don't mean to bring us in fair and equal. They mean to walk over us and treat us as they treat you. Haw, haw 'soldiers and gentlemen' bossing everything— muddling everything, spoiling our railways, spoiling our trade, snubbing all our promise, breaking our hearts — with a few moneylenders here and there to help 'em. That's part of their pretty ways. They will insult any good white man who isn't and doesn't want to be rich, and they will truckle to any nigger who understands twenty per cent. Your Colonies in Columbia wouldn't stand it. *You* wouldn't stand it, if you hadn't to do so. You know you'd barricade the streets of Brumosa to-morrow if you got your hands on the guns and were sure the Barbarossa and Saltaria people would stand off while you settled 'em. Only you're so thundering loyal and politic. You hate 'em, and so do we! We won't have 'em in Marantha! We will burn our towns first! We'll make our country a desert before we stand that! Better be shot than stifled. It's no war against Aurelia ——"

"It's a class war."

"Yes. And so was the revolt of your Colonies in Columbia a hundred years ago."

"*They* don't think it was now."

"They've jabbered the truth away. But the Columbia war of Independence was just a war against privilege, and so is this. And what a man of your class has to do on the side of privilege ——"

"I'm an Aurelian," said Esau.

"You're a fool," said Smith, and drummed impatient fingers on the table.

"Try that for a year, anyhow," said Smith.

"I'll try it for two," said Esau.

"And then ——?"

"Still Aurelian," said Common.

Smith stood up. "Here is the address of an agent of mine," he said. "Whenever you want your passage to Marantha he'll give it you." He hesitated with a card in his hand. "Even if the war has begun. Of course, this address at any rate is confidential ——"

"Of course." said Esau. "But I sha'n't come, for all that."

"My dear man! Your country will be licked into a cocked hat, and *then* — it will hump its back and say 'No, thank you,' to a man of your sort. They'll make a ninth-class kingdom like Portugal of this Empire before they let your sort in. They'll put a Jew or a Gilchrist nigger in before they let *you* in. You're the uttermost foreigner, you're a lower middle-class Aurelian. And then you ——. Ugh."

And Smith turned himself about to find his hat. . . .

So soon as Smith had left him, Esau set his brains to work to demonstrate his loyalty to the country that was his own. He had a vision of a great series of articles on the national military inefficiency that he would write, articles of such capable and pitiless demonstration that it would be impossible for any sane person to deny the necessity of reform, and of reform in the direction that he would indicate. *Variorum* copies of these articles still exist in manuscript. Three even reached type. They were sent to prominent magazines, they went as letters to politicians. The burthen of them all was that the Army was bad, officers ignorant and untrained, men ignorant and untrained, arms defective, staff defective; ill-reading for Aurelian eyes. It became evident Esau was a Pro-Maranthian. One scheme Esau proposed for the brigading of volunteers was adopted without acknowledgment in a mangled form by the War Office, and a well-connected Colonel patented one of Esau's suggestions for transport vehicles. The rest of his criticism and proposals were as the voice of one whose head is in a sack.

And meanwhile the slow interchange of diplomacy broadened that little issue between Marantha and Aurelia, that little difficulty of the Custom House added to itself other difficulties and still other difficulties, until the Marantha question had clambered from obscure corner paragraphs in the newspapers to the possession of a daily column, and until that column had shifted from position to position until it was the dominant column every day. . . .

[*Here the fragment ends. The impossibility of keeping up the tone of careless geniality dawned upon the author.*]

17

The Wild Asses of the Devil

I

THERE was once an Author who pursued fame and prosperity in a pleasant villa on the south coast of England. He wrote stories of an acceptable nature and rejoiced in a growing public esteem, carefully offending no one and seeking only to please. He had married under circumstances of qualified and tolerable romance a lady who wrote occasional but otherwise regular verse, he was the father of a little daughter, whose reported sayings added much to his popularity, and some of the very best people in the land asked him to dinner. He was a deputy-lieutenant and a friend of the Prime Minister, a literary knighthood was no remote possibility for him, and even the Nobel Prize, given a sufficient longevity, was not altogether beyond his hopes. And this amount of prosperity had not betrayed him into any un-English pride. He remembered that manliness and simplicity which are expected from authors. He smoked pipes and not the excellent cigars he could have afforded. He kept his hair cut and never posed. He did not hold himself aloof from people of the inferior and less successful classes. He habitually travelled third class in order to study the characters he put into his delightful novels; he went for long walks and sat in inns, accosting people; he drew out his gardener. And though he worked steadily, he did not give up the care of his body, which threatened a certain plumpness and what is more to the point, a localized plumpness, not generally spread over the system but exaggerating the anterior equator. This expansion was his only care. He thought about fitness and played tennis, and every day, wet or fine, he went for at least an hour's walk. . . .

Yet this man, so representative of Edwardian literature— for it is in the reign of good King Edward the story begins— in spite of his enviable achievements and prospects, was doomed to the most exhausting and dubious adventures before his life came to its unhonoured end. . . .

Because I have not told you everything about him. Sometimes — in the morning sometimes — he would be irritable and have quarrels with his shaving things, and there were extraordinary moods when it would seem to him that living quite beautifully in a pleasant villa and being well-off and famous, and writing books that were always good-humoured and grammatical and a little distinguished in an inoffensive way, was about as boring and intolerable a life as any creature with a soul to be damned could possibly pursue. Which shows only that God in putting him together had not forgotten that viscus the liver which is usual on such occasions. . . .

The winter at the seaside is less agreeable and more bracing than the summer, and there were days when this Author had almost to force himself through the wholesome, necessary routines of his life, when the south-west wind savaged his villa and roared in the chimneys and slapped its windows with gustful of rain and promised to wet that Author thoroughly and exasperatingly down his neck and round his wrists and ankles directly he put his nose outside his door. And the grey waves he saw from his window came rolling inshore under the hurrying grey rain-bursts, line after line, to smash along the undercliff into vast, feathering fountains of foam and sud and send a salt-tasting spin-drift into his eyes. But manfully he would put on his puttees and his waterproof cape and his biggest brierwood pipe, and out he would go into the whurry-balloo of it all, knowing that so he would be all the brighter for his nice story-writing after tea.

On such a day he went out. He went out very resolutely along the seaside gardens of gravel and tamarisk and privet, resolved to oblige himself to go right past the harbour and up to the top of the east cliff before ever he turned his face back to the comforts of fire and wife and tea and buttered toast. . . .

And somewhere, perhaps half a mile away from home, he became aware of a queer character trying to keep abreast of him.

His impression was of a very miserable black man in the greasy, blue-black garments of a stoker, a lascar probably from a steamship in the harbour, and going with a sort of lame hobble.

As he passed this individual the Author had a transitory thought of how much Authors don't know in the world, how much, for instance, this shivering, cringing body might be hiding within itself, of inestimable value as "local colour" if only one could get hold of it for "putting into" one's large acceptable novels. Why doesn't one sometimes tap these sources? Kipling, for example, used to do so, with most successful results. . . . And then the Author became aware that this enigma was hurrying to overtake him. He slackened his pace. . . .

The creature wasn't asking for a light; it was begging for a box of matches. And what was odd, in quite good English.

The Author surveyed the beggar and slapped his pockets. Never had he seen so miserable a face. It was by no means a prepossessing face, with its aquiline nose, its sloping brows, its dark, deep, bloodshot eyes much too close together, its V-shaped, dishonest mouth and drenched chin-tuft. And yet it was attractively animal and pitiful. The idea flashed suddenly into the Author's head: "Why not, instead of going on, thinking emptily, through this beastly weather — why not take this man back home now, to the warm, dry study, and give him a hot drink and something to smoke, and *draw him out*?"

Get something technical and first-hand that would rather score off Kipling.

"It's damnably cold!" he shouted, in a sort of hearty, fore-castle voice.

"It's worse than that," said the strange stoker.

"It's a hell of a day!" said the Author, more forcible than ever.

"Don't remind me of hell," said the stoker, in a voice of inappeasable regret.

The Author slapped his pockets again. "You've got an infernal cold. Look here, my man — confound it! would you like a hot grog? . . ."

2

THE scene shifts to the Author's study — a blazing coal fire, the stoker sitting dripping and steaming before it, with his feet inside the fender, while the Author fusses about the room, directing the preparation of hot drinks. The Author is acutely aware not only of the stoker but of himself. The stoker has probably never been in the home of an Author before; he is probably awestricken at the array of books, at the comfort, convenience, and efficiency of the home, at the pleasant personality entertaining him. . . . Meanwhile the Author does not forget that the stoker is material, is "copy," is being watched, *observed*. So he poses and watches, until presently he forgets to pose in his astonishment at the thing he is observing. Because this stoker is rummier than a stoker ought to be —

He does not simply accept a hot drink; he informs his host just how hot the drink must be to satisfy him.

"Isn't there something you could put in it — something called red pepper? I've tasted that once or twice. It's good. If you could put in a bit of red pepper."

"If you can stand that sort of thing?"

"And if there isn't much water, can't you set light to the stuff? Or let me drink it boiling, out of a pannikin or something? Pepper and all."

Wonderful fellows, these stokers! The Author went to the bell and asked for red pepper.

And then as he came back to the fire he saw something that he instantly dismissed as an optical illusion, as a mirage effect of the clouds of steam his guest was disengaging. The stoker was sitting, all crouched up, as close over the fire as he could contrive; and he was holding his black hands, not to the fire but *in* the fire, holding them pressed flat against two red, glowing masses of coal. . . . He glanced over his shoulder at the Author with a guilty start, and then instantly the Author perceived that the hands were five or six inches away from the coal.

Then came smoking. The Author produced one of his big cigars — for although a conscientious pipe-smoker himself he gave people cigars; and then, again struck by something odd, he went off into a corner of the room where a little oval mirror gave him a means of watching the stoker undetected. And this is what he saw.

He saw the stoker, after a furtive glance at him, deliberately turn the cigar round, place the lighted end in his mouth, inhale strongly, and blow a torrent of sparks and smoke out of his nose. His firelit face as he did this expressed a diabolical relief. Then very hastily he reversed the cigar again, and turned round to look at the Author. The Author turned slowly towards him.

"You like that cigar?" he asked, after one of those mutual pauses that break down a pretence.

"It's admirable."

"Why do you smoke it the other way round?"

The stoker perceived he was caught. "It's a stokehole trick," he said. "Do you mind if I do it? I didn't think you saw."

145

"Pray smoke just as you like," said the Author, and advanced to watch the operation.

It was exactly like the fire-eater at the village fair. The man stuck the burning cigar into his mouth and blew sparks out of his nostrils. "Ah!" he said, with a note of genuine satisfaction. And then, with the cigar still burning in the corner of his mouth, he turned to the fire and *began to rearrange the burning coals with his hands* so as to pile up a great glowing mass. He picked up flaming and white-hot lumps as one might pick up lumps of sugar. The Author watched him, dumbfounded.

"I say!" he cried. "You stokers get a bit tough."

The stoker dropped the glowing piece of coal in his hand. "I forgot," he said, and sat back a little.

"Isn't that a bit — *extra*?" asked the Author, regarding him. "Isn't that some sort of trick?"

"We get so tough down there," said the stoker, and paused discreetly as the servant came in with the red pepper.

"Now you can drink," said the Author, and set himself to mix a drink of a pungency that he would have considered murderous ten minutes before. When he had done, the stoker reached over and added more red pepper.

"I don't quite see how it is your hand doesn't burn," said the Author as the stoker drank. The stoker shook his head over the uptilted glass.

"Incombustible," he said, putting it down. "Could I have just a tiny drop more? Just brandy and pepper, if you *don't* mind. Set alight. I don't care for water except when it's superheated steam."

And as the Author poured out another stiff glass of this incandescent brew, the stoker put up his hand and scratched the matted black hair over his temple. Then instantly he desisted and sat looking wickedly at the Author, while the Author stared at him aghast. For at the corner of his square, high, narrow forehead, revealed for an instant by the thrusting back of the hair, a curious stumpy excrescence had been visible; and the top of his ear — he had a pointed top to his ear!

"A-a-a-a-h!" said the Author, with dilated eyes.

"A-a-a-a-h!" said the stoker, in hopeless distress.

"But you aren't ——!"

"I know — I know I'm not. I know. . . . I'm a devil. A poor, lost, homeless devil."

And suddenly, with a gesture of indescribable despair, the

apparent stoker buried his face in his hands and burst into tears.

"Only man who's ever been decently kind to me," he sobbed. "And now— you'll chuck me out again into the beastly wet and cold. . . . Beautiful fire. . . . Nice drink. . . . Almost home-like. . . . Just to torment me. . . . Boo-ooh!"

And let it be recorded to the credit of our little Author, that he did overcome his momentary horror, that he did go quickly round the table, and that he patted that dirty stoker's shoulder.

"There!" he said. "There! Don't mind my rudeness. Have another nice drink. Have a hell of a drink. I won't turn you out if you're unhappy— on a day like this. Have just a mouthful of pepper, man, and pull yourself together."

And suddenly the poor devil caught hold of his arm. "Nobody good to me," he sobbed. "Nobody good to me." And his tears ran down over the Author's plump little hand — scalding tears.

3

ALL really wonderful things happen rather suddenly and without any great emphasis upon their wonderfulness, and this was no exception to the general rule. This Author went on comforting his devil as though this was nothing more than a chance encounter with an unhappy child, and the devil let his grief and discomfort have vent in a manner that seemed at the time as natural as anything could be. He was clearly a devil of feeble character and uncertain purpose, much broken down by harshness and cruelty, and it throws a curious light upon the general state of misconception with regard to matters diabolical that it came as a quite pitiful discovery to our Author that a devil could be unhappy and heart-broken. For a long time his most earnest and persistent questioning could gather nothing except that his guest was an exile from a land of great warmth and considerable entertainment, and it was only after con-siderable further applications of brandy and pepper that the sobbing confidences of the poor creature grew into the form of a coherent and understandable narrative.

And then it became apparent that this person was one of the very lowest types of infernal denizen, and that his rôle in the dark realms of Dis had been that of watcher and minder of a herd of sinister beings hitherto unknown to our Author, the

Devil's Wild Asses, which pastured in a stretch of meadows near the Styx. They were, he gathered, unruly, dangerous, and enterprising beasts, amenable only to a certain formula of expletives, which instantly reduced them to obedience. These expletives the stoker-devil would not repeat; to do so except when actually addressing one of the Wild Asses would, he explained, involve torments of the most terrible description. The bare thought of them gave him a shivering fit. But he gave the Author to understand that to crack these curses as one drove the Wild Asses to and from their grazing on the Elysian fields was a by no means disagreeable amusement. The ass-herds would try who could crack the loudest until the welkin rang.

And speaking of these things, the poor creature gave a picture of diabolical life that impressed the Author as by no means unpleasant for any one with a suitable constitution. It was like the Idylls of Theocritus done in fire; the devils drove their charges along burning lanes and sat gossiping in hedges of flames, rejoicing in the warm dry breezes (which it seems are rendered peculiarly bracing by the faint flavour of brimstone in the air), and watching the harpies and furies and witches circling in the perpetual afterglow of that inferior sky. And ever and again there would be holidays, and one would take one's lunch and wander over the sulphur craters picking flowers of sulphur or fishing for the souls of usurers and publishers and house-agents and land-agents in the lakes of boiling pitch. It was good sport, for the usurers and publishers and house-agents and land-agents were always eager to be caught; they crowded round the hooks and fought violently for the bait, and protested vehemently and entertainingly against the Rules and Regulations that compelled their instant return to the lake of fire.

And sometimes when he was on holiday this particular devil would go through the saltpetre dunes, where the witches' brooms grow and the blasted heath is in flower, to the landing-place of the ferry whence the Great Road runs through the shops and banks of the Via Dolorosa to the New Judgement Hall, and watch the crowds of damned arriving by the steam ferry-boats of the Consolidated Charon Company. This steam-boat-gazing seems about as popular down there as it is at Folkestone. Almost every day notable people arrive, and, as the devils are very well informed about terrestrial affairs — for of course all the earthly newspapers go straight to hell — whatever else could one expect? — they get ovations of an almost under-

148

graduate intensity. At times you can hear their cheering or booing, as the case may be, right away on the pastures where the Wild Asses feed. And that had been this particular devil's undoing.

He had always been interested in the career of the Rt. Hon. W.E. Gladstone. . . .

He was minding the Wild Asses. He knew the risks. He knew the penalties. But when he heard the vast uproar, when he heard the eager voices in the lane of fire saying, "It's Gladstone at last!" when he saw how quietly and unsuspiciously the Wild Asses cropped their pasture, the temptation was too much. He slipped away. He saw the great Englishman landed after a slight struggle. He joined in the outcry of "Speech! Speech!" He heard the first delicious promise of a Home Rule movement which should break the last feeble links of Celestial Control. . . .

And meanwhile the Wild Asses escaped — according to the rules and the prophecies. . . .

4

THE little Author sat and listened to this tale of a wonder that never for a moment struck him as incredible. And outside his rain-lashed window the strung-out fishing smacks pitched and rolled on their way home to Folkestone harbour. . . .

The Wild Asses escaped.

They got away to the world. And his superior officers took the poor herdsman and tried him and bullied him and passed this judgement upon him: that he must go to the earth and find the Wild Asses, and say to them that certain string of oaths that otherwise must never be repeated, and so control them and bring them back to hell. That — or else one pinch of salt on their tails. It did not matter which. One by one he must bring them back, driving them by spell and curse to the cattle-boat of the ferry. And until he had caught and brought them all back he might never return again to the warmth and comfort of his accustomed life. That was his sentence and punishment. And they put him into a shrapnel shell and fired him out among the stars, and when he had a little recovered he pulled himself together and made his way to the world.

But he never found his Wild Asses and after a little time he gave up trying.

He gave up trying because the Wild Asses, once they had got

out of control, developed the most amazing gifts. They could, for instance, disguise themselves with any sort of human shape, and the only way in which they differed then from a normal human being was — according to the printed paper of instructions that had been given to their custodian when he was fired out — that "their general conduct remains that of a Wild Ass of the Devil."

"And what interpretation can we put upon *that*?" he asked the listening Author.

And there was one night in the year — Walpurgis Night — when the Wild Asses became visibly great black wild asses and kicked up their hind legs and brayed. They had to. "But then, of course," said the devil, "they would take care to shut themselves up somewhere when they felt that coming on."

Like most weak characters, the stoker devil was intensely egotistical. He was anxious to dwell upon his own miseries and discomforts and difficulties and the general injustice of his treatment, and he was careless and casually indicative about the peculiarities of the Wild Asses, the matter which most excited and interested the Author. He bored on with his doleful story, and the Author had to interrupt with questions again and again in order to get any clear idea of the situation.

The devil's main excuse for his nervelessness was his profound ignorance of human nature. "So far as I can see," he said, "they might all be Wild Asses. I tried it once ——"

"Tried what?"

"The formula. You know."

"Yes?"

"On a man named Sir Edward Carson."

"Well?"

"*Ugh!*" said the devil.

"Punishment?"

"Don't speak of it. He was just a professional lawyer-politician who had lost his sense of values. . . . How was *I* to know? . . . But our people certainly know how to hurt. . . ."

After that it would seem this poor devil desisted absolutely from any attempt to recover his lost charges. He just tried to live for the moment and make his earthly existence as tolerable as possible. It was clear he hated the world. He found it cold, wet, draughty. . . . "I can't understand why everybody insists upon living outside of it," he said. "If you went inside ——"

He sought warmth and dryness. For a time he found a kind of

150

contentment in charge of the upcast furnace of a mine, and then he was superseded by an electric-fan. While in this position he read a vivid account of the intense heat in the Red Sea, and he was struck by the idea that if he could get a job as stoker upon an Indian liner he might snatch some days of real happiness during that portion of the voyage. For some time his natural ineptitude prevented his realizing this project, but at last, after some bitter experiences of homelessness during a London December, he had been able to ship on an Indiaward boat — only to get stranded in Folkestone in consequence of a propeller breakdown. And so here he was!

He paused.

"But about these Wild Asses?" said the Author.

The mournful, dark eyes looked at him hopelessly.

"Mightn't they do a lot of mischief?" asked the Author.

"They'll do no end of mischief," said the despondent devil.

"Ultimately you'll catch it for that?"

"Ugh!" said the stoker, trying not to think of it.

5

Now the spirit of romantic adventure slumbers in the most unexpected places, and I have already told you of our plump Author's discontents. He had been like a smouldering bomb for some years. Now, he burst out. He suddenly became excited, energetic, stimulating, uplifting.

He stood over the drooping devil.

"But my dear chap!" he said. "You must pull yourself together. You must do better than this. These confounded brutes may be doing all sorts of mischief. While you — shirk. . . ."

And so on. Real ginger.

"If I had some one to go with me. Some one who knew his way about."

The Author took whisky in the excitement of the moment. He began to move very rapidly about his room and make short, sharp gestures. You know how this sort of emotion wells up at times. "We must work from some central place," said the Author. "To begin with, London perhaps."

It was not two hours later that they started, this Author and this devil he had taken to himself, upon a mission. They went out in overcoats and warm underclothing — the Author gave

the devil a thorough outfit, a double lot of Jaeger's extra thick—
and they were resolved to find the Wild Asses of the Devil and
send them back to hell, or at least the Author was, in the
shortest possible time. In the picture you will see him with a
field-glass slung under his arm, the better to watch suspected
cases; in his pocket, wrapped in oiled paper, is a lot of salt to use
if by chance he finds a Wild Ass when the devil and his string of
oaths is not at hand. So he started. And when he had caught and
done for the Wild Asses, then the Author supposed that he
would come back to his nice little villa and his nice little wife,
and to his little daughter who said the amusing things, and to
his popularity, his large gilt-edged popularity, and— except for
an added prestige — be just exactly the man he had always
been. Little knowing that whosoever takes unto himself a devil
and goes out upon a quest, goes out upon a quest from which
there is no returning ——

Nevermore.

18

Answer to Prayer

THE Archbishop was perplexed by his own state of mind. Maybe the shadow of age was falling upon him, he thought, maybe he had been overworking, maybe the situation had been too complex for him and he was feeling the reality of a failure without seeing it plainly as a definable fact. But his nerve, which had never failed him hitherto, was failing him now. In small things as in important matters he no longer showed the quick decisiveness that had hitherto been the envy of his fellow ecclesiastics and the admiration of his friends. He doubted now before he went upstairs or downstairs, with a curious feeling that he might find something unexpected on the landing. He hesitated before he rang a bell, with a vague uncertainty of who or what might appear. Before he took up the letters his secretary had opened for him he had a faint twinge of apprehension.

Had he after all done something wrong or acted in a mistaken spirit?

People who had always been nice to him showed a certain coolness, people from whom he would have least expected it. His secretaries, he knew, were keeping back "open letters" and grossly abusive comments. The reassurances and encouragements that flowed in to him were anything but reassuring, because their volume and their tone reflected what was hidden from him on the other side. Had he, at the end of his long, tortuous and hitherto quite dignified career, made a howler?

There was no one on earth to whom he could confide his trouble. He had always been a man who kept his own counsel. But now, if only he could find understanding, sympathy, endorsement! If he could really put things as he saw them, if he could simplify the whole confused affair down to essentials and make his stand plain and clear.

Prayer?

If anyone else had come to him in this sort of quandary, he would have told him at once to pray. If it was a woman he would have patted the shoulder gently, as an elderly man may do, and he would have said very softly in that rich kind voice of his, "Try Prayer, my dear. Try Prayer."

Physician heal thyself. Why not try prayer?

He stood hesitatingly between his apartments and his little private oratory. He stood in what was his habitual children's-service attitude with his hands together in front of him, his head a little on one side and something faintly bland and whimsical about him. It came to him that he himself had not made a personal and particular appeal to God for many years. It had seemed unnecessary. It had indeed been unnecessary. He had of course said his prayers with the utmost regularity, not only in the presence of others, but, being essentially an honest man, even when he was alone. He had never cheated about prayer. He had felt it was a purifying and beneficial process, no more to be missed than cleaning his teeth, but his sense of a definite hearer, listening at the other end of the telephone, so to speak, behind the veil, had always been a faint one. The reception away there was in the Absolute, in Eternity, beyond the stars. Which indeed left the church conveniently free to take an unembarrassed course of action. . . .

But in this particular tangle, the Archbishop wanted something more definite. If for once, he did not trouble about style and manner. . . .

If he put the case simply, quite simply, just as he saw it, and remained very still on his knees, wouldn't he presently find this neuralgic fretting of his mind abating, and that assurance, that clear self-assurance that had hitherto been his strength, returning to him? He must not be in the least oily — they had actually been calling him oily — he must be perfectly direct and simple and fearless. He must pray straightforwardly to the silence as one mind to another.

It was a little like the practice of some Dissenters and Quakers, but maybe it would be none the less effective on that account.

Yes, he would pray.

Slowly he sank to his knees and put his hands together. He was touched by a sort of childish trustfulness in his own attitude. "Oh God," he began, and paused.

He paused, and a sense of awful imminence, a monstrous awe, gripped him. And then he heard a voice.

It was not a harsh voice, but it was a clear strong voice. There was nothing about it still or small. It was neither friendly nor

154

hostile; it was brisk.

"*Yes*," said the voice. "*What is it?*"

They found His Grace in the morning. He had slipped off the steps on which he had been kneeling and lay, sprawling on the crimson carpet. Plainly his death had been instantaneous.

But instead of the serenity, the almost fatuous serenity, that was his habitual expression, his countenance, by some strange freak of nature, displayed an extremity of terror and dismay.

19

The New Faust

A FILM STORY

A PLEASANT dining-room in Park Square, London. The room
has an air of refinement and wealth. Two gentlemen are seated
at dinner, while an admirable butler, Mutimer, waits un-
obtrusively. One, the host, Mr. Elvesham, is an old gentleman
of seventy-one. His hair is grey and thin and his hand is
tremulous. He has a hard, discontented, wrinkled face and a
characteristic way of lifting his chin when he speaks. Although
he is proud of his fine hands they are veined and shrivelled, and
he lifts his left (adorned by a diamond ring) in an elegant
artificial gesture, that has now become second nature.

The age of his visitor is less certain. He is a dark, aquiline-
faced gentleman, with a small moustache, a Disraeli tuft and
thick, slightly oblique eyebrows. His straight hair, brushed
back over the pointed ears, looks as if it were dyed black. When
presently he gets up and moves about, he is a little lame, and his
peculiar boots suggest that he may even be slightly club-footed.

ELVESHAM speaks: "I can't tell you, Dr. McPhister, what a
pleasure it is to catch you for dinner. You flit to and fro and one
never knows where you are."

McPHISTER: "The pleasure is all mine. It is always interesting to meet you and see how things are with you. As for me, I'm
always — as the proverb has it — going to and fro in the earth
and walking up and down in it. We — we psychiatrists have to
keep moving. How is it with you since we last met?"

ELVESHAM: "None the younger, Dr. McPhister."

McPHISTER: "Time, like an ever flowing stream, bears all its
sons away. They fly forgotten, as a dream flies at the opening
day! How true, how unintentionally true, these hymns can be!
. . . And what a rich store of memories vanishes when a man
dies! It has always seemed a pity to me that it was impossible to
carry on those memories — beyond bodily decay. I've worried
about it no end. It's been one of my many little quarrels with the
Order of Creation. Because, you know, Man *is* the rebel of child
creation. Such a waste! *Such* a waste! But now, you know, *now* it
is no longer impossible."

156

ELVESHAM: "What do you say? No longer impossible to carry on memories — after death? To die and still remember?'

McPHISTER: "Practically that."

ELVESHAM: "But how?"

McPHISTER, slowly and impressively: "I was in a private hospital in Belgrade only a few days ago assisting at some of the most remarkable experiments in the world — a transfer of memories from brain to brain."

ELVESHAM: "A transfer of memories. I don't understand."

McPHISTER: "What an excellent savoury this is! Your cook gets better every time I come here. You know, he isn't afraid to make the stuff *hot*."

ELVESHAM: "But this transfer of memories from brain to brain! That opens the most extraordinary possibilities."

McPHISTER: "I thought you would see that."

ELVESHAM: "But why not the whole thing — the whole memory system?"

McPHISTER: "Why not?"

ELVESHAM: "But a man—— What is a *man*? What is he but a system of memories?"

McPHISTER sips his wine and speaks with disingenuous deliberation: "That at any rate is the Behaviourist doctrine."

ELVESHAM: "And so— if I could shift my memories out of this rather worn and tired old brain of mine into another— younger and fresher — it is *I* who would shift. . . ."

McPHISTER: "You are quick on the uptake. That is exactly what is possible now. An old man can begin afresh in a younger brain."

ELVESHAM: "Nonsense!"

McPHISTER: "Fact."

ELVESHAM: "Imagine what it means!"

McPHISTER: "*Can* you imagine it?

ELVESHAM: "I think I can — in a dazzled sort of way."

McPHISTER: "You'd find yourself in a young body. . . ."

ELVESHAM: "With all my knowledge and experience."

McPHISTER: "With all your knowledge and experience. That is the thing that appeals to my imagination. And when you have worn out your second body — then again, you could begin afresh. . . ."

ELVESHAM: "Why do you bring this to me? Why not do it for yourself?"

McPHISTER: "Circumstances — too complex to explain."

157

ELVESHAM: "But what sort of circumstances? I know so little about you — although we have this habit of meeting."

McPHISTER: "My position in the world — is a peculiar one. . . . I have always had a great pity and sympathy for Man — for my fellow men I should say. But the point is that I could not conduct this experiment upon myself."

ELVESHAM: "But you could upon me?"

McPHISTER: "Yes. You see — someone who knows about it must stand by."

They are interrupted by the butler, who clears the savoury and brings cigarettes and coffee. A clock on the mantel strikes nine. Elvesham is excited by this new idea and does not care to talk of what is on his mind in front of the butler.

While the conversation goes on Elvesham's memories go back, first to his childhood, and he pictures a little fellow in a plaid frock running down a garden path in pursuit of a bird or a butterfly. From boyhood he recalls a youngster in knickerbockers playing with bricks and toys on a nursery floor. School, and he remembers writing at a well-worn schoolroom desk and then in shorts going out, not too confidently, into the field with a football team. College, and he sits deep in an armchair in a Cambridge study and reads. . . .

McPHISTER'S voice breaks into his thoughts: "Then you began to think seriously of what you were going to do with your life — and at the same time you began to dream of romance — and women."

ELVESHAM: "Yes — it all came with a rush. As it does to all young men."

There are memories of the young man in the National Gallery pausing to look at Leonardo's *Our Lady of the Rocks*, at the Velasquez *Venus*, at a Greuze. Then a couple of girls pass and he turns to look at them. They glance back at him artlessly. One is very pretty and as they go out of the room he hesitates and follows rather vaguely. Then he talks with another girl in an orchard. He dares to kiss a third — in the conservatory outside a ball-room. Then he is being a masher in the Empire Promenade and he is accosted and talks to a prostitute.

ELVESHAM: "It was all very swift. I wanted pleasure, but also I wanted success. I was ambitious. I was a good business organiser." (He is seen in a business office with two elder men). "I took up one thing after another as opportunity came rushing upon me. I never seemed to concentrate. I fell in love."

158

McPhister: "Several times."

Elvesham: "Yes, several times. But there was one girl. . . ."

McPhister: "Lovelier than anybody."

Elvesham: "Lovelier than anybody. How did you know?"

McPhister laughs: "She always is."

Elvesham remembers cutting two names on the bark of a tree. "Mary Farlake. Tom Elvesham." He shows the names to Mary Farlake, who is in 1893 costume. He sees her sitting in the fork of a tree while they kiss. After kissing they separate and look with an intent scrutiny at each other. Then they are in a very late Victorian room together. He walks up and down, explains something defensively and she does not like his explanation.

Elvesham: "Yes — yes — for me she was lovelier than anyone. She was more *real* to me. Closer. She mattered more to me than anything else. She became engaged to me — and then we fell out. She criticised me. She hesitated to give herself to me. We quarrelled, she never seemed sure of me. She didn't like some of my business deals. She didn't understand. It's a queer thing — she was all the world to me and yet I resented her importance."

McPhister: "Not queer at all. That's the common way. There never was love of woman without doubt, jealousy and a struggle since the world began."

Elvesham: "Sometimes I thought I was all the world to her. And yet we parted. The things we parted about seem trivial now. In comparison with parting. Perhaps I was hard in business."

McPhister: "One *must* be hard in business."

Elvesham: "But was that her affair?"

McPhister: "Exactly. Was it her affair? Love is a usurpation — always."

Elvesham: "There's no accounting for these things. She married a small landowner, and went to live at Barchesham. I happened to take the castle there only a year ago, but I found that she had been dead some years. She thought I did not love her enough and yet, come to think of it, she has influenced all my career. I went on working and growing rich and influential very largely on account of her."

McPhister: "Just to show her."

Elvesham: "Just to show her."

McPhister: "There have been other women?"

Elvesham: "Any amount of them. But none of them

mattered in quite that way. For a time I was frantic to console myself. A rich man need never want for women. They hang about me still. But I never married any of them. As you probably know I got and developed a great concession in Rumania and another in Sweden. Rushing about — seeing people — fixing things. The years slipped by unnoticed. Lord! It's all gone by like a dream."

The two men are now standing up from the table. McPhister leans on the mantelshelf and Elvesham, preoccupied by his memories, stands brooding over the debris of the dinner-table.

McPHISTER: "And here you are! You have lived life round. And you are dissatisfied. You don't like the way things are coming to an end. You were *rushed* through it. I agree with you. The Order of Creation gives too brief a run to men. I am no friend of the Order of Creation. I am for circumventing His limitations. And now? Now perhaps we have a chance of doing something better. Suppose I *were* to help you to take fifty years more of vitality. And after that yet another fifty years. And then still more. Suppose I did manage to make you a sort of unending man. What would you *do* with those added years, Elvesham?"

ELVESHAM: "*Do* with them?" He looks up. "With fifty years more of youth and energy, without fatigue, without this constant sense of limited time that torments me, I could *eat* the world."

McPHISTER: "I'm not so sure of that. I've watched men live. I've watched men die. But I've never seen them start anything really new. You are certain you wouldn't just go round the squirrel's cage again?"

ELVESHAM: "I've learnt my lesson."

McPHISTER: "And what would you do?"

ELVESHAM: "Something bolder, finer, more decisive."

McPHISTER: "You'd go on? Unscrupulous and assured? Yes — yes. What would you *do*?"

ELVESHAM: "Take power."

McPHISTER: "And how? You are to be a young man again — with all your old memories — and your present wealth. I cannot imagine what a man, any man, would do in such a case. How would you take power?"

ELVESHAM: "The world is full of unrest and discontent. I should begin in America or Western Europe. I should buy one or two important newspapers. Perhaps more. I should start a

youth movement, with myself— a youth with a mature brain—
as leader."

McPHISTER: "Go on."

ELVESHAM: "I should become a young Cæsar. The hope of
youth everywhere."

McPHISTER: "Yes?"

ELVESHAM: "Before they knew what they were doing they
would have put Power into my hands. See what lesser men have
done."

McPHISTER: "And then?"

ELVESHAM: "Discipline for the world. *Mastery!*"

McPHISTER: "And when your time was drawing near and
you were growing old again?"

ELVESHAM: "I should make a religion of it. Like the Dalai
Lama in Tibet, my successor would be chosen secretly. And in
him I should live again, the Phœnix-Master."

McPHISTER: "You warm my heart. This is what Napoleon
might have wished to be! A serialised Napoleon. Each instal-
ment bigger than the last. Heaven Himself at last will be afraid
of you. And if I were to win this endless life for you, you promise
me to do all that?"

ELVESHAM: "I feel I could show you great things."

McPHISTER: "No loitering with women by the way. No love,
no weakness."

ELVESHAM: "Who have I got to love now? All that is past.
That goes and never returns."

McPHISTER: "Are you sure?"

ELVESHAM: "Sure."

McPHISTER: "You promise me you will tower up to Heaven
with a heart of steel?"

ELVESHAM: "I could go on and tower up to Heaven now, if I
had not to grow old and die. I have only begun to realise my
possibilities." He passes his hand over his brow. "What are we
talking about? You fill me with fantastic thoughts. You intox-
icate me with this possibility. Are you a hypnotist?"

McPHISTER: "An experimentalist, Mr. Elvesham. Curiosity
my master passion. I wanted to see how you would react to this
suggestion. You understand that you would have to make an
exchange. You have *that* clear? That's essential. No memory, no
mind can exist without a brain and a body, nowadays. You
must get someone to swap brains with you. The other person—
the owner of the young brain —*that* set of memories would have

161

to take your place. There's your brain ripe and ready to transfer. But that other might not be so eager to leap into that sound and well-preserved, but — may I say it? — elderly fabric."

ELVESHAM: "That's the catch. Consent."

McPHISTER: "*One* catch. Not the only one."

ELVESHAM: "But how can we find that young man?"

McPHISTER: "Difficult. But not impossible. In a world of money and urgent needs — Oh! I know possible types."

ELVESHAM: "Tell me. Would it be necessary to explain *exactly* to the young man we choose what was to be done? I mean, couldn't we represent the whole thing as a *partial* transfer? A little dangerous perhaps but no more than dangerous. . . ."

McPHISTER: "I've thought of that. But I wanted *you* to think of it first. You mean we might change by a trick. *That* might be done. Think of all that there is at stake."

ELVESHAM: "At one moment you make this thing seem possible, almost practicable, and then it recedes beyond hoping." He is suddenly despondent. "And then I know we shall never find that young man. But it is *all* a preposterous dream. We've been talking nonsense. What nonsense we have been talking!"

McPhister seems to be thinking hard. "Now *where* have I seen someone? Quite recently. . . . Ambitious — impatient."

On a beautiful river reach in the South of England, under a high moon, a rowing boat is being paddled slowly up-stream. In the distance are lawns, trees and a large white mansion. Two lovers sit side by side in the steering seat. The oars are shipped and the man keeps the boat moving by an occasional stroke of the boat hook-paddle he holds in his hand. He is a handsome, intelligent-looking young man of twenty-seven. His name is Arthur Reston. The girl, Marguerite Swift, is twenty-one, very lovely, broad-browed, broad-faced, grave and sweet. They talk softly to one another:

ARTHUR: "How sweet you look in the moonlight! I've been in love with you, darling, since you were fourteen, and all that time you have been growing lovelier and lovelier. All too good for me you were then, and all too gooder you've got."

MARGUERITE: "Seven years. A lovely dream. You know — I knew you loved me *years* before you said a word."

ARTHUR: "I lived for a year or so — on the chance of just seeing you look at me. You know you would never *look* at me —

162

openly. You had a sort of pussycat, downcast way with you, so that one was never quite sure. . . ."

MARGUERITE: "Well, I chose science for my degree because of you. I used to watch you. When I was still at school the girls suspected something because I was always so eager to hear anything of you."

ARTHUR: "And now what are we going to do?"

MARGUERITE is silent for a moment and ripples her hand in the water: "I want to go on working and studying with you."

ARTHUR: "And that's all?"

MARGUERITE's hand becomes still. She answers after another pause. "No."

ARTHUR: "Of course not. We want to be lovers out and out. We want to go out into the world and live a better life than this humdrum college routine. I've been finding out Barchesham College for some time. Darling, I'm discontented. On this lovely night — on your birthday."

MARGUERITE looks at him with her steady eyes: "Who can you grumble to except to me? I know. You've been fretting. I know you so well, dear. I've wanted you to tell me."

ARTHUR: "These little colleges, these little provincial colleges are impostures. I want to get away — and take you away."

MARGUERITE: "Go on."

ARTHUR: "They're not large enough. There's no mental vitality here. The place pretends to be a home of learning. Really it's a teaching sweat-shop. For the glory of the governors and the satisfaction of local pride. I've got a scheme for research and I can't find time for it, I can't find freedom for it — there isn't the apparatus I want. I *can't* go on like this. Marguerite! What am I to do? Am I to live and die a fruitless little small-college don?"

MARGUERITE: "You won't do that, my dear."

ARTHUR: "But the years are passing! How am I to get out of this? I've the brains to do real work — yes — but when it comes to finding time and material . . .? I need the sort of laboratory you'd find in Cambridge or London. I need — for the apparatus I dream of — money."

MARGUERITE: "What sort of money?"

ARTHUR: "Two thousand pounds and freedom. And time. Time to experiment and then try again."

MARGUERITE: "And then ——?"

ARTHUR: "I know what I have in mind. In three years the

world would be at my feet. The world that counts, anyhow. At *our* feet, darling."

MARGUERITE: "And here am I — useless and unhelpful."

ARTHUR: "Think of all the money there is in the world! Think of the men who go down to the city and get thousands. Here's this old Elvesham, who lives here in Barchesham Castle. He's rolling in wasted opportunities like a dog in the manger. The things he might set going. He could take his cheque book and launch me with a flick of the pen . . . Oh, what's the good of grousing. Here we are."

The boat is now near a landing-place with a small boathouse and trees. Arthur stands up and goes forward to paddle the boat in among the others. There is a dark shadow that suggests a human being standing up by the boathouse under the tree.

"Hullo!" says Arthur, "lend a hand there."

Dr. McPhister dissolves into the lights and shades under the tree.

MARGUERITE, half-rising from her seat: "You want me to lend a hand?"

ARTHUR: "I thought there was someone there. But it's no one. Just a shadow."

He jumps ashore with the painter and pulls the boat in for Marguerite to land.

MARGUERITE stands in the boat with Arthur holding her hand: "*I* thought I saw someone there."

She lands and Arthur Reston ties up the boat. They stand side by side in the moonlight. They forget about the stranger.

MARGUERITE: "This lovely world! This lovely night! It makes one feel nothing is impossible."

ARTHUR: "Nothing is impossible for the discontented."

MARGUERITE: "Oh, Moon, Goddess of the Silver Sky! Give him opportunity."

ARTHUR: "Listen, old Moon. Old Aunt Moon with the great round face. Escape and opportunity — the prayer of the young. Can you deny it for Marguerite even if you deny it for me?"

Elvesham is in his dress shirt, trousers and dressing-gown, in his big well-furnished London bedroom. The bedroom looks out on a London park. He is walking up and down the room meditating and talking to himself.

ELVESHAM: "Absurd that I should be excited by a fairy story

of this sort. Greedy we human beings are for life — life and *more* life."

The telephone bell rings.

"Yes — who is it? Oh! it's *you*, McPhister. Yes, this is Elvesham. What is it? . . .

"*What!* You've found the young man already! You haven't been gone from this house forty minutes and you've *found* him. . . .

"Oh, you've *thought* of him. You knew him before. That's different. . . .

"See him. I'd certainly like to see him.

"*Come down and see him.* Where? *Barchesham?* Why! but, my dear sir, I rent a house there — Barchesham Castle. Yes. Yes. All the easier to come down to Barchesham. Yes. But——? It's a hundred and seven miles. *Come* down you say. Where on earth *are* you, McPhister? What do you mean by *come down*?

"Oh, go down — go down to-morrow. That's different. You're at your London hotel, of course. I'd certainly like to see the proposed new body . . . . Friday afternoon . . . . Yes I can wait that long. I want to think. I'm impatient, yes, but I'm *afraid*."

He puts down the receiver. Then he is struck by an afterthought and picks it up again: "McPhister! Dr. McPhister!" But McPhister is off the line.

ELVESHAM: "Nuisance. Don't know his number. Don't know his address. Queer chap, the doctor. Quick worker. Oh, but the whole of this thing is impossible. I'm dreaming it. To be born again — practically. To begin life over again!"

A typically English scene, a cricket field in a town park. A cricket match is in progress: Barchesham College v. Second Cheshamshire. Spectators grouped about the pavilion. Village elders sit on a form. Small boys squat on the roller and lie prone on the grass.

Mr. Elvesham and Dr. McPhister are in chairs in the front of this pavilion, and with them is Principal Jeddles, of Barchesham College.

ELVESHAM: "I want to know more of the local life of Barchesham. I am getting very much at home up at the Castle. I may even live down here for good."

MCPHISTER: "We're particularly interested in your research work at the college."

Jeddles, who has kept one eye on the game, interrupts to shout: "Well hit, sir! Well hit!"

He turns to Elvesham: "Yes, that's the young man. That was a fine open slog. He'd be a great cricketer if he had time for practice. But he is trying to be three things at once. He is a good teacher. Popular. He's a good sportsman. And he has a sort of vanity— I don't know, it may not be vanity— that he ought to do research work. We have this disposition to do research work here on the part of the younger men. They will not be contented with life as it is. That lean young man who is batting with him, Professor Spike, is always inoculating mice and rabbits— with all kinds of diseases. I don't quite like it."

McPhister: "Surely inquiry — research, are things to encourage."

Jeddles: "I'm not so sure of that. As the Principal of the College I have to weigh one thing against another. Mediæval history is my subject and naturally I look first at the cultural side. I doubt if these experiments upon animals make for popularity."

Elvesham: "Still if the young man has a gift ——"

Jeddles: "So hard to determine. My conception of this college is a centre of culture, of gracious living— not a centre of unrest. My disposition is to turn the attention of our donors and founders to tangible things. Look, for instance, at those handsome buildings." (We are shown some extremely pretentious pseudo-Gothic piles.) "The Sir Joshua Smirke Hall; the Bludsole Memorial Wing. In their own distinctive way they are our equivalents of Magdalen Tower at Oxford or King's College, Cambridge. They will make atmosphere for generations of undergraduates. They will give them a background of elegance and aloofness. And they make the pious donor's gift a perpetual monument to his generosity, Mr. Elvesham. I have dreamt at times of seeing the college with a chapel worthy of it, before I die. Our benefactors would be perpetuated in marble and stained glass. . . . When you buy buildings you know what you're getting, Mr. Elvesham."

McPhister: "I can assure you it isn't the immortality of bricks and mortar that Mr. Elvesham is after."

There is a great outburst of clapping about them.

Jeddles: "Boundary! That's the winning hit! That settles it."

The match is over, and the cricketers return to the pavilion. Triumphant march of Spike and Reston in their pads and flannels to the pavilion amidst applause. Everyone is moving.

Jeddles: "Let me introduce you, Mr. Elvesham and Dr. ——"

McPhister: "Dr. McPhister."

Jeddles: "— Dr. McPhister, to our two ah!— intellectuals."

Elvesham says to Arthur and Spike: "We have heard of your work here. My friend, Dr. McPhister, is all for stripping the fruit from the tree of knowledge, and he is egging me on to help ——"

McPhister: "In fact we want to know what your difficulties are here."

Spike, with his eye on the Principal, whom he does not wish to offend: "Difficulties! There's nothing to complain of. I'd like a little more time to myself. Perhaps two assistants— to train. I may get those among the students. But mice and guinea pigs are cheap and you'd be surprised how little my disease-germs ask for their services."

McPhister: "That's not quite the same with *your* work, Mr. Reston."

Arthur: "No."

McPhister: "You want equipment?"

Arthur: "I want a lot of expensive stuff. Don't I, Dr. Jeddles?"

Elvesham: "I'm not a man of science myself. Dr. McPhister is the man to discuss things with you, Mr. Reston. He'll understand your difficulties better than I shall. Would you mind telling him a little about your work?"

Jeddles: "Let them talk. Mr. Reston knows how to ask. Meanwhile I pray you, Mr. Elvesham, give me five minutes for my beautiful unfinished swimming bath."

Jeddles leads off Elvesham. McPhister takes Arthur by the arm and leads him to the scorers' table in the tent, leaving Spike alone.

McPhister: "So far, Mr. Reston, it is all plain sailing. I don't think there need be any difficulty about that two thousand pounds— or even a little more. I've no doubt you're on to a very hopeful line of inquiry." Reston refrains by an effort from jumping with joy. "But for everything in this life — there is a quid pro quo. I want to tell you of something in which you can be a great help to Mr. Elvesham and myself. In its way it is also research."

He pauses. "Go on," says Reston. "Anything in reason."

McPHISTER: "It's peculiar. It's a mental experiment. The question is whether a group of mental impressions — memories — can be shifted from one brain to another."

ARTHUR: "Telepathy. I don't believe in it."

McPHISTER: "It's rather more than that. It's an exchange of memories. We have an idea that in a properly arranged field of force, two brains which have had suitable hypnotic treatment, may exchange — oh, a considerable body of their impressions."

ARTHUR: "Sounds quite impossible to me. Bad analogy with electrical induction — nothing more."

McPHISTER, with a gesture: "I'm open-minded. But our friend here is very keen on its being tried."

ARTHUR: "And he wants to tie up a participation in that experiment with a little matter of two thousand pounds."

McPHISTER: "Exactly. But that's for your research also."

ARTHUR: "M'm." He stands up regarding McPhister very thoughtfully. "I don't suppose it would take up much time and my name needn't be implicated. It seems a lot of money."

McPHISTER: "There are risks. At least Mr. Elvesham thinks there are."

ARTHUR: "For example?"

McPHISTER: "You are going to put your brains in a field of considerable intensity. You may float your mind off its anchorage, so to speak. We want you to be clear about that before you consent."

ARTHUR: "Float my mind off its anchorage?"

McPHISTER: "A certain detachment."

ARTHUR: "I don't mind so long as you don't electrocute me or boil my head."

McPHISTER: "All the same, this experiment *may* affect your individuality for a time. That's where I'm interested."

ARTHUR: "And when do I get my two thousand pounds?"

ELVESHAM: "In advance. All that shall be seen to."

ARTHUR: "I'll take the risk. Better disaster in pursuit of knowledge than sitting down in toilsome uselessness in Barchesham for the rest of my life."

McPHISTER: "Better disaster! How I agree with you!"

ARTHUR: "Man was made to take risks."

McPHISTER: "Life was made to take risks."

Elvesham and his lawyer, Mr. Siddonson, in one of those dark and frowsty rooms in Lincoln's Inn dear to solicitors.

Siddonson is a stoutish, short man, deferential but wary in his manner, rather proud of his diplomatic ability and surprised at nothing. "Go on, Mr. Elvesham."

ELVESHAM: "This young man, you must understand, is a sort of relation of mine — closer than many people suppose."

SIDDONSON: "I *quite* understand."

ELVESHAM: "Then we'll leave it at that. Now he and I are going to do a little experiment. Very good of him. A sort of rejuvenation business — blood transfusion and all that."

SIDDONSON: "Wonderful. And naturally you want to provide against any risk."

ELVESHAM: "He's pretty stout and strong. It's myself I'm anxious about. Sometimes these — these blood transfusions affect the mind. If everything doesn't go well — I may be left a little groggy and queer."

SIDDONSON: "Let's hope nothing of that sort ——"

ELVESHAM: "Anyhow we have to provide."

SIDDONSON: "Nothing should be left to chance I agree."

ELVESHAM: "No. Then what I want to do is to give this excellent young man — in conjunction with yourself — the *fullest* powers to handle my property, draw money, incur liabilities. I begin to find responsibilities rather wearisome. And we'll tear up that old will of mine and make him my heir."

Elvesham, Arthur and McPhister pass through the large bedroom of Elvesham in Barchesham Castle. McPhister leads the way and Elvesham and Arthur follow. In the centre of the dressing-room they come to a broad divan, like a surgeon's operating couch, but wide enough to hold two men. Over this are great reflectors capable of throwing an intense light on their faces and shoulders. A small neon light tube throbs softly, but there is no other exposure of apparatus. On a table close at hand are several medicine bottles and a couple of measuring glasses. There is a large clock dial at the back. Black curtains can be drawn round the couch. The windows of the room and their wooden shutters are closed and the room is lit with electric light in contrast with the sunshine of the bedroom.

McPHISTER: "It has taken this time to assemble because we did not want anyone to know of this but ourselves. Everything has been made in London and brought down here bit by bit."

ARTHUR: "You make a lot of secrecy about it."

ELVESHAM: "No one knows about this — not even the

servants. Perhaps we have exaggerated the mystery of it all."

ARTHUR: "It makes it almost — occult."

ELVESHAM: "And how do you feel about it all? No wish to draw back?"

ARTHUR: "On the whole, I am amused. What do you think, Mr. Elvesham, are you likely to get out of all this?"

ELVESHAM: "Well, I can hardly say. It's McPhister there who is the great panjandrum."

ARTHUR: "I guess unless he electrocutes us by accident nothing will happen. What current have you got there?"

McPHISTER: "It's time to get ready."

ELVESHAM: "I haven't seen your pretty young lady, Miss Swift, about these last few days."

ARTHUR: "She's gone to Clifford's Beaches with her Mother. I'm to join her the day after to-morrow — if all goes well."

They move back into the bedroom, and later return to the dressing-room, Arthur and Elvesham in white pyjamas. They both move gravely under McPhister's directions. He hands them a dark drink. Then they lie down side by side on the operating table. Their faces have become still and intent as if they have been hypnotised. The light is at first intense and then it dies away and comes again. The face of Elvesham displays great tension. Before he becomes rigid he glances once at Arthur quickly and apprehensively. Arthur's expression is that of a courageous young man resolved to go through with a strange, unreasonable but unavoidable experience. McPhister bends broodingly over them and his shadow falls upon them. He touches a lever. He looks up at the clock dial and then at the pulsating neon light. All this is done in absolute silence. Then he sweeps the black curtains together and stands still, listening. There is a faint throbbing in the air, which increases for a few seconds and dies away again. Then he pulls back the curtains and the faces of the two men are seen again. But it is the young man's face now which is intent and almost peevish. The older man's face has become that of a tranquil sleeper.

The old man lies still. The young man stirs, wakes and sits up abruptly.

He stares at McPhister. He is now Arthur 2, the changed Arthur.

McPHISTER, elated: "Well, who are you? What's your name?"

ARTHUR 2: "Thomas Newton Elvesham."

McPhister: "Not *now*."

Arthur 2: "*What?*"

McPhister: "The thing is done. You are in your new body, Elvesham. You are Arthur Reston — and yourself. . . . Look at him. That old carcass will need a long rest. How do you feel? I tell you the thing is done."

Slowly, incredulously, guiltily Arthur 2 stares at the comatose Elvesham 2, shrinks away from him and stands up. There is something faintly senile in his pose and movements.

McPhister: "Go and dress. Begin your new life."

Arthur 2: "And *him?*"

McPhister: "He may sleep for days. Go."

Arthur 2: "Was I like *that* — so old and worn out?"

McPhister: "He's got to have a rest. He hasn't your vitality. You weren't quite so bad as that."

Arthur 2: "But what is to be done with him?"

McPhister: "Leave that to me. No one must see you here." He points to the open door. "Get your clothes and go."

Arthur 2 walks out still dazed, leaving McPhister by the side of the couch. McPhister broods darkly.

He seems to wake up from deep thought. "And now what will they do? This is a new riddle for the powers above."

He walks to the bell and rings it. Wilkins, the Barchesham Castle butler, appears in the doorway. He is the small, active type of butler — not in the magnificent Mutimer style. He is evidently astonished at what he sees, and betrays it.

McPhister: "Mr. Elvesham has had rather a trying operation. Will you carry him to his bed in the next room? And when he has had his sleep clear all this apparatus away."

He watches the frankly astonished butler.

McPhister: "Everything is all right with him. But he may sleep for days. Do nothing to disturb him. I am the operating doctor. Leave him absolutely quiet."

Wilkins: "I'd better get the footman to help."

McPhister: "Certainly."

Wilkins: "I knew nothing about this."

McPhister: "It wasn't your business to know."

He walks past the staring butler out into the bedroom. He passes across the bedroom into a broad passage. He walks a little way down the passage, looks over his shoulder to see that he is unobserved, and — vanishes.

He just vanishes.

A stone staircase on the west front of Barchesham Castle. Tall windows from a study give on this staircase. Arthur 2 appears at the windows unattended. He has put on his ordinary clothes again. He comes out to the top of the stairs, stands and surveys the prospect. "A pretty place. . . . But you may have it."

He stretches out his arms, expands his chest, lifts his face to the sky. Then he lifts his chin as did Elvesham in the opening scene. "This body is a fair exchange for all the stately homes of England. A-a-ah!"

He looks about him. "And now I suppose for the get-away. Let me see, where do I live? 19 Dewsbury Street. Where's Dewsbury Street? I ought to have looked that up before. Never mind. I'll find it. I'd hate to ask the way to my own lodgings."

He comes down the staircase and walks across the lawn. "The *feel* of it," he says. He repeats the rather affected gesture of the elegant hands that Elvesham 1 used at the dinner-table. He looks at his hands.

"Rather larger. Not quite so fine. But by Heaven, *young*!"

He crosses Barchesham Park, comes out of the park gates, on to the high road.

He talks to himself: "This is the grandest idea that has ever come to man. The greatest experiment. I am a pioneer in earthly immortality. A new race. Men who neither die nor age. We'll *breed* young louts to carry our minds for us — on and on and on and up and up. We'll go on for ever — renewing and extending ourselves. . . ."

He is so lost in these splendid ideas that he wanders into the middle of the road. A powerful car appears round a bend, travelling at seventy miles an hour. The chauffeur hoots and then, seeing this will not avert a disaster, claps on his brakes. The car swerves violently and skids. The car misses Arthur 2 by an inch or so and piles up on the bank against a tree-stump, with the explosion of one tyre, a smash of glass and screams from inside the car.

Arthur 2 clutches his heart and staggers to the roadside. "The idiot might have killed me. Me!"

A gentleman struggles out of the car and helps out a lady. "Are you hurt, my dear? Faint? Come and sit down here."

The chauffeur struggles out from behind a wheel that has pinned him. He is distracted. He is a bantam of a man and he is holding a damaged wrist. "I couldn't help it, sir. That blithering fool!" Then his feelings explode in rage against Arthur 2. He advances upon him. Arthur 2 gives ground before him, stepping back into the road.

CHAUFFEUR: "You silly idiot! You silly mug! I ought to have mown you down."

ARTHUR 2: "You might have killed me!"

CHAUFFEUR: "Killing you would have been a useful bit of work. Look at that car. And you! Not even *hurt*."

A car comes by on the opposite side of the way. Arthur 2 jumps apprehensively to the grass.

CHAUFFEUR: "You can get out of the way fast enough now, blight you! Ugh, you *Muck*."

He turns towards his master and mistress. "Any help I can give," he says with his back to the audience.

ARTHUR 2: "Accidents will happen. Can *I* help?"

CHAUFFEUR turns upon him frantically. "Get *out*! Get *out*! Before I spoil your silly face."

ARTHUR 2 stands disconcerted. Then he makes a rather elderly gesture of helplessness and walks away. Then suddenly he sees the humour of it and begins to laugh. "That's queer that was. Funny if I'd been killed. Oh, too funny. The laugh would have been on me." Grows serious again. "Safety first, Mr. Reston. You carry Cæsar and all his fortunes and don't you forget it. . . . And now for 19 Dewsbury Street and the unknown landlady."

On the way we see him hesitating at a crossing. A car has pulled up on account of him.

DRIVER: "Oh, *come on*! Hop it!"

Arthur 2 crosses. He moves with deliberation. He has none of the insouciance of a healthy young man.

The sitting-room of Arthur Reston at 19 Dewsbury Street, Barchesham. It is the room of a junior don who mingles a certain amount of sport with his scientific work. There are more books than the abundant shelves will hold. There is a writing-table littered with papers, two modern slide rules, a box of mathematical instruments, and above it are a few papers of notes fixed up by pins. There is a bat and a cricketer's bag. There are two photographic enlargements of Marguerite. There is a bowl of flowers but no pipe racks. A few silver cups adorn the mantelshelf. A pleasant-faced landlady holds the door open and Arthur 2 enters and looks around rather like a visitor to a show house.

Arthur 2: "So this is *my* room."

Landlady: "Of course it's your room, Mr. Reston. Why you should go stalking past me without a word into the downstairs drawing-room beats me altogether."

Arthur 2 considers her gravely for a moment. Then he decides upon his course of action. "The fact is I'm just a little dazed. Something has happened to me."

Landlady: "You haven't been drinking, Mr. Reston?"

Arthur 2: "No. I think I'd best tell you. I've been doing something much more foolish. I've been trifling with hypnotism — mesmerism — you know?"

Landlady: "You *do* look a little starey-like."

Arthur 2: "I am. That old man Elvesham, that rich old man who has just taken the castle, persuaded me just to try. . . . He's mad. Anything he says isn't to be believed. He's a danger——"

Gesticulates with hands to suggest hypnotic passes.

Arthur 2: "It's left me in a dream. I can't *remember*. I shall come round presently, Mrs. — Mrs. ——? I can't remember your name. Isn't it extraordinary? I can't. No."

Landlady: "Sandilands, my name is. And you haven't been above calling me Sandy at times."

Arthur 2: "I think — if I could have some tea, Mrs. Sandilands. If I could sit down here quietly and just think — I'd find myself — bit by bit. Coming here, I was almost knocked down by a motor-car. Quite a close shave. I've got to pull myself together. The reckless way they drive nowadays is disgraceful. They set no value whatever on human life. . . ."

Mrs. Sandilands betrays a little surprise at this last opinion. It seems to her not quite the sort of thing her Mr. Reston would say. "I'll get you a nice cup of tea, Mr. Reston," she says, looking at him for an instant before leaving the room.

Arthur 2 walks to the hearthrug: "That's all right. Sandilands, eh? She likes me. Good to be good-looking again. And now to find out about myself. Pockets first. Ah, here's money! Five, six, seven, eight, ten and sixpence. Cheque-book anywhere? How about handwriting?"

He takes a sheet of paper and we see him writing, "Thomas Newton Elvesham." "Tut, tut," he says. Then he writes, rather laboriously, "Arthur Reston." "H'm," he considers. "I don't know his signature. That may be inconvenient."

He finds a sheet of paper on which is written, *Note on a New Type of Vibration in Suspended Particles by Arthur Reston*." He compares his own "Arthur Reston." The handwriting is entirely different.

He soliloquises. "Funny little difficulty. How can I meet it? I can go to the bank. Sign before witnesses. I can pretend to have writer's cramp, bad wrist. But wait a moment! If I want a cheque or so from my dear old friend Elvesham this will be convenient. And he can't even alter that will I made. M'm. Yes he can — before witnesses."

He stands up and looks about the room. A cup on the mantel attracts him and he reads the signature.

"Cup for the high jump. I'll have to learn to jump all over again. Lord, how I used to hate jumping!" He looks at his other cups. "Swimming. Diving. Now shall I be able to swim?"

Later Mrs. Sandilands is putting tea things on the table and Arthur 2 is intent upon his papers, so avoiding conversation with her. She lingers as if she would like a word or so. As she leaves the room he says, "Thank you, Mrs. Sandilands. Thank you," over his shoulder.

He thinks with his eyes on the closed door. "It's going to be interesting — and difficult — this business of impersonation."

He stands in front of the enlargement of Marguerite. "Especially with *you*, my dear. . . . Gods! you might be Mary born again!" He takes up both portraits so as to hold one in either hand. "I'll get it all right this time. This is going to be worth while. You'll find your lover improved, I think. Something a little less shy and crude, my dear, than I used to be. Or he is. Lovely thing you are. I think I'd better get down to Clifford's Beaches and get busy with you right away. Little you realise the old scores we have to settle, my dear."

He moves towards the bell and stops short.

"Confound it, I've got to pack my own bag, I suppose."

He returns to the portrait of Marguerite.

"How lovely women can seem! I never really escaped you — and this time you shall not escape me. I've learnt a bit since the old days. They've waited to be married! *He* waited. We won't have it like that *now*, my pretty darling. No."

Clifford's Beaches is not a conventional watering-place with stucco boarding houses, a mile long parade, a pier and so forth. The hotel nestles against the woods; there are bungalows and houses up the hill slope and there is a short esplanade with a shelter, a run down for boats and so forth. Farther along the coast there is a rocky cove.

Here Marguerite and another girl are swimming, while Marguerite's mother sits under a sunshade reading among the rocks. Both girls swim well. A small boy appears with a telegram and hands it to the mother. She reads and waves it and the two girls come out of the water.

MOTHER: "He's coming by the afternoon train."

MARGUERITE turns to her friend: "He's never sent a telegram before. He's getting thoughtful. Nice of him. I didn't think he'd come until to-morrow. Is the telegram for me, Mummy?"

MOTHER: "Darling, I wouldn't have opened it. It's just addressed 'Swift.'"

MARGUERITE makes a face: "Now why didn't he address it to me and put a nice little word in. I suppose he sent it in a hurry."

At the chief entrance to the Clifford's Beaches Hotel the porter appears, looks away off as if expecting arrivals, and then becomes obsequious and turns the door for someone from within the hotel. Dr. McPhister appears in a grey golfing suit and carrying a putter. He wears boots designed to correct a slight malformation of his feet. He also glances in the same direction as the expectant porter, considers what he shall do, and then seats himself in one of the chairs, pulling the canopy forward so as to shade his face.

Arthur 2 arrives in station bus. He is the only new-comer. He is wearing a rather worn tweed suit, slightly baggy at the knees, and a cap. The bus porter hands him down and then takes a very old valise from the bus. He exchanges a critical grimace with the hotel porter.

Arthur 2 intercepts the grimace.

He speaks, and as he does so he makes the slightly finical gesture characteristic of old Elvesham. And his manner has the confidence of a rich man accustomed to be welcomed by hotels.

"That's my bag all right— treat it respectfully. Are you fairly full here?"

HOTEL PORTER: "I doubt if there's any single rooms left, sir." Sarcastically: "There's a suite, I know — the Prince's suit."

Bus Porter lifts his eyebrows and becomes aware that Arthur 2's trousers are slightly frayed at the edges.

ARTHUR 2: "I expect the suite will do. If it's airy. Oh, hullo! How did you get down here?"

McPHISTER: "I came by air. Always my favourite method of

176

travel. I came here because among other things I play golf. My lameness makes me slow but I have the devil's own luck. I like the game. It brings out all the evil that there is in a man. But why are *you* here. . . . Not on account of Miss Marguerite Swift by any chance?"

ARTHUR 2: "That young woman has gripped my imagination."

McPHISTER: "The devil she has! This is disconcerting."

ARTHUR 2: "She is so like Mary."

McPHISTER: "Maybe she *had* to be!"

ARTHUR 2: "I thought this sort of thing was over for me. But it isn't."

McPHISTER: "Don't tell me you've renewed your youth just to begin running after women again. You're not just *repeating* life, remember. You're going on to a new stage in life. That's the essence of our experiment. Long life and a greater life."

ARTHUR 2: "I shan't be running after women here. She'll take no running after. This peach is ripe on the wall. It would be stupid to leave it."

McPHISTER shrugs his shoulders in confidence to himself: "And after you've gobbled your peach, then what?"

ARTHUR 2: "Oh, the great world, the new stage of life — vigour to a hundred and twenty. I spent all my first life in accumulating means, and I found myself too old to use those means. We have altered all that." McPhister nods approval. "Now I start to conquer the world — to walk over it — the unknown protégé of the late Mr. Elvesham."

McPHISTER: "Not so *late* as all that. He is — you must remember — still alive."

ARTHUR 2: "Well, what can the poor devil do?"

McPHISTER: "Suppose he came down here?"

ARTHUR 2: "In that repulsive body? He'll keep away from her if he has any self-respect."

McPHISTER: "Love looks not with the eye but with the mind."

ARTHUR 2: "I'll risk its scrutiny."

McPHISTER: "But here she is. Coming to meet you."

ARTHUR 2: "Leave it to me. *How* she carries herself!"

McPHISTER: "Like a healthy, well-built young woman."

ARTHUR 2: "No. There's something about that girl! Mary moved just like that."

McPHISTER: "He's *got* it. This comes of young blood in an old memory. And so he's going to discover the mystery and divinity of women all over again. Just as though he has never been disillusioned."

Arthur 2 descends the hotel steps and approaches Marguerite. McPhister remains inconspicuously watchful. His expression is hostile and curious.

She brightens at the sight of him and takes both his hands in both of hers. "Darling, you're looking well and proud. Did everything go well?"

They both hesitate and kiss. It is not quite the usual kiss and she apprehends this faintly. There is a sort of disingenuous fatherliness in his bearing.

ARTHUR 2: "Go well?"

MARGUERITE: "The experiment?"

ARTHUR 2: "Everything, my dear, went marvellously."

MARGUERITE: "And Mr. Elvesham is going to help your research? It's too lovely."

ARTHUR 2: "Better. He is going, he says, to identify himself with my ambitions. I have a lot to tell you, my dear. Now it is all over I can tell you just what has happened. I didn't tell you much before. Did I?"

MARGUERITE: "You made a mystery of it."

ARTHUR 2: "I thought so. Now we can talk."

MARGUERITE: "In a quieter place."

The hotel porter appears with an interrogative expression on the steps.

ARTHUR 2: "I'll take that suite. Send my bag up. I'll see to all that presently."

MARGUERITE, struck by something: "*Suite?*" She looks puzzled but says no more at the time.

In a sheltered corner under the cliffs Arthur 2 talks and Marguerite listens to him at first with eager and affectionate attention. But presently her face betrays a slight perplexity.

ARTHUR 2: "Oh! Something between psychic research and hocus-pocus. *I* don't pretend to understand it. I don't think he did — not even the doctor, the specialist."

MARGUERITE: "Who was this doctor?"

ARTHUR 2: "*I* don't know. He spoke English very well, but he had a foreign look about him."

MARGUERITE: "Did you look up his qualifications?"

ARTHUR 2: "Never thought of anything of the sort. But as I say, the general effect was hocus-pocus; telepathy in it and all that sort of thing. Rather a strain on us both — what with drugs, hypnotism, magnetic-field all mixed up together."

MARGUERITE: "That sounds so queer."

ARTHUR 2: "It *was* queer. It strained *me*. And it upset the old fellow altogether. *I'm* still so dazed I hardly feel myself yet. But *he* ——! You've heard of these cases — when men forget who they are — forget their own names."

MARGUERITE: "But what sort of experiment was this? You said drugs? What sort of drug?"

ARTHUR 2: "Sorts you wouldn't know about, my dear — oriental drugs."

MARGUERITE, faintly incredulous: "Oriental?"

ARTHUR 2: "Yes. That was it. Like hashish — one of those *oriental* drugs. They're tremendous things, those oriental drugs. I shall be all right again soon."

MARGUERITE: "But you said hypnotism and magnetism."

ARTHUR 2: "Those were quite accessory. The oriental drug's the idea. The great thing, my dear, is I've got the two thousand pounds. We're no longer poor and helpless. We can dare to make love. Yes. The world begins again for us."

MARGUERITE: "Old Aunt Moon has answered your prayer."

ARTHUR 2: "Old Aunt Moon. Why Aunt Moon?"

MARGUERITE: "Don't you remember? That night you prayed to the Moon? Old Aunt Moon with the great round face?"

ARTHUR 2: "Of course! I prayed to the Moon and she's answered my prayer."

MARGUERITE: "But that old man? Did you wake up? Did you come to — and *leave* him?"

ARTHUR 2: "He's got his servants there. There was that foreign doctor I told you about. Quite a big swell, I think. What could *I* do? I should just have been in the way."

MARGUERITE: "I'm trying to recall that old man. It's queer how *present* he seems to me. He didn't *look* senile or silly. He had a hard resolute face and hard searching eyes. Greedy eyes. He wasn't — feeble."

ARTHUR 2: "Not so feeble — before the experiment. No. But the thing is, it was too much for him — and that's really the end of his story. And here we are, my pretty one, with the moments simply flying. . . ."

He makes to embrace her. She resists him for a moment, tries to hold his eyes with her own, and then yields her lips to his. He kisses her and holds her hungrily. His hands seem eager to take possession of her. This isn't quite the respectful love-making she is accustomed to and she struggles out of his arms again.

MARGUERITE: "Dearest! This is a public place. And — I don't know."

ARTHUR 2: "Sweetheart, you're not going to be coy with me. Haven't we waited long enough for love?"

MARGUERITE: "You're different, Arthur. You're not yourself. That drug ——! And the old man you've left behind."

ARTHUR 2, giving way to his impatience: "Confound the old man I've left behind. I've left him behind. He took his chance and he lost. He's done for. He's finished. He's like an old coat that is thrown away. But I am only beginning. I want to live, my dear. I want to love. And I want *you*. And always you keep me waiting. It has always been like that. Mary — the difficult! Mary the inaccessible!"

MARGUERITE: "Mary! What do you mean, Arthur? Why are you calling me Mary?"

ARTHUR 2: "You *are* Mary to me."

MARGUERITE: "But why? You've never called me Mary before."

ARTHUR 2, realising the situation: "I have never called you Mary! In my heart I have a thousand times."

MARGUERITE: "But why?"

ARTHUR 2: "It's been a secret fancy of mine. Your hidden name. I've thought of you as a Madonna. Often and often. I've never told you that. It was my clumsy way of reconciling myself to your remoteness and coldness."

MARGUERITE: "My coldness! It is as if someone quite different were talking to me. What has this drug done to you, Arthur?"

At Clifford's Beaches Arthur 2 and McPhister are dining. Arthur 2 addresses the maître d'hôtel: "Just a bottle of your excellent Brauneberger and one — no, two liqueur glass of Kirsch, the peel of an entire cucumber — not just scraps — and a few big lumps of ice. So?"

Maître d'hôtel departs in a state between deference and surprise at the incongruous savoir faire of this untidy, ill-dressed young man.

McPHISTER: "And how does the love-making go?"

ARTHUR 2: "It doesn't *go* — it crawls. Never before did I realise that infinite leisureliness of young people. And their

180

complicated lack of straightforwardness."

McPhister: "That is an interesting variant to headlong youth. Complicated lack of straightforwardness — that's good!"

Arthur 2: "I thought nowadays young people were rather frank. I thought they *knew everything*, as people say, and were perfect young terrors. Well, McPhister, it isn't so."

McPhister: "It never was so."

Arthur 2: "She doesn't know her own mind."

McPhister: "That comes late in life for everyone — if ever it comes. That is where you are going to be so interesting."

Arthur 2: "She will and she won't. She comes forward and she recoils. Whenever I press the love-making she sheers off and wants to talk of our future home together — and everything else in the world but love."

McPhister: "I know. A curious diffidence. It used to be called maiden modesty, fastidiousness — a deliberation."

Arthur 2: "Deliberation. Aren't I her accepted lover?"

McPhister: "She is looking ahead for her whole life. She doesn't understand this impatience of yours."

Arthur 2: "She's so like Mary. Mary used to hold me off like that — cool and gentle. *Exasperating!*" The conversation is interrupted by the maître d'hôtel and two waiters. They serve melon and bring Arthur's wine cup. A little is poured for him and the maître d'hôtel waits for his nod of approval. It is obvious he finds something elusively odd about both of them. "When I want to make love she talks of *research*. This absurd young prig seems to have spent his time and hers talking about mathematics and physics. And now I've got to pretend —— McPhister, what on earth is a goniometer?"

McPhister: "A harmless thing for measuring the angle of crystals."

Arthur 2: "Well, it seems the college goniometer isn't good enough for us. One of the first things we have to buy with our two thousand pounds is a new and better goniometer. . . . Did you ever hear of such — *love talk!*"

McPhister: "You'll have to learn it up, Elvesham — I mean Reston — this goniometer business. And this new mathematical Love Talk. Delightful for you to have these interests in common. Most of the men in love I have to deal with complain of the lack of interesting talk they encounter in between their gusts of passion."

ARTHUR 2: "She's suspicious about me. That is one reason why she puts me through my scientific paces. She smells a rat. Queer, isn't it?"

McPHISTER: "You mustn't fancy things."

ARTHUR 2: "And she sticks to it, asking me what *exactly*, in scientific terms and all that, was the experiment I did at Barchesham. They teach women too much science nowadays. Makes them neither one thing nor the other."

McPHISTER: "What have you told her?"

ARTHUR 2: "Oriental drug. It didn't go for a moment. *What* oriental drug? Seems she *knows* about most oriental drugs."

McPHISTER: "Blood transfusions would have been much better — something at once generous, modern and matter of fact."

ARTHUR 2: "And she's got sentimental about me — I mean about Elvesham. She seems to think I deserted him. She thinks Elvesham was benevolent— interesting— wise even. I seem to have made a great impression upon her in that other carcass of mine. . . . If only she *knew*! I'll get level with all this yet."

McPHISTER: "Level! I wanted you to soar."

After dinner they go out to a grassy terrace of the hotel, overlooking the sea. The place is lit by electric lights in swinging pseudo-marine lanterns. Arthur 2 and McPhister occupy comfortable wicker-chairs and there are coffee and liqueurs on a conveniently placed table.

McPhister in the evening light has become slightly more Mephistophelean in appearance. He talks.

McPHISTER: "I must confess I find you disappointing, Elvesham."

ARTHUR 2: "Reston."

McPHISTER: "Elvesham, between ourselves. Here we are, making a wonderful experiment. You are having a new lease of life. You begin with the experience of seventy-one years, with a prospect of living perhaps fifty years more. And then, if you like, a further prolongation. Think of it. And what do you do? Do you go on with that splendid career we talked about? Do you take hold of life with both hands? No — you come down here in pursuit of a pretty young woman with a sweet face — and you seem to be thinking of nothing else."

ARTHUR 2: "I *want* her."

McPHISTER: "Evidently — but *why*? You remind me of that miserable creature, Faust. He too couldn't leave a pretty girl alone. You know the old story."

ARTHUR 2: "I love her."

McPHISTER: "Nonsense. Men of seventy don't love. They want. Do any men really love? Everlastingly you talk of love, but that is different. You want her to love you. You want her to go down at your feet. You are already beginning to be spiteful and malicious about her, because you discover she has a certain independent personality of her own. You want to overcome her resistances. You want the sexual triumph — and then . . .?"

ARTHUR 2: "But the point is — she is Mary Farlake over again. It is not just love-making I want — it is Mary."

McPHISTER: "And if you get your — Mary — Marguerite."

ARTHUR 2: "Then I could go on."

McPHISTER: "To what? Another woman. After *his* Marguerite, Faust wanted Helen of Troy. Have human beings no imagination beyond sex? Why not begin with Power. Can't you forget this Mary? Can't you forget? Is every human mind curled up round some personal attachment like a pearl round a bit of grit? You, with a reasonable prospect of limitless life, of leaping from one body to another, of going on and going on, why do you not take possession of the world? Is this indeed Man, the rebel child of Earth? I have looked to you to rise against fate, gather power and scale the heavens. And when I put the scaling ladder into your hands ——!"

ARTHUR 2: "Scaling ladder? Sometimes you say strange things, McPhister."

McPHISTER: "Well, perhaps I'm not quite an ordinary being — but let that pass. It exasperates me to see the incurable littleness and spiritlessness of man. Will you *none* of you escape from this love story?"

ARTHUR 2: "How can I escape? Here I am with young blood again! It will have its way in spite of you."

McPHISTER: "Let it have its way. But you are falling in love. Don't fall in love. Don't let another personality get a hold upon yours. Keep love in its place."

ARTHUR 2: "And how?"

McPHISTER: "There are millions of young women in the world as lovely as she is. Forget her before she obsesses you altogether."

ARTHUR 2: "But what do you mean?"

McPHISTER: "A rational love, not this unlimited stuff."

McPhister stands up and looks round. He makes a pass like a

conjurer and both he and Arthur 2 vanish from the scene. The terrace, table, chairs remain. A waiter comes and stares about.

"Funny! I didn't see them *go*," he remarks, and begins to clear away the coffee things.

The scene changes to a large and brilliantly lit hall, full of men and women in evening dress. They are excited; they eat and drink and chatter and make love. A variety turn is in progress. Arthur 2 and McPhister are in evening dress like the others. They sit at a table with champagne, and two charming young women, a blonde and a brunette, are making up to them, and incidentally sipping most of the champagne. One, the fair one, concentrates on Arthur 2 with ardent eyes and a whispering charm, and the other, dark, plays a rather graver rôle with McPhister. "Prizes," comes a voice, and the fair girl who is concentrating on Arthur 2 stands up very cheerfully and says "*Me?* I've got a prize!" The two girls go to get their prize, leaving Arthur 2 and McPhister at the table.

McPhister: "Now here's love in its proper place. You love and you pay and off you go to the serious business of life."

Arthur 2: "That's rational enough."

McPhister: "I thought you'd see that."

Arthur 2: "Only love isn't rational. I wish Marguerite were here."

McPhister: "Marguerite! And the goniometer?"

Arthur 2: "Yes — and the goniometer. I'm as badly hit as that. I tell you she has got into my blood, and I don't want anyone else. And the things that vex me only provoke me more."

McPhister: "Can't you take everything else that life offers you now and leave that girl at Clifford's Beaches alone. I don't want this new lease of life of yours to be mortgaged from the outset. I want to make a great man of you. Remember— Power! I want you to scale the heavens, not climb Romeo's balcony. I ask you— don't go back to her. It is the most dangerous thing you can do. You will get worse and worse. You will give way to fits of irrational honesty and self-abandonment. You may even come to confess to that girl. And will *she* give herself away to *you*? *No*. Women give their bodies but the men give their souls. There is an infinite reserve in every woman."

Arthur 2: "These things don't seem to matter just now."

McPhister, in expostulation to fate: "Oh, what have I done? Given this man fifty years more of life and vitality and all he can do with it is to play the young lover again! The pitiful limitation of man! The pitiful limitation! The want of imaginative power! I wonder at times if the creatures really *have* souls! Or whether I'm not being swindled altogether! I thought we were opening a new phase of life, clear-headed and more creative than the Creator, and I find nothing but a renewal of that old imperative I have always detested. Is there to be no escape for men for ever from this omnipresent eternal delusion of Love? *Must* you centre on it? *Must* you gravitate about it? Don't you see that this second life begins to be a mere echo of your first — a second round of the old course? Is it worth while to live again for that?"

A darkened bedroom in Barchesham Castle. A four-poster bed. A sleeper is seen indistinctly. He mutters: "Marguerite! Dear Marguerite!"

Then he yawns and talks to himself: "I'm tired. Damnably tired. But it's all right. I've got the money. Two thousand pounds. And I'm alive. . . . Wonder what the time is?"

Suddenly he sits up. It is Elvesham 2. He looks about him in great perplexity. "What room is this? How did I get here? After the experiment? I don't remember."

He sits in profound perplexity. He glances at his pyjama sleeves. He begins to have a faint realisation of the state of affairs. He moves his mouth and looks as though he had tasted something disagreeable. He whispers: "God! What has happened?"

With an expression of dismay he puts his fingers to his mouth and his face changes to infinite horror. His voice is almost tearful. "Oh, my *teeth!* Where are my *teeth*?"

Then he glances at the shrivelled hand he is holding close to his face. "Oh — these hands!"

He gets half out of bed. "What has *happened* to me? Disease? What? What has *happened* to me?"

Across the room he sees himself dimly in a mirror. He tumbles clumsily out of bed and stumbles towards it. "I'm like — that old man! My God, is this part of the experiment? I'm *infernally* like him."

He wanders round the room examining things on the toilet-table and bedside-table. He discovers a tumbler with false teeth in it. "But this is *horrible* — unspeakably horrible!"

He returns to the mirror. Then he feels his toothless mouth again. "False teeth!" Fumbling, he puts them in.

Then he stands hesitating at a bell. Finally he rings. Wilkins appears.

ELVESHAM 2: "Who are you? What's your name?"

WILKINS: "Wilkins, sir — as usual."

ELVESHAM 2: "And who am I?"

WILKINS: "Well, sir, you're Mr. Elvesham. Who else should you be? And you've had a nice long sleep. You've been sleeping since yesterday afternoon. Such a sleep, sir."

ELVESHAM 2: "Yesterday afternoon? What happened then?"

WILKINS: "Perhaps you're confused, sir. You had a slight operation. Don't you remember, sir? I think you must have had some sort of gas."

ELVESHAM 2: "Where was the operation — here?"

WILKINS: "No, sir — in there."

ELVESHAM 2 walks slowly to the dressing-room and stares at the apparatus: "I begin to remember. . . . Why didn't you wake me before?"

WILKINS: "The doctor, sir, said you were not to be disturbed. On no account."

ELVESHAM 2: "What doctor?"

WILKINS: "The dark gentleman."

ELVESHAM 2: "Where is he? I want to speak to him."

WILKINS: "He's gone, sir."

ELVESHAM 2: "Where did he go?"

WILKINS: "We didn't see him go, sir. He just went. You want something a bit refreshing, sir. Shall we say coffee, sir — or tea. Or even perhaps a cocktail. You could have it in the little parlour while I put out your clothes. Lounge suit, I presume, sir."

ELVESHAM 2 considers: "Coffee? Cocktail? Where *is* the little parlour?"

WILKINS smiles deprecatingly: "Through that door, sir, of course."

ELVESHAM 2: "Through that door. Very well."

The little parlour is a finely furnished room with old china and some good pictures. Wilkins has already laid a table for tea. Elvesham 2 stares unseeingly out of the window and then turns to the tea-table.

ELVESHAM 2: "This is just *horrible*. But, by Jove, it's marvellous too! I'm the sort of young man who falls naturally into a trap. Barchesham College — to this. Out of the frying-pan into the fire. From frustration to senility — not a bad description of a respectable life. But this — this isn't possible. A trap. A trap. . . . I wonder if I'm beaten. Ugly and monstrous. . . . Still . . . What's been done can be undone. . . . Queer it feels . . . nasty, uncomfortable, dirty old body."

"What has to be done? Get on the track of Dr. McPhister. That's the trouble. They may both have skipped. I suppose old Elvesham went off to collect my things. That's why he paid the two thousand pounds. I suppose he has a banking account. I suppose his cheques can be traced. After all, I suppose I've got some money here. Probably I'm not badly off so far as money goes."

Sits down and pours out coffee. "Ugh! These stringy old hands!"

WILKINS appears. "Your clothes are all ready, sir."

ELVESHAM 2: "Stop a minute, Wilkins."

He stands up and takes the measure of the little butler. "Wilkins, I like your face. I'm in trouble. You've got to help me. You think I've had an operation."

WILKINS: "A slight operation, sir."

ELVESHAM 2: "Well, it wasn't. It was an experiment."

WILKINS: "An experiment. Very good, sir."

ELVESHAM 2: "It was an experiment all out. A rather dangerous experiment. With the mind. You'll find me quite another man. My mind is a little dazed. My memory's all at sixes and sevens."

WILKINS: "The doctor, sir, said your mind might be a little dazed. He said you might have fancies."

ELVESHAM 2: "I haven't got fancies — don't get that into your head. What sort of fancies?"

WILKINS: "He said you might fancy you were somebody else."

ELVESHAM 2: "*Did* he? I see. No, there's nothing in *that*. But my memory, Wilkins, is bleached white."

WILKINS does his best to understand. "Yessir — bleached white — kind of blank, sir."

ELVESHAM 2: "So the strange doctor left no address. And now tell me, have I a lawyer? What's his name?"

WILKINS: "Why, Mr. Siddonson, of course. He was here last week."

ELVESHAM 2: "Siddonson. Not a common name. He won't be hard to find. Where do I live in London?"

WILKINS: "Sussex Terrace, sir."

ELVESHAM 2: "And do you go to and fro?"

WILKINS: "No, sir. Mr. Mutimer is in charge of the London establishment."

ELVESHAM 2: "Any cars here?"

WILKINS: "The usual two, sir."

ELVESHAM 2 walks to the door of the dressing-room and surveys the experimental installation.

ELVESHAM 2: "Don't touch any of this. We may want it again."

WILKINS: "The doctor, sir, said it was to be all cleared away."

ELVESHAM 2: "Never mind what the doctor said. I'm master here, anyhow. Where's the key of this room? In the door? Good. I'll take it when I come out."

A burly young man walks in with an air of authority.

YOUNG MAN: 'I didn't know you was awake, sir. You shouldn't have got up without *me*."

ELVESHAM 2: "Who are you?"

YOUNG MAN: "Well, I'm the trained attendant, sir. From the County Mental Home. Dr. McPhister thought you might need a little care."

ELVESHAM 2: "You drink beer too early in the morning, young man. You smell of beer. Look me in the eye. Am I in need of what you call a little care?"

YOUNG MAN: "You look all right to me, sir."

ELVESHAM 2: "And I am all right. And see here!— you pack your bag and go back to the County Mental Home and say I sent you. . . . Nobody has certified me. . . . Wilkins, clear this lout off the premises."

Wilkins obeys, and the young man goes.

ELVESHAM 2: "So that's the game. Mad? Fancies about being somebody else. They counted on that. Bit obvious, Elvesham. But it's going to be difficult. If I tell this story—— If he outfaces me. No. Delusional insanity. I've got to watch my steps. Clever, but not *too* clever."

Wilkins reappears.

ELVESHAM 2: "Wilkins, where's my bureau?"

Wilkins leads the way back to the parlour. Elvesham 2 tries a drawer. "Locked. You don't know where my keys are?"

WILKINS: "Haven't you got them, sir?"

ELVESHAM 2: "No."

He pulls up short and stares at the date indicator on his desk.

ELVESHAM 2: "The sixteenth — the sixteenth? What was it

about the *fifteenth*? By Jove! I ought to have been at Clifford's Beaches yesterday."

For the first time he thinks of Marguerite. "Marguerite! What's going to happen about Marguerite? If that swine goes after her! But he'd never be such a fool. And yet I remember — he looked at her. He kept looking at her. . . ."

The little esplanade at Clifford's Beaches in front of the Grand Hotel. Marguerite is sitting in a canopied chair with a book. A clock on the hotel shows three in the afternoon. She is inattentive and glances ever and again at the hotel. She cannot understand the disappearance of Arthur. A station car arrives and he descends. He looks towards the esplanade and Marguerite waves to him. He comes forward eagerly and stands beside her chair. There is a certain constraint between them and they do not kiss.

MARGUERITE: "Well? And where have you been, Mr. Arcturus? You vanished yesterday afternoon."

ARTHUR 2: "I went to London in a temper."

MARGUERITE: "So?"

ARTHUR 2: "Because I'm in love and you tantalise me beyond endurance."

MARGUERITE: "And what did you do in London?"

ARTHUR 2: "I went on with my temper."

MARGUERITE: "And now you've brought it back with you?"

He sits down beside her. ARTHUR 2: "Darling, don't you *understand* love is impatient — love is a fever?"

MARGUERITE: "Love, my dear, isn't a fit of temper."

ARTHUR 2: "I went to London thinking of you, I thought of you all the time, desiring you, and here I am, a storm of impatience."

MARGUERITE leans forward and scrutinises him. "You look tired and fretted, my dear. There is a sort of strain in your face. I've never seen you looking so old. That drug or experiment or whatever it was, has left you jangling. Let's take a boat and dive and swim. That will bring you back to coolness again."

ARTHUR 2 is stricken with doubt: "Dive and swim!"

She stands up and he stands up, too. "If I'm in this fever ought I to swim? To-day? I might get a chill."

She is astonished. "*Get a chill!* What an *elderly* expression!"

They go to change. Presently they are off the shore in a boat, and Marguerite dives gracefully from the stern. Arthur 2 stands up, by no means sure of himself. He makes an awkward flop into the water and is immediately in difficulties.

Both Marguerite and the boatman are incredulous at his inability. Marguerite, who is some distance away, treads water and cries: "Darling! Don't splash about like that!"

ARTHUR 2, swallowing water and clutching: "I can't. I can't."

BOATMAN: "Float, sir. Float for a bit."

ARTHUR 2: "Help. I can't do it."

The boatman realises things may be serious and pulls round to assist. Marguerite swims back to help. With some difficulty Arthur 2 is got aboard the boat again. He clutches the side and is manifestly incompetent. But he is more frightened and ashamed than exhausted. He makes some clumsy attempt to help Marguerite back into the boat.

MARGUERITE: "All right, dear. I can manage." She swings up over the stern and immediately concentrates on Arthur 2. "What happened to you? What *is* it?"

ARTHUR 2: "A sort of vertigo. I seemed to go all to pieces. It's that confounded experiment!"

MARGUERITE becomes all tenderness and solicitude. She sits up in the boat and Arthur 2 lies at her feet resting against her knees, and she takes his head and runs her hand soothingly through his hair. "Poor tired little Arcturus. And his hair is all wet. And his head going round and round. And they made him dive and swim." To the boatman: "We'll go ashore. Right on the beach here. Mr. Reston isn't well."

Arthur 2's expression becomes one of extreme contentment. Then Marguerite helps him up the beach where they rest. She sits and he lies prone close to her. She has a Japanese sunshade with which she shades his head.

ARTHUR 2: "My dear, it is not altogether this experiment which has disturbed me. That has just released things that were there all the time. Love deferred maketh the body go sick. Now that we are free— with all this money— with all these prospects — Darling! I've waited for you so long. You don't know how long. . . ."

MARGUERITE: "Sweetheart, let me whisper." She speaks very softly. "Do you think that I have neither dreams nor desire. D'you think that I'm not sometimes impatient?"

ARTHUR 2: "It's good to hear you say that. Thank you for that."

MARGUERITE: "If you want, darling, I'm ready to marry you. Quite soon. I'm ready to be yours altogether. I'm ready and more than ready. It could be done now — in such a little while."

ARTHUR 2 sits up: "Marry! My *dear*. The parson and the relations, the cards and the reception. I can't wait for all that. Let us slip off together somewhere. Now. We've got this money. The adventure of it. The glorious feeling of defying the world. Say you will come. And then I should feel you really loved me. Love, my darling, is a desperate thing or it is nothing. Heaven alone knows how badly I need your love."

While these last sentences are being spoken a shadow has come into the foreground of the picture. It moves noiselessly until it lies across both the recumbent bodies and then it stays still. They become aware of this new presence almost simultaneously. They turn round to face it. With her, astonishment passes into recognition. With him, recognition is immediate and fear and anger follow.

Elvesham 2 is standing very still and looking down at them. He is wearing a white linen suit. His hands are in his pockets. He speaks without apparent excitement. "So here you are," he says softly.

ELVESHAM 2: "I've been looking for you" — slight pause — "Reston, all the afternoon."

Arthur 2 sits up and then stands up. Marguerite kneels up watching them both.

ARTHUR 2: "What on earth are you doing down here?"

ELVESHAM 2: "Just seeing what *you* are doing down here."

ARTHUR 2 bites his lips perplexed: "I don't want you to talk to us. Marguerite!" He speaks in a lower voice: "This man is mad. He is obsessed by a fantastic delusion."

ELVESHAM 2 lays his hand on Arthur 2's shoulder, and presses on his to restrain him. "If anyone has fantastic delusions, my lad, it is you. I am your old familiar friend, Elvesham, and I mean nothing but good to you both."

ARTHUR 2: "I ask you not to listen to him Marguerite."

MARGUERITE: "But why shouldn't I listen?"

ELVESHAM 2: "Yes, why shouldn't she listen? Do be reasonable. You are practically my adopted son. We all belong together. Won't you both dine at my table in the hotel this evening?"

ARTHUR 2: "We can't. I'm engaged to someone else."

ELVESHAM 2 to Marguerite: "But *you're* not engaged? Are you

191

in the hotel? Whom are you staying with?"

MARGUERITE: "I'm in lodgings with my mother. . . . Here *is* my mother."

Marguerite's mother appears, carrying a wrap. "Darling, I've been looking for you everywhere. I've got your wrap for you — before the evening gets chilly. Did Arthur have a nice swim? Oh, isn't that Mr. Elvesham from the Castle?"

ELVESHAM 2: "Sure it is, as the Irish say, Mrs. Swift, and I'm asking your charming daughter and you to dine with me at the hotel."

MARGUERITE'S MOTHER: "Well, but that would be *nice!*"

ELVESHAM 2: "Then we'll take that as settled. Eight o'clock. And meanwhile, Reston, my lad, since you cannot dine with us, you and I will have a little chat together."

Elvesham 2 and Arthur 2 walk off together to another part of the esplanade.

ELVESHAM 2: "Elvesham, you're not a particularly wise old man, are you? Just a bit greedy to want my girl as well as my body, eh? So you had to come down here and give yourself away to the one person who was most likely to find you out."

ARTHUR 2: "Now look here, Elvesham. I don't know what you're talking about. My name is Arthur Reston. I have always been Arthur Reston, and I am going to be Arthur Reston until the end of the chapter. You are insane. You are suffering from a delusion that we have changed bodies."

ELVESHAM 2: "So. And that's the attitude you're going to take."

ARTHUR 2: "It's how things are."

ELVESHAM 2: "But if I fall in with the idea that I *am* Mr. Elvesham, and if I say nothing to throw a doubt on that, how will you persuade people I'm suffering from any delusion at all?"

ARTHUR 2: "That will satisfy me completely. If you stick to it."

ELVESHAM 2: "I wonder if it *will* satisfy you. You see, I am going to be your great friend and patron now, that wealthy old humbug, Elvesham, always at your side, always watching over that body you have stolen from me. I don't think you've reckoned with that possibility. You may find me a considerable hindrance. I'm going to be always between you and *my* Marguerite. Yes — I know — you love her. But so do I. She's *my* Marguerite and don't you forget it. Don't you forget it."

He takes Arthur 2 by the arm in an almost fatherly way. "I have been thinking over this situation you have created, thinking harder perhaps than you have done. I've not such a bad intelligence, you know, 1938 pattern, and not 1885. Perhaps it has been built up by scientific work and all that on a better foundation than yours. You don't know what you want. You *think* you are gaining a wonderful extension of life."

ARTHUR 2 realises he is falling into acquiescence: "I don't see why I should have to listen to all this extraordinary stuff."

ELVESHAM 2: "You know why you listen well enough. You might have taken — and what a wonder it would have been! — fifty active years beyond the seventies. But you have let an old man's envy of mere youthfulness get the better of you. You are not taking a new chapter in life. You are just being a young man over again — desire for love — all the old story. Why couldn't you leave Marguerite alone? No, no, no. Don't break away. You have to hear me out. You're in your own trap. Always I shall be standing in wait for you. Somehow — I don't know how yet — somehow I shall compel you to admit this first experiment has failed — somehow I shall squeeze you back out of that body of mine into your own."

ARTHUR 2: "I suppose I must listen to your ravings!"

ELVESHAM 2: "Well, what else can you do, you frowsty old thief of life — what else can you do? You put your head in a trap. . . . You won't think better of it, will you? And throw the game up *now?* — take old age *decently* as an old man should."

ARTHUR 2: "No."

ELVESHAM 2: "You've got my body and you mean to keep it."

ARTHUR 2: "Yes. To be plain with you — *yes*."

Arthur 2 and Dr. McPhister dining. They are more than halfway through their dinner and Arthur 2 is drinking nervously, he had already had rather too much for a young physique, which reacts more quickly to alcohol than an older one. Both men are in dinner jackets.

Marguerite, Marguerite's mother and Elvesham 2 at a distant table. The three have just come in and the maître d'hôtel shows them their seats. Marguerite glances at Reston as she sits down, but the lovers exchange no greetings.

ARTHUR 2: "There we are. I thought we'd have him put away in an asylum and everything would go well. And here he is, malignant, revengeful and most infernally cool-headed."

McPHISTER: "Every experiment is liable to the unforeseen. That is what experiments are. Hunts for the unforeseen."

ARTHUR 2: "Oh, *don't* philosophise. What are we to do?"

McPHISTER: "I am nothing if not a philosopher and all my interest in this affair is philosophical. You must let me deal with things my own way. I warned you not to pursue this girl here. I did at least warn you of that. I told you plainly I was helping you on to a new stage of human life, to wider opportunities, to enlargement. But you must turn back to adolescence again, to mating and the love delusion. Has a life-time taught you nothing? Is that old cycle of mating and love and struggle and personal competition all that is possible to humanity? Beyond that nothing?"

ARTHUR 2, with a touch of boredom: "Well, what else is there?"

The two men rise from their places to go to the darkened terrace outside. A wind is blowing and the lanterns swing about and the shadows dance. A few couples are nearer the lighted hotel windows and McPhister and Arthur 2 are rather isolated.

McPHISTER: "After all, that old body isn't so very strong — it must die soon."

ARTHUR 2: "And meanwhile he can hold me in a state of subjection. He knows exactly what he is doing. It may be — for years."

McPHISTER: "Every wrong you do a man makes you his slave."

ARTHUR 2: "Even now he may be inside there — making suggestions to her — hinting things against me. . . ."

McPHISTER draws a general conclusion: "If you *must* do wrong to a man — I should say — wrong him outright and finally."

ARTHUR 2: "You mean?"

McPHISTER: "Don't leave a lot of him about."

Elvesham 2, who has parted from Marguerite and her mother, appears at the corner of the hotel, and strolls to the parapet of the terrace, and stands, lit by moonlight and lantern light, looking out over the sea. His face, we note, has changed since the experiment. His eyes are steadier and his expression more steadfast and thoughtful. His mouth is firmer. He strolls slowly along the terrace with his hands in his pockets, passing McPhister and Arthur 2 without seeing them.

McPHISTER's dark face comes close to Arthur 2's. He whis-

194

pers slowly: "There goes your man, Elvesham."

ARTHUR 2: "Well?"

MᶜPHISTER: "He seems to be going for a walk — alone."

Arthur 2 stares at his own feet with an expression of extreme perplexity. He arrives at a decision.

MᶜPHISTER: "Well?"

ARTHUR 2: "I think, I, too — will go for a walk."

MᶜPHISTER is left alone meditating. He drums on the table thoughtfully and peers after Arthur 2 and Elvesham 2, and shakes his head: "The experiment is going wrong — from bad to worse!"

Elvesham 2 walks along the cliff edge, deep in thought. One hears very faintly the slow lapping splash of the swell against the cliff below.

ELVESHAM 2: "Things look dim but magical and there is a sort of stillness. . . . I wonder if these ears are a little deaf. . . ." He goes to the extreme edge of the cliff and looks down. "High tide. I ought to hear the wash of the sea. It is calm, but one ought to hear. Yes, I must be a little deaf, though I seem to get what people say. Gods, the serenity! The world through an old man's eyes has a loveliness of its own." Pause. "And I was praying to you, old Aunt Moon, not three weeks ago! But not quite for this . . . no. . . ."

Arthur 2 appears creeping up behind him, looking left and right. He hesitates and then stoops swiftly like a charging football player and thrusts Elvesham 2 forward. Elvesham twists round and clutches at the turf so as to see his assailant before he goes over the cliff edge. As he clings Arthur 2 stoops down to him and strikes at his face. Elvesham 2 falls, leaving Arthur 2 crouching at the cliff edge, dismayed by the vigour of his own action. Splash!

Arthur 2 hears the splash. "That settles that." But he still peers down. "Lord he's trying to swim. *Much* he'll swim!"

He takes another look and then stands up. "Better get away. . . . No — not down the cliff path — inland and by the field. . . ."

Elvesham 2 swims stoutly in the moonlight. He floats with the utmost economy of energy. He is getting his clothes off as he swims. But he finds it hard work. He spouts water. "Can I do it? Rotten old lungs," he gasps.

A skiff appears with a girl — Marguerite's friend — a boatman and two middle-aged men in bathing costumes.

ELVESHAM 2: "Hi. Help! Help!"

Eventually he is hauled into the boat and he faints.

ONE OF THE MEN: "Get him some brandy. He's exhausted. How did he get into the water?"

THE OTHER MAN: "He must have dived or fallen from the cliff."

Crowd at the boat landing place. Elvesham 2, still insensible, is carried up to the little shelter. Arthur 2 is seen coming towards the group.

ARTHUR 2: "What! Man drowned! You've found him already. Who can he be?"

AN OLD BOATMAN: "*He's* not drowned."

In the shelter by the boat landing, Elvesham 2 is coming to. One of the men from the boat gives him brandy.

A BYSTANDER: "But how did you get into the water?"

ELVESHAM 2, weakly: "Eyesight bad. Walked clean over the cliff edge. Moonlight very deceitful."

He discovers Arthur 2 in the crowd. "Hullo, Reston!"

ARTHUR 2, coming forward: "Elvesham! What induced you to jump into the water?"

ELVESHAM 2 to Arthur 2: "All right. All right."

Pause while he gathers strength. He addresses Reston. "I know exactly where I am now — exactly. Mr. Reston here, is — friend of mine. But I want someone else. Where's my man — what's his name? — Wilkins." (Wilkins appears.) "Ah! I knew you wouldn't be far off."

ELVESHAM 2: "Wilkins, don't leave me. Don't leave me for a moment. Put me to bed. God! This *feeble* heart!" He faints again.

Next morning; he is propped up by pillows in his bed and his face looks white and transparent. Arthur 2 stands sullenly at the foot of the bed.

ELVESHAM 2: "I think it very impulsive and clumsy of you. This old body you've given me won't last a year. They talk of a young man in a hurry. You are an old man in a hurry." Rubs his cheek. "That was a nasty punch you gave me. And unnecessary."

ARTHUR 2: "I don't know what you are talking about."

ELVESHAM 2 looks at him gravely and smiles. "I suppose you must keep up this sort of thing. Why should you? I don't intend to send that body of mine to prison or to hurt it in any way. I don't want to bring the name of Reston into disgrace. I mean to get it back. But I shan't give you away. What are you afraid of? Why are you so impatient?"

ARTHUR 2: "I'm not impatient. What have I to be impatient about?"

ELVESHAM 2: "Now don't you know that you must pick up more about your new self before I go — or you won't *join on*. If you want to take my place you *must* understand the research on which you are supposed to be so intent. Your old nineteenth-century memories stuffed with stale ideas and wrong ideas about matter and force and so on. I doubt if you have any real grasp of four dimensional geometry. You must bring yourself up-to-date. Clear all that old clutter from your wits and get in the new conceptions. If you *won't* die you must learn — and learn over again. You're stale. *All* old men are stale. Marguerite knows far more of modern physics than you do. I'm only trying to help you. But you'll have to come with me to the Barchesham Laboratory, while I train you. Every day. You can't get out of that."

ARTHUR 2: "Every day I'm to work in that beastly little laboratory of yours with *you*!"

ELVESHAM 2: "From ten to four. It's work I *love*. You've got to stand it."

WILKINS appears. "Miss Marguerite Swift."

ELVESHAM 2: "Show her in. Don't go, Reston. She'll think it funny if you go."

Arthur 2 shrugs his shoulders, takes a stride or so up and down the room and stands looking towards the door.

Marguerite enters with a bunch of white roses. She seems slightly surprised to see Arthur 2 in the room. She takes the other side of the bed so that there is no close greeting with Arthur 2.

MARGUERITE, with a faint flavour of reproach: "I didn't see you this morning, Arthur."

ARTHUR 2: "Where were we to meet?"

MARGUERITE: "If you don't know, I can't *tell* you. I've brought you some flowers, Mr. Elvesham, and come to see how you are."

Elvesham 2 glances from one to the other with a faint smile of gratification at their misunderstanding.

ELVESHAM 2: "You see, Reston was here before you."

MARGUERITE: "You're not talking of any more experiments?"

ELVESHAM 2: "What do you think, Reston?"

ARTHUR 2: "I've done with them."

ELVESHAM 2: "Not just one more try?"

MARGUERITE: "I forbid it. I don't know what it's done to you, Mr. Elvesham, because I didn't know you at all before, but I'm very dissatisfied with Arthur — very dissatisfied. It's strained his nerves. It's *altered* him."

ELVESHAM 2: "Don't lose heart, Marguerite dear. Keep him in his place and up to the mark and he'll come back all right one day — never fear. But to tell you the truth, that was a silly experiment of ours and no one can regret it more than I do. What lovely wild roses these are!"

ARTHUR 2: "There are better roses than that along through the woods beyond the cliff. You ought to see them, Marguerite."

ELVESHAM 2: "You must take her there. Yes. But first — do you mind if we have a little talk?"

MARGUERITE: "We came to talk — if you're strong enough."

ELVESHAM 2: "Well, to be frank, aren't you two young people thinking of marriage?"

ARTHUR 2: "We are."

MARGUERITE: "When you have quite recovered, Arthur."

ELVESHAM 2 smiles cheerfully at Arthur 2. *"He'll* recover," he says.

MARGUERITE: "I know he'll recover."

ELVESHAM 2: "But, Marguerite. You know I'm a solitary man, a lonely old man. I doubt if this old body of mine — it's a rather overstrained old body, Reston — will last much longer. I want to do all I can, my dear, for our young friend here. I believe in him. He's a wonder. He's got an old head on young shoulders. He'll go far. But you're a darling too, my dear. If I were a young man I'd tell you I was in love with you. Well — is it selfish of me? — if I asked you not to marry and go away for just a little while? Eh, Modge of the Hill?" He takes her hand.

MARGUERITE is surprised and then snatches her hand away. "When did he tell you he called me Modge of the Hill?"

ELVESHAM 2: "Reston, when *did* you tell me you called her Modge of the Hill?"

ARTHUR 2: "It slipped out the other night."

ELVESHAM 2: "Of course, it slipped out the other night."

MARGUERITE: "But it's such a silly name to tell — anyone."

ELVESHAM 2: "But I'm not anyone, my dear. And did you by

chance call *him* old Stodge of the Hill? By way of repartee?"

MARGUERITE: "But how did you know?"

ELVESHAM 2: "I like to think of attractive people having fanciful names. If I were your lover I should always be thinking of names for you and saying little things to please you. I'd love to have a silly little language that only you and I understood. But that's all dreaming. It's wonderful how all this love business lingers in the imagination after we ought to have grown out of it completely. I haven't forgotten. But never mind that now. The strange thing about Reston there is that since this experiment he has forgotten all your names and all the little language you used to use with him. You try him."

ARTHUR 2: "Oh but — *nonsense!*"

ELVESHAM 2: "You try him, my dear — you try him. When you go to see those roses. It will all come back some day — but not yet. And of course you can't marry him until he remembers the little language and all the ways you had of calling one another. Can you? It wouldn't be decent. You can't be dear to each other without these very dear little things. But I can't go on talking. I'm tired. That plunge in the sea was rough on my poor old body, Reston. But you two have a talk together — and promise me."

ARTHUR 2: "But what can he know of love — and the impatience of love?"

MARGUERITE: "He seems to know quite a lot about love, Arthur."

ELVESHAM 2: "More than you have ever forgotten, Arthur. I was young once. Sometimes it seems only a few days ago that I was young. But the sunshine out there is calling you both. How I would love to be with you, Marguerite, and watch that pretty face of yours when you see those wild roses."

A woodland walk upon the Barchesham Castle estate. The time is late October. Leaves are beginning to fall and a glimpse of fields in the distance shows stubble being ploughed.

Arthur 2 is in gaiters and carrying a gun. He walks through a drift of newly fallen leaves and kicks them spitefully. Behind his back McPhister, dressed in ordinary walking costume, appears suddenly from nowhere — and hurries to overtake him. Arthur 2 turns at sound of his approach.

MCPHISTER: "Hullo, Faust, how goes it?"

ARTHUR 2: "I wish you'd remember my name is Elvesham —

I mean Reston. Where have *you* sprung from?"

McPhister: "Just to see how the great experiment is going on."

Arthur 2: "It isn't going on. It's stuck. It's paralysed."

McPhister: "Why don't you do something to get away from this close little tangle here? Why don't you travel? Why don't you begin your new career?"

Arthur 2: "He won't let me. He keeps me here a prisoner. He will hardly let this body of his out of his sight for fear that I should do it a mischief."

McPhister: "And the great love affair?"

Arthur 2: "He knows her mind. He and she become more and more easy and confidential with each other and she and I realise more and more our fundamental estrangement."

McPhister: "You still want her?"

Arthur 2: "More than ever, and I cannot get a word with her."

McPhister: "But things cannot go on like this. That old body is so aged and feeble ——"

Arthur 2: "It isn't so ill as it ought to be."

McPhister: "Perhaps Christian scientists are right after all, and the mind has an influence over the body. It would be amusing if his body began to get younger and yours began to age. He certainly isn't as ill as he ought to be."

Arthur 2: "He takes great care of himself. And of me. He's so infernally temperate. He drinks nothing but milk until dinner time — milk — *glasses of milk!* He insists on my playing *croquet* with him. McPhister, it's a game for the *damned.*"

McPhister: "I've noticed that."

Arthur 2 goes on with his grievances: "He keeps me here. He stints me of money. He keeps me in training. He lets me drink nothing but milk, too. And all that lovely wine of mine spoiling at Sussex Terrace. He's sent away my cook— simply to exasperate me — and got a good plain cook."

McPhister: "I know those good plain cooks. I travel, you know, in England and Scotland and Ireland as well as abroad."

Arthur 2: "He is constantly scheming to make me play cricket. I *daren't* play cricket. I never *did* play cricket. If I played it now it would give the whole show away. And a ball might kill me at any moment. They throw the ball about at cricket in the wildest way. I ask you, McPhister, how long have I to wait?"

McPhister, abruptly: "Do you never go shooting together?"

McPhister vanishes. He is standing beside Arthur 2 at one instant and the next he is not there.

ARTHUR 2: "Shooting? Once or twice, yes. Bad shots, both of us. He got nothing and I peppered a few rabbits and a bird . . . . *Shooting*? Now what are you putting into my head McPhister?"

He turns to look at the doctor. He stares with astonishment and stands gaping about him.

ARTHUR 2: "I could have staked my life on the fact that I was talking to McPhister. Have I just been talking to myself all this time? My imagination is beginning to play tricks with me. That idea of shooting. . . ."

A bridle path leading to a glade in the Barchesham woods. One sees down a long shady vista to a small party sunlit in the distance, moving about in the glade. Elvesham 2 is sitting on a log and two middle-aged sportsmen are with him. There are two keepers with sticks. They are waiting for the rest of the party. Two footmen come carrying a hamper. They put it down to rest.

FIRST FOOTMAN, HOOPER: "Phew! hot for October, Jinks."

JINKS, referring to the hamper: "Pretty 'eavy to-day — for five guns."

HOOPER: "It's this extra milk in its ice-jacket. If you'd told me a year ago that Mr. Elvesham would take to drinking glass after glass of milk and never touching nothing alcoholic but a glass of 'ock for dinner, I'd 'a' called you a silly ass."

JINKS: "And the way he makes that young man drink milk and be'ave 'imself — I never did."

HOOPER: "Curious about that young Mr. Reston. Picks him up — makes him his heir and all that — and *tyrannises* over him. You'd think it was pure luck if you was made heir to all this."

JINKS: "I *should*."

HOOPER: "And look at it. Soaks 'im in milk — flirts with his girl."

Jinks makes a cluck of protest.

HOOPER: "Well, he *does*. Goes to the college every day and holds his nose down to them scientific researches of his. I tell you it's a slavery."

JINKS: " 'E's all right to everybody else."

HOOPER: " 'E's improved. Before your time, before he picked up young Mr. Reston, the old gentleman was very nearly unbearable. But now 'e gets it all and we . . ."

JINKS: " 'E gives us a *nice* time. He's *jolly* to the servants. He's kind to everyone."

HOOPER: "Perhaps it's drinking that milk."

JINKS: "Oh, gee!"

HOOPER: "Well, we've got to be charitable, Jinks. Even milk may have merits. I never see a man so changed."

The sound of a shot from the glade. Commotion. Arthur 2 and another young man have joined the party. Wilkins is with them and a boy carrying two birds, and Arthur 2, holding his gun dangerously on his arm, has contrived by a clumsy movement to fire it off accidentally at a range of a couple of yards point blank at Elvesham 2's side. Elvesham 2 rises from the log on which he is sitting and falls forward on his face. Arthur 2 starts back in assumed horror. Everyone is stunned for the moment. Wilkins is the first to get to Elvesham 2's side and to try to lift him.

Elvesham 2 is the centre of interest. His side is blackened but there are no signs of shot. He is insensible. Wilkins kneels by him and has turned him over on his back.

WILKINS: "It's his heart. He's fainted but he's not hurt."

ONE OF THE MIDDLE-AGED SHOTS: "Let's see. I'm something of a doctor still. Get some cold water— ice." He comes round to the other side of Elvesham 2 and produces a businesslike brandy flask.

ARTHUR 2: "My God! My God! I'll never handle a gun again." He shows the other young man. "It's this sleeve of mine caught the trigger."

HOOPER to Jinks, arriving breathlessly: "Go back and get water and ice from the hamper. *Hurry!*"

ARTHUR 2: "Where did the shot go? Did it miss him? Isn't he shot?"

WILKINS, kneeling up beside Elvesham 2's body and speaking with a Cockney intensity of significance: "Naw! Mr. Reston, he *isn't* shot."

ARTHUR 2, dismayed: "*Not shot?*"

He glances swiftly at the man next to him, pulls himself together and says "Thank God!"

THE MIDDLE-AGED GENTLEMAN, who is something of a doctor: "It's just a faint. It's shock — nothing more. Astonishing escape."

WILKINS: "Mr. Reston, you got to thank *me* for not being a murderer here and now."

ARTHUR 2, centre of attention: "Murderer!"

WILKINS: "Well, *ommicide* if you like! You see — I was

watching you this morning and I never see anyone 'andling a gun more dangerous than *you*. Always seemed to be pointing it at someone — mostly Mr. Elvesham. So I took the liberty of loading you some of Mr. Elvesham's cartridges and taking away yours."

THE SECOND MIDDLE-AGED GENTLEMAN: "What difference did *that* make?"

WILKINS, expository: "Oh, you know since Mr. Elvesham took to drinking milk and all that, he didn't seem to like *killing* things. He went out shooting with his shooting parties because he didn't want to be unneighbourly and a spoil-sport and all that, but he had a special sort of blank cartridge made for him — looking all right and sounded all right, but it hadn't no shot at all. See? And that's what I give to young Mr. Reston to-day."

ARTHUR 2: "I've got to be grateful to you. Wilkins, I won't forget — all my life."

THE SECOND MIDDLE-AGED GENTLEMAN: "Lucky escape for *you*, young man."

ELVESHAM 2 recovers consciousness. He stares at the sky for a second. He looks at Wilkins and smiles faintly. "So he got me, Wilkins?"

WILKINS: "No, sir — blank shot."

Elvesham 2 tries to understand that.

FIRST MIDDLE-AGED GENTLEMAN: "Who do you mean, *got* you?"

ELVESHAM 2's face shows a returning intelligence. He smiles at Arthur 2. "Just an old joke of mine with Wilkins. Who *did* shoot me?"

ARTHUR 2: "It was *my* gun, sir."

ELVESHAM 2: "You're a clumsy lad, Arthur — clumsy lad. I'll have some more of that brandy. I'll be all right in five minutes. Where are those fellows with the lunch?"

Hooper and Jinks remember their duties and go off briskly to fetch the hamper.

Arthur 2 kneels beside Elvesham 2 as if in a mood of remorseful devotion.

ELVESHAM 2 in an intense undertone: "You silly old ass. If you get that body of mine hanged or sent to gaol —— I've a great mind to disinherit you here and now."

Scene changes to the hall of Barchesham Castle. The shooting party has come in for early cocktails before dispersal. They stand about in the awkwardness of departure. Elvesham 2, who has recovered so that he is only a little painful over his ribs, calls out "Wilkins! Another glass of milk. And one for Mr. Reston . . . . Good-bye, Colonel Greenly; good-bye, Mr. Wisdom. You leave us at our horrible potations. The great milk cure. Drink More Milk."

Outside shot of the Castle entrance. The guests get into a rather old car while Elvesham 2 and Arthur 2 wave good-bye. Then Elvesham 2 turns to Arthur 2 with something very like a grin on his face, in spite of the fact that he feels a twinge at his side.

ELVESHAM 2: "Forgive the impertinence of an old man addressing a young man old enough to be his grandfather, but you're losing your nerve. This business with the gun! My *dear* fellow! I find it hard to keep your secret. Really I do. The servants don't like you here. They think you're an interloper. Naturally. They're watching you all the time. Don't you realise that! You know *now*, as things are, even if I die a natural death, there'll be an inquest and all sorts of suspicions about you. I think seriously about changing my will and leaving everything to Marguerite. Won't you wait a year? I doubt if this old body will *last* a year. For a man of your experience you're absurdly impatient."

ARTHUR 2, in a state of nervous misery: "Can't you make things a little *easier* for me?"

ELVESHAM 2: "Now that's a lovely question — a *lovely* question. Coming from you. Give me back my body, Mr. Body-Snatcher, and then see how easy I'll make things for you."

ARTHUR 2: "This practice of imprisoning me in the laboratory every day with you while you do your scientific work, is driving me mad. I'm not accountable for my actions."

ELVESHAM 2: "You — with your old-fashioned mind — don't understand how interesting science is. And after all, it's Reston's work — your work. *You* will get all the credit for it. You'd better try to understand it. You'll have to pretend to understand it when I'm dead and gone."

A biological and bacteriological laboratory, not a very well-equipped one, in the Barchesham College. Professor Spike and a woman assistant, both in white overalls, are going about the laboratory in a gravely disconsolate state. They are looking for something that has been mislaid. They are looking in the hopeless way in which people search a room that has already been searched several times. They come face to face.

WOMAN ASSISTANT: "They've gone, Professor Spike. And that's all about it."

PROFESSOR SPIKE: "Enough typhoid to kill all Barchesham."

WOMAN ASSISTANT: "What are we to do — tell people?"

Professor Spike makes the hopeless gesture of a thoroughly unpractical man.

ELVESHAM 2 comes in. He looks ill and he walks with none of the youthful springiness that has hitherto characterised his gait since the experiment. "Hello, Spike, I'm knocking off. I'm feeling a little tired. A cold or something. I'm going home — perhaps to bed. But the master mind is staying behind to carry on the work."

He walks past Professor Spike, who hesitates and then says: "Mr. Elvesham!"

ELVESHAM 2: "Yes, old man?"

PROFESSOR SPIKE: "I'm not a practical man, sir. Do you remember at the cricket match when first you came here you asked if I wanted anything for my research work. I had to consider the feelings of Principal Jeddles and practically I said I didn't. Great pity. What I want, sir, is a lock-up laboratory to work in — instead of this, that I have to share with two other people. It isn't a laboratory so much as a highway."

ELVESHAM 2: "I'm sorry if I'm invading you, Spike."

SPIKE: "It's not that. But I'm in a frightful fix. I've had something stolen."

ELVESHAM 2: "What?"

PROFESSOR SPIKE becomes confidential: "Typhoid fever!"

ELVESHAM 2: "How?"

PROFESSOR SPIKE: "Tubes like this." Shows a small corked tube. "Ten of them. What am I to do? What on earth am I to do, sir? Enough to infect the county water supply and start an epidemic."

ELVESHAM 2: "That's serious, Spike. You *are* in a mess."

PROFESSOR SPIKE: "Tell the police?"

ELVESHAM 2: "Mustn't start a panic."

PROFESSOR SPIKE: "Private detectives?"

ELVESHAM 2: "More sense in that. You're in a nasty mess, Spike. Let me think it over — my wits are a bit muddy to-day. I don't know why. If I get an idea I'll telephone."

In the hall of Barchesham Castle Elvesham 2 goes to the hall table where there is a glass of milk. Wilkins appears as Elvesham 2 drinks it.

ELVESHAM 2: "Does Mr. Reston get his milk? I never see a second glass here nowadays."

WILKINS: "Mr. Reston has his milk sent to his room now."

ELVESHAM 2: "And he drinks it there?"

WILKINS: "That I can't say, sir. Everybody hasn't your absorbin' passion for milk, sir."

Exit Wilkins.

ELVESHAM 2 puts down his glass thoughtfully. Then his eye catches something at the back of the still unlit hall fire. He becomes curious and walks towards the fireplace.

He picks up a small glass specimen tube broken and turns it round to a small label of stamp paper bearing the letters B.T.

ELVESHAM 2: "Bacillus typhosus. Looks to me as though I am done."

He reflects. "Yes, that's why I feel so queer. I've got it. I've *taken* all right. He wins.

"Now what am I to do? What am I to do? Die. I shall die all right. I've got no strength left to fight it. Die as decently as possible. What shall I do? Leave everything to Marguerite? Set Siddonson on to him for forgery? What good will that do? But he mustn't marry her. Will she? . . . I must think fast — before this fever gets a complete hold on me. . . ."

He goes into the little parlour of the castle. "No way out that I can see. No. Unless — Wait a moment! Wait a moment — one little gleam of hope. One thing ——" He moves his hand as if checking points in a scheme. "If I can carry off that."

He suddenly takes up the telephone.

Back in the hall where the fire is now lit, Elvesham 2 sits down deep in thought. ARTHUR 2 comes in: "You telephoned for me?"

ELVESHAM 2 stands up with his back to the fire. "I wanted to look at you."

ARTHUR 2: "Is that all?"

ELVESHAM 2, scrutinising him: "You don't look well. You look worried and troubled about the eyes. You are ill."

ARTHUR 2: "I thought *you* were feeling ill."

ELVESHAM 2: "That's gone. A touch of cold, and a dose of quinine has cured it. But you are really ill, old chap. You are in for trouble."

ARTHUR 2: "What trouble?"

ELVESHAM 2: "Typhoid. They say it goes harder with a young body than with an old."

206

ARTHUR 2: "But what makes you think *I* have typhoid?"

ELVESHAM 2, smiling: "*This*." He holds out the little broken tube.

ARTHUR 2, after start of recognition: "What's *that?*"

ELVESHAM 2: "Elvesham, you are an *old fool*."

ARTHUR 2: "What do you mean?"

ELVESHAM 2: "I told you the servants didn't like you. The faithful Wilkins has kept his eye on you. You have been putting this infection into my milk. He has seen you doing it, I think, Elvesham. And every day he has changed *my* milk for yours."

ARTHUR 2: "You mean ——? It's absurd!"

ELVESHAM 2: "I saw him doing it this morning. I asked him why he did it and he wouldn't say. Very discreet man, Wilkins. Suggests everything and says nothing. But I thought you would have done things better than this, Arthur."

Arthur 2 has no doubt that Elvesham 2 is telling the truth. He walks down the room, cursing silently. Elvesham 2, holding himself erect by an effort, watches him with an expression of serene triumph.

ELVESHAM 2: "What is the period of incubation for typhoid? *I* don't know. But it's probably about time you began to feel feverish and rotten. You're bit by your own bacteria. How do you feel?"

ARTHUR 2 comes back towards the fireplace and sits down abruptly. "I can't face typhoid."

ELVESHAM 2: "They say you're insensible most of the time. It looks worse than it is. The danger is the relapse."

ARTHUR 2: "I can't *face* typhoid."

ELVESHAM 2: "It's amusing to think that I shall probably go to *your* funeral. Or at least it ought to be amusing. All the same, I hate to think of your dying in that nice body of mine. I've taken care of *your* old carcass, far better than you've done for mine. It's fitter than when you got out of it. Why not change back even now? Then I'll take on the typhoid and fight it to the best of my ability and you can go into training for the next experiment. Eh?"

ARTHUR 2: "We can't change back without McPhister."

ELVESHAM 2: "He'll turn up. He always does turn up. *There!* What did I tell you?"

McPhister walks in through the open front door.

ELVESHAM 2: "McPhister, you've come in the Nick of time. The Old Nick of time. Here's Elvesham wants to change back again and try all over again with somebody simpler. He has got typhoid by drinking germs he meant me to drink. That body there is dying of typhoid. I ask you, McPhister, was it worth while to try to prolong an ass like that for fifty years?"

McPhister: "Or any such ass!"

Elvesham 2: "All the apparatus is ready there! Everything is ready. I saw to that."

His face is lit. He has never looked so youthful as he does at this moment of escape.

In the dressing-room the two men are lying in their pyjamas as before. The black curtain is drawn over them. There is a three-quarter length of McPhister brooding over the situation and then he turns round to draw the curtain back.

At once Arthur 1 sits up beside the prostrate, insensible body of Elvesham 1. The characters are reversed. Arthur is really a young man now through and through and Elvesham is truly old. McPhister stands regarding the two.

Arthur: "Bring him round. I've got something to tell him."

McPhister: "But he needs rest. The man's heart is hardly beating. He's near the ebb."

Arthur: "Oh, let him ebb. Wake up, Elvesham! Wake up!"

Elvesham is awakened with difficulty. He passes his hand over his eyes and blinks.

Arthur: "I've got something to say to you that won't keep. Elvesham! About that typhoid. I think I ought to warn you. It was disgusting of me, I admit, but I told you a lie about the glasses of milk being changed. I told you a lie. See how you've corrupted me! That body you're *in*, is the infected body. You'd better do something about it. That's all."

Arthur stands up and asks McPhister: "What *ought* he to do, Doctor?"

McPhister: "Go to bed, I suppose. I'm losing interest in him."

Elvesham sits up weakly and listens to them with a drawn, distressful face.

Arthur: "As one experimentalist to another, I don't think you've been particularly brilliant in this case. Why did you pick on *me*?" He turns so as to address both Elvesham and McPhister. "What you wanted was an able-bodied mental defective. I think there's a good lot to be said for the idea of handing on memories in this way. Oh, a lot. In the county asylum here you ought to be able to find — just what you want. A body to let. But you'll have to hurry up. That body of yours, Elvesham, is in a shocking state. Pushing it over the cliff didn't do it any good. I've been giving it a lot of rough wear. The gun accident was a shock. I didn't let on at the time, but it was. The heart's rotten. Lord! how bad it felt at times. But who am I to give advice to my seniors? You old cronies had better have a good talk about it. I want to find Marguerite. I don't know how you've left things between me and Marguerite. I suppose my clothes are next door."

He walks out of the room and Elvesham is left with Mc-Phister.

ELVESHAM: "I'm dying. There'll be no other experiment. One lives — *once*."

McPHISTER: "No time left now — no."

ELVESHAM: "But isn't there still time? Couldn't you? A mental defective——? There is something in that idea of his."

McPHISTER: "There's no more time. And besides, if you *had* time, would you do any better? You may not be convinced of that, but I am."

ELVESHAM: "And the deeds and the will — no time — no energy to alter them. That young fool *wins* all round."

McPHISTER: "No — you lose. . . ."

ELVESHAM: "You *cheat*! But now I know who you are and what you are. The mockery of life."

McPHISTER: "Yes — Mephistopheles, the laughter in the shadow — the mockery of life! It's pleasant to throw off one's incognito for a moment. Well, well. We've played our little game. You've had your second time on earth, Dr. Faustus Elvesham."

Elvesham is sinking down in his chair and his face becomes leaden and expressionless.

McPHISTER leans over him, peering down at him: "Come, old bundle of habits and stale memories and faded yet ineradicable instincts. You've made your great experiment and much good it has done you. *How* you've failed me! *How* you've failed me! You and your loves and desires. Little you are, like all your kind. Little and unstable. I thought you might go on from life to life and scale the skies. You didn't want to scale the skies. Not for a moment. . . . One might as well expect the stick of a rocket to scale the skies. Tried and found wanting, you petty soul. You couldn't even stick to the new body I gave you. You mechanism. You animal. You ape. Come."

He moves so as to hide Elvesham almost completely. He becomes a black shape like a velvet pall brooding over the old man. Only Elvesham's fine wrinkled white hand, resting on the chair arm, is visible. On his finger is his diamond ring. It clings twitching to the chair-arm for a moment. It makes a last effort to hold on. It relaxes and falls limp.

The front entrance of Barchesham Castle, Marguerite approaches. The figure of Arthur appears from within and he stands awaiting her. She hesitates and approaches.

ARTHUR: "Can you give me a minute, Miss Swift, before you go in? Something very important has happened— and I want to be the first to tell you."

SHE looks at him with hard distrust. "Has something happened to Mr. Elvesham?"

ARTHUR: "Yes."

MARGUERITE: "Then let me go in and see him."

ARTHUR: "Please, not for a moment. I have something very difficult to tell you."

MARGUERITE: "Is he ill?"

ARTHUR: "He has changed suddenly. He and I have changed suddenly."

MARGUERITE: "What do you mean — *changed*?"

ARTHUR: "Marguerite, haven't I been changed since that queer experiment? Haven't I been changed altogether?"

MARGUERITE stands on the steps looking up at him. "Yes."

ARTHUR: "Was I horrible?"

Marguerite nods reluctantly.

ARTHUR: "I've come back. I've changed back. I am the old Arcturus you loved and who loved you for seven years."

MARGUERITE: "But ——"

ARTHUR: "I am restored to myself."

MARGUERITE: "But then — what has happened to Mr. Elvesham?"

ARTHUR: "Will you come into the hall and talk with me for ten minutes in spite of everything that has happened?"

Marguerite does not move.

MARGUERITE: "He is dead?"

ARTHUR: "Yes. He is dead." He leads her to a seat in the hall.

MARGUERITE: "And he was so kind, he was so gentle and understanding with me."

ARTHUR: "I'm glad you found him so. Since the experiment."

MARGUERITE: "I don't know how I could have lived through these last three months if it had not been for him."

ARTHUR: "Dear Marguerite, dear Daisy Star, was I as frightful as that?"

MARGUERITE: "Yes."

ARTHUR: "And that hard old man with the greedy eyes, who is lying dead upstairs now, took over all my tenderness?"

MARGUERITE looks at him earnestly. "You *have* changed back Arthur. You talk almost as you used to talk. You look at me — as you used to look. Arthur, what does it mean? Let me tell you something I have had on my mind. I have dreamt such strange things lately that my world has been upside down. Everything has changed. You seemed so cruel, so pitiless and hard and at the same time so cowardly and mean. . . I was afraid of you. I said to myself, Arthur is Arthur no longer. And then — I had a dream. I had a dream, my dear, and I seemed to see everything. It was mad and yet in a way it explained. . . ."

ARTHUR: "It explained — the experiment."

MARGUERITE: "Yes, that experiment."

ARTHUR: "What you dreamt was the truth. For a time I was that old man and he me. Unthinkable folly — a cheat and a trick — but so it was."

MARGUERITE: "He — he was truly you?"

ARTHUR: "Yes, and I — I — was the old man you learnt to trust and tried to protect."

They both stand up and for a moment or so they scrutinise each other mutely. Then she becomes radiant.

MARGUERITE: "I knew it. I knew it. Even before my dream I knew it. It is *you* I have loved all along. I could tell you, darling, through a hundred changes and disguises. I loved you young and I loved you old. I have always loved you and I shall love you to the end of our days. My dear!"

As she speaks in the background of the hall appears McPhister. They do not observe him. He regards them malevolently for a moment and says: "The old old story. The destined round. The little human life. . . . They seem to like it."

He shrugs his shoulders, turns about with a gesture of infinite disgust and vanishes.

The lovers, unaware of his intense disapproval, cling to each other, as lovers have done since the world began.

MARGUERITE, joyfully: "We are ourselves, my dear, we are ourselves. We'll never be anyone else."

Bibliography

1 The Man with a Nose, *Pall Mall Gazette*, 6 February 1894
2 A Perfect Gentleman on Wheels, *Woman at Home*, April 1897
3 Wayde's Essence, *New Budget*, 18 April 1895
4 The Queer Story of Brownlow's Newspaper, *Strand Magazine*, Vol. 83, 1932
5 Walcote, *Science Schools Journal*, December 1888–January 1889
6 The Devotee of Art, *Science Schools Journal*, November–December 1888
7 A Misunderstood Artist, *Pall Mall Gazette*, 29 October 1894
8 Le Mari Terrible, *New Budget*, 23 May 1895
9 The Rajah's Treasure, *Pearson's Magazine*, July 1896
10 The Presence by the Fire, *Penny Illustrated Paper*, 14 August 1897
11 Mr. Marshall's Doppelganger, *Gentlewoman*, August 1897
12 The Thing in No. 7, *Pall Mall Budget*, 25 October 1894
13 The Thumbmark, *Pall Mall Budget*, 28 June 1894
14 A Family Elopement, *St. James's Gazette*, 3 March 1894
15 Our Little Neighbour, *New Budget*, 4 April 1895
16 The Loyalty of Esau Common, *Contemporary Review*, February 1902
17 The Wild Asses of the Devil, Chapter 8 of *Boon, The Mind of the Race, The Wild Asses of the Devil and The Last Trump*, 1915
18 Answer to Prayer, *New Statesman*, January 1937
19 The New Faust, *Nash's Pall Mall*, December 1936